Queen & Emperor

Queen & Emperor

A NOVEL OF THE MUGHAL EMPIRE

Tony Raosto

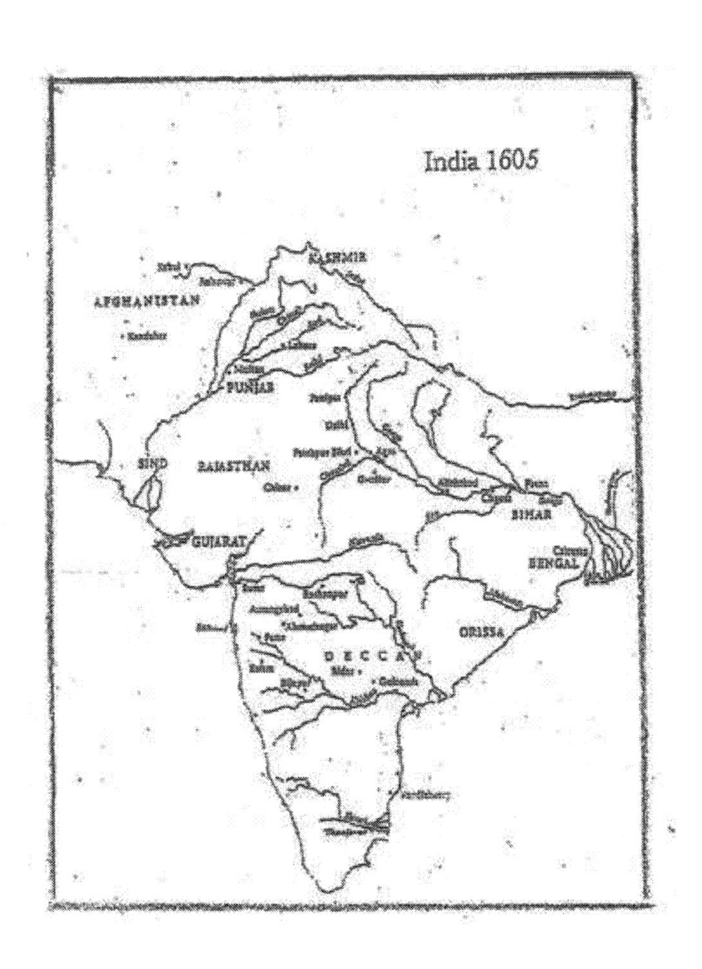
India 1605
KASHMIR
AFGHANISTAN
PUNJAB
SIND
RAJASTHAN
GUJARAT
BIHAR
BENGAL
ORISSA
D E C C A N

tonyji03@yahoo.com

ISBN-13: 9781546484943
ISBN-10: 1546484949

For my daughter Jessica.

PROLOUGE

Agra, 1603

HE HAD THE STERN VISAGE and high cheekbones of the Central Asian. The blood of both Tamerlane and Genghis Khan flowed in his veins. He was called Akbar the Great. He was the greatest ruler India would ever know, and he was dying.

White-haired beneath his turban and dazzling in his jeweled robes, the emperor stood at his balcony at Agra Fort and looked down at the mass of people on the field below. Akbar was a conqueror, a master of politics, and a just ruler. With his every motion, the crowd responded with applause and shouts of approval. By tapping his right palm twice to the heart, he confirmed his love of Islam and of the people. And the crowd roared, echoing across the expanse of the land and the river a resounding cry: "*Padshah Sala'mat*"—health to the emperor.

At the very moment when the sun lit the horizon, the elephants of Prince Salim and his son Khusro rode out before Akbar's balcony. Under iron prods, the elephants took turns genuflecting before the emperor. A half hour earlier, both animals consumed buckets of water fortified with palm wine, and the drunken creatures now rose and raised their trunks to trumpet loudly and belligerently. In the slant light of dawn, the elephants' long shadows swept over the churning crowd.

Salim's elephant, caparisoned in red, was the larger beast, but Khusro's, in yellow, was mounted by a master handler from the tribal regions. His presence had evened the betting odds.

Akbar struck down his hand. The elephants charged, and the earth trembled. They met head on. Jungle screams and the dull thumps of flesh upon flesh carried across the maidan. Ivory gnashed and pillars of gray leg struck into the earth like driven piles.

Salim's elephant swung his tusks and gashed the smaller creature's forehead. The wounded beast shuddered and his head spun away, showering the audience with crimson dots. A man ran despairing, wiping blood from his eyes.

Salim's elephant charged and knocked Khusro's *mahout* from his perch. Ringing with ankle pbells, he stomped the man's chest. The elephant, as if admonishing the audience, raised the dead man's body and shook it before them like a rag doll.

Khusro's elephant galloped in panic to the river, and the crowd, excited by the sight of blood, ran howling alongside the loping winner. The air rang with shouts of victory as Salim's elephant bulled his rival into the muck of the riverbank, then raised his trunk in a scream of triumph. To Salim's supporters, the victory was an omen of his inevitable rule. They hoisted the prince and paraded him before the emperor's balcony.

Akbar inclined his head slightly, but it was enough to convey his congratulations.

As the conquering elephant approached the royal balcony, the mahout prodded him to kneel. He swept his hand elegantly to his forehead in the *kornish*, the traditional salute to the emperor. Dressed only in white turban and loincloth, his dark legs dangled from the elephant's shoulders. His arms throbbed at his sides. He dropped his head and submitted to the applause of the crowd and a shower of silver rupees. Then the mahout slid from his mount, pressed his hands together, and bowed. He backed his animal away from the balcony as he gathered his coins from the sand.

"The astrologers say that no event can happen below that is not written above. Must we then believe that Allah favors your father?" said Aziz Khan, Khusro's father-in-law. They were standing at the riverbank among a group of nobles watching the rival mahout bow before the emperor. In the contest for the dying Akbar's crown, the court's astrologers had declared that the winner of the elephant fight could claim the favor of heaven.

"Nonsense," Khusro said. "Allah favors the bold. I will raise an army!"

"Praise God!" cried Aziz.

War was the way the Mughals had always selected their kings, and lust for the throne had always obliterated all sense of kinship. The saying went that a king should consider no one his relation.

The assembled nobles felt that the dissolute Salim, addicted to both wine and opium, would be a catastrophic choice for the empire. They would prefer even the headstrong Khusro to an unstable Salim. They bowed to Khusro in their brilliant turbans and wind-blown robes, and in so doing cast their vote for war.

CHAPTER 1

THE NEWS HAD JUST COME: Khusro's elephant had lost. There was commotion throughout the harem. The libraries, baths, schoolyards, and kitchens that made up the grand household of the zanana were abuzz with questions: If the fight were a true augury, would Akbar, indeed, crown Salim King? What if instead, despite the astrologer's predictions and the loss of the fight, Khusro was crowned emperor? Everything in their lives depended on the answer to these questions and on the character of the new emperor.

A servant had brought Ruqaiya Begum the news as she was flying her pigeons on the roof of Agra Fort. Sone of her birds had settled on the white dome of the palace. A single black pigeon stood on its gold crescent finial overlooking the dwellings, Mosques, and bazaars of Agra town to the left. And to the right, the Doab—the vast tract of fertile land between the Yamuna and the Ganges. Along the curved line of the Yamuna shore were the white mansions and abundant gardens of Mughal royalty.

The birds lived in an elegant, hexagonal building with a tiled roof and windows of filigreed wire. Espaliered deciduous trees clung to its pink walls. Set in the garden's soil were scattered plantings of tulip and nasturtium. Violets and pansies grew there as well along with giant sunflowers at the borders. At the center of the garden was a small marble pavilion where the ladies sat on a thick Persian rug drawing on the velvet snake of a huqqa.

There were hawks in the air and Ruqaiya was rattling a wooden canister of hemp seed to tempt her birds back into the coop. The Pigeons had just returned from a flight to Lahore and Maryam Makani, and Salima Begum sat and watched as she whistled and gently cajoled until all the birds had been confined. Then she joined the ladies in the pavilion.

The three begums constituted the informal ruling body of the *zenana*, the grand dames of the seraglio. Under their authority, the harem's eunuchs and armed female guards kept Akbar's city of women orderly and guarded the treasure, secret documents, and seals held in its vaults. The queen mother had called a meeting on the rooftop where they would not be observed.

"What can be done?" said Maryam.

"I imagine that some of these poor birds will have to be turned around to send news of the fight to Lahore and Delhi," said Ruqaiya

" No, not about the fight darling, the succession,

"We will do what we have always done, engage the Emperor's mind," Salima said.

"But, does anyone know what the Emperor's mind is," Ruqaiya said. The opium she had been savoring gave an unusual calm to her voice.

"Yes, of course, we do. He favors Khusro," Salima said, with a smile.

"If this is true, we have our work cut out for us," Ruqaiya said. The women, who were in various states of intoxication, sat cross-legged around the opium pipe. It had been a trying morning, and they were anxious to find a strategy before the sun should rise to its zenith.

"My dear Ruqaiya, unlike other women of the harem, you can trust me not to be persuaded by that boy's good looks. He is my grandson after all. I suppose it would be unkind to call him mad, but the truth is, I have serious reservations about his sanity," said Maryam Makani. She wore a simple gown of teal silk, and her golden chains and medallions flickered in the morning sun.

It was breezy and cool on the roof and would be for another hour or so. When the sun rose to its full height the marble tiles which glazed the roof's surface would grow unbearably hot and no matter how much opium the women smoked or how much water a servant might splash, the women could not walk the tiles in their customary bare feet.

"He has lost the fight, and, as the astrologers say, Allah will not grant him the crown," said Salima. Of the three, she was the one who had been consuming the most afim. That morning, as soon as she had heard of the outcome of the elephant fight, she had rushed to the comfort of her pipe.

"But Akbar might still confirm him," said Salima, hopefully.

"Yes, it's possible. Since when has Akbar followed the wishes of Allah?" Ruqaiya said.

Akbar had often been in opposition to the dictates of the Muslim clergy, especially when they had framed their mandates as the wishes of Allah.

"Then we must make a plan that will put him on the right path," said Maryam.

"You know what they say about men's stomachs leading directly to their hearts?

In this case, we must aim for his mind. And what could be more persuasive than a sumptuous Mugalai feast made in the harem's kitchens? I propose a dinner where we can give his thoughts a bit of a cuddle." said Ruqaiya. Salima had stayed silent, while the queen mother voiced her agreement.

"A cuddle? My dear, you have always had the most distinct way with words. But, I do agree with you. And we have a majority. Two out of three. Salima, will you join us?" said Maryam. Salima nodded her head, reluctantly acknowledging defeat.

"Three out of three then. The matter is closed. Akbar will have his dinner, and we shall have our emperor," said Maryam, stepping out of the pavilion and moving toward the coop. She was nearly eighty, but her long elegant legs strode with the grace and sexual authority of a twenty-year-old. Her bright face was blessed with high cheekbones and full lips and her dark eyes glimmered in vivid contrast to the white of her complexion. Even at this age, men found her attractive. She was not only beautiful but infinitely wise and worldly as well. There were few people in the empire who were as tough minded and experienced as she. In every sense she was the Rajmata, the Queen Mother.

The rajmata's mind flooded with memories. She thought about that small desert town. When she had arrived she was filthy, her delicate face had been wrapped in a coarse cloth and her juba was grimy from the turbulent sand. Only the gems set in Humayan's turban had suggested that this party might be more than ordinary. Humayan had ridden into town upon a camel—a mount considered inappropriate for a noble. He had given his horse to Maryam when her own bare ribbed mare had collapsed from starvation.

"Humayan's amirs had so despised me that no one would lend me another horse although I was their queen. Albeit, I was a young queen only 19, and I admit, not yet worthy of the name. We had spent twelve days crossing that infernal desert, running for Kabul. We were in a state of near starvation, subsisting on berries and un-cooked millet. Water too, was scarce in that land—the local people had choked the desert wells with sand to thwart our advancing army (such as it was). I thought I would die. It was during Ramadan and although Allah, in his mercy, exempts travelers from the fast, we had experienced abstinence much greater than what was required by our Holy Quran. Our circumstances were such that our fast lasted not only throughout all the days but after sundown as well. Only the thought of my coming child had kept me from despair. I was eight months pregnant. My body ached to see my son (my Lord husband, a talented astrologer, had accurately predicted that it would be a son). My husband also divined in a dream the name Jalall-ud-Muhammad Akbar (Great) which proved prophetic. Our son became a great king that would unite India into an empire that would encompass most of the sub-continent. He is known as Akbar the Great.

Humayan and I would have to suffer to regain the Empire that had been lost to that Afghani horse trader Shah Suri. And, make no mistake, it was the both of us who suffered. In war, women as well as men endure the hardships. The book of Heaven is inscribed with both our names and so should be the book of history.

After our son was born, our intention was to cross the Hindu-Kush and enter Persia, a trip so perilous that Humayan insisted we leave our six month old Akbar with his cousins in Umekot. But, I had protested.

'I cannot abandon him my Lord he is only a baby,' I said.

'You would have him freeze in the mountains? What mother does that? You must hold yourself as a queen and not succumb to the emotions of a peasant. That is unseemly,' he said.

'Ya Allah, I am not a peasant,' I cried, straightening and speaking to Humayan ardently, 'but I love my son.' and then I broke into full-fledged weeping.

'Do you think my love is less? In the name of Allah, take heart, we shall have him back when these tribulations have finished,' my husband said, gathering himself to speak in his strongest voice.

I had not wanted to marry Humayan. It was Hindal his handsome younger brother that I had cherished. We had become close, for I had attended many parties at his palace set by his mother Dildar Begum. Ironically, they were organized to acquaint me with her other son, Humayan. But it was Hindal that captivated me.

Together, Hindal and I resisted Dildar's imperative that I marry Humayan. To put her off I had declared: 'I shall marry someone; but he shall be a man whose collar my hand can touch, and not one whose skirt it does not reach.' But she and Humayan were determined. Humayan was taken with me or so he said and without a doubt he needed my Persian connections. Perhaps he would find my pale Persian skin useful as well. In any case, Dildar Begum, that master intriguer, would not permit Hindal to marry me. She insisted I marry her elder son, the one destined for the throne. Eventually, she got her way. I was only seventeen and vulnerable to the suggestions of a forceful older woman.

Initially, I had refused even to meet Humayan, but for months he pursued me, appearing at even the most insignificant social events with his bejeweled swords and perfumed robes, reciting Hafez and Rumi in his melodic Persian and casting his romantic gaze through eyes lined with the blackest khol. While he was not as handsome as his younger brother, I must admit that he charmed me. There is a reason he was called *Insan-i-Kamil* (The Perfect Man). So, truth be told, I went into this marriage, not entirely against my will.

The Rana Prasad, that most gracious king, had given us asylum at his palace in the oasis town of Umekrot. Perhaps he did this because he knew It was the town in which I was born, or that he had a premonition of my son's future greatness. Or it could be a reaction to the Hadith of the Prophet that said:

'whoever gives food to a fasting person to break his fast, shall have his sins forgiven, and he will be saved from the Fire of Hell, and he shall have the same reward as the fasting person, without his reward being diminished at all.' And the Prophet, peace be upon him, also had said that: 'When Ramadan starts, the gates of heaven are thrown open and the gates of hell closed, and the devils chained.' Whatever the reason, by Allah's mercy, the Rana, although a Hindu, had taken us in from the desert and treated us with respect and kindness—may God grant him long life!

From the parapets of the Rana's fortress we could see the fearful silhouettes of Shah Suri's camels, curving against the blue void of the desert sky. They had pursued us relentlessly across this barren land. Now, with matchlocks and long lances, they massed on the sand hills rising before the fortress, intent on killing my husband, the lawful king of Hindustan, and to murder his heir and me for good measure.

When night fell, they lit their campfires, and by their extent we could gage Suri's numbers:

'Five thousand I reckon, more if they lay hidden beyond the hills,' my husband said, 'they surround and outnumber us. They stalk the fortress walls around us looking for opportunities.'

They all had agreed: the amirs and the Rana and Humayan that our position was untenable. That opportunities for attack would inevitably present themselves and that all interests were best served by Humayan's party making a run for Persia where I had relatives.

In the end, our escaping party numbered only 30—all that were left that still loved the King. It was, as my husband had later declared: 'the lowest point in my life.' And it was mine as well.

We left on the Night of Power when Allah offered the most protection and Shah Suri's men, following the Prophet's admonition, turned their palms to the stars and recited special prayers throughout the night. Humayan would later insist that the angel Jibril had descended and made us all invisible. How else to explain the miraculous evasion of the Pathan sentries? My own belief was that Allah had chained those devils in prayer. Whatever the truth, we evaded Suri's men and the following day, we galloped across the burning Thar desert and high up into mountains. A week later, we found ourselves at the frozen Hindu Kush, the mountainous gateway to Persia. I was cold, colder than I had ever been before. I was born a princess pampered by a palace full of servants devoted to my wellbeing, and who professed to love me. I had never been exposed to such torments of weather. My husband did his best to comfort me, but he was preoccupied with his other charges, his 30 followers and their animals, not one of them, man or beast without complaint.

When we arrived at the pinnacle poised to begin our descent to warmer weather, the following day, we found that the wind had stripped the mountain bare. We had only twigs to burn. All night long, my husband and I huddled in our drafty tent and fed them carefully to a meager fire while the wind howled and whipped the snow outside.

The next morning, by Allah's mercy, the sun came up clear and bright, casting it's light and heat along the mountain trails. Our animals, yawning clouds of steaming air, were saddled to go down to where enough fuel could be found for breakfast and a blazing fire. Two days later we crossed the border into Persia"

Along with the emperor's wives, the seraglio housed the emperor's female relatives: his aunts, cousins, sisters, mother, and grand-mothers as well—all in separate apartments.

Although all the zanana women who weren't slaves, servants, kin or concubines were officially the wives of Akbar, a good portion of them remained virgins. There were so many women in the harem—nearly five thousand—that the emperor, try as he may, couldn't possibly attend to them all. And he did try.

"It will be good to have the emperor among us for a change," said Ruqaiya, "especially for the younger women."`

"Ah, you do remember," said Maryam.

"Mother, your son is unforgettable," said Ruqaiya," and if you were not his parent, I would provide some succulent details."

"Ah, but I have details of my own. My son, I am told, can satisfy 20 women at a time," she said with pride.

"Yes, that is the truth mother, but only when he has swallowed one of those *Vajikarana* mixtures, then he would have the sexual vigor of a horse. He could bring many more to orgasm, by painting his organ or the ladies' privates with one of those *dravana* salves. I believe that the court biographers say he can climax over a hundred.

"A true king," the emperor's mother said.

"Our emperor of love, deserves a toast, does he not?" said Ruqaiya who was looking for an excuse to extend her elevated mood.

"Oh yes," said Salima coming out of the pavilion, it is my duty to salute our king. And you mother?"

"By all means," said the Rajmata.

When a servant arrived with a flask of honey wine, the women drank until on top of their opium intoxication they all, became drunk.

Then the three inebriated, opiated women leaned over the balustrade of the roof looking down at the banks of the Yamuna. They could see Salim's distinctive palki slipping past.

"There he is, the emperor-to-be," said Salima slurring her words.

"Our future," said Maryam, she too slurred her words.

"He is good looking, but Khusro is handsomer.... more handsome," Salima drawled.

"Agreed, but I daresay that neither of them will be looking in your direction when night falls." said the queen mother.

"Yes, but I am not too old to hope," said Salima her eyes drooping with the opium. The other ladies laughed softly and drunkenly.

"Look, there is Khusro," said Ruqaiya. They were high up but could still identify the figures below.

"Even from this height he is handsome," said Salima.

"Oh, Salima, careful, lest you let your Nafs overcome your reason," said Maryam Makani, "remember, also, that you have already voted, and I will not allow you to rescind. You must turn the restless camel of your mind toward heaven."

"It was just a bit of wistfulness," said Salima "Of course, you are right mother."

When Salima returned to her apartment, she drank another goblet of sweet wine. Still drunk and suffused with opium, the longing that had possessed her earlier welled up again, and she went to the drawer where she kept her lingerie.

"Borte, come here," she called to the Tartar tribeswomen who guarded her door.

"Explore again, shall we?" she said, "would you like to?"

"Yes, very much so, your highness, as always," she said.

"Then, I will help you strap it on." She took from her drawer from among others of teak and Ivory, a golden phallus set with smoothed opals at its tip. It glimmered in the sunlit room. When the phallus was in place, Salima bent over and with her head on the divan and her buttocks in the air and lifted her crimson gown. The guard pushed it into her with extended, well-lubricated strokes. The phallus was so long and thick that Salima could barely accommodate it, but the pleasure was deep and satisfying, and the opals did their job of titillating her insides as the guard plunged deeper and harder until Salima screamed with joy and orgasm. It was not over. Salima ordered that the guard perform once more and again after that. When they were both exhausted they lay in each other's arms, she in gossamer silks and the guard in the black robes of the palace guard. Salima let her hand slide to the other woman's sex and stimulated her to orgasm. Then she kissed her fingers.

"I'm beginning to think that you might be better than a man," Salima said, "surely you last longer."

"I am happy to please you, Highness," said Borte,

"But do I please you, darling?"

"In many ways, but I do prefer a man if you will forgive me,"

"Yes, they squirt, don't they? That is delicious. I suppose that I prefer men too, but it has been so long, and I am growing old. Is it fair that the emperor should have many choices, but I have none?"

"I cannot judge. In my country, Alhumdillah, women have freedom of choice."

"With no restriction?"

"Very few. When I go home, I will find a lover."

"I wouldn't know how to deal with such freedom."

"You will come with me. I will show you. Do you ride?"

"Of course, but age has blunted my taste for adventure."

"Nonsense, you are not old, and Tatar men are devilishly attractive."

"Oh yes, I know," said Salima smiling.

She had lain there on that very divan thinking about the freedom that Borte described, thinking about men in general and the emperor in particular, recalling his embrace. When she was younger, the emperor would visit her often and her days were light and happy. She had been lucky. She knew that many of Akbar's wives represented political liaisons in whom he had only a lukewarm interest if any—poor souls condemned to a loveless existence. Consequently, the harem was a sexual tinderbox, a palace of unfulfilled longing. And forbidden, of course, were all expressions of love and sex outside the emperor's purview: greengrocers could not deliver carrots, leeks, white radish, cucumber, bitter melon, etc. unless they were cut into small pieces and could not be used for erotic purposes.

It was death for a eunuch to kiss or caress one of the emperor's wives and likewise, the woman would be subject to the same penalty. Doctors, workmen and other men who had legitimate business in the harem were carefully scrutinized. There were spies everywhere. Despite these dangers, there were still women who would risk all for romance. Liaisons with eunuchs were not unheard of, despite the risk. The more adventurous women would, sometimes, devise schemes to smuggle lovers into the harem or to arrange outside trysts.

"When will you go home Borte?" said Salima.

"I'm obliged to be in service for three years more."

"Ya Allah, by that time I will truly be old!" cried Salima, "but I might still go."

She had no intention of leaving. She had spent nearly her whole life in the harem. She knew nothing of the outside world, and she was frightened of it. The idea of escaping the zenana was pure fantasy.

"You will begin a new life."

"Yes, I shall consider it," Salima said, and suddenly bored with the conversation stood up and frowned, smoothed her gown and with an imperious finger pointed toward the door, indicating that their session had concluded and that Borte should re-assume her post at the apartment's entrance.

"Kuda Hafez," said the Begum and, as Borte strode out of the apartment, smiled the stiff smile reserved for social inferiors.

Despite the sexual repression, the harem was an exuberant place to live, enlivened by the wit, intelligence and free-spirited singing and dancing of the elite women who lived there—the cream of the empire, the daughters of the Nawabs and Rajas of the vast Indian sub-continent.

The zanana was also a place of learning and creativity. Some of the women studied philosophy, science, mathematics and a few produced admirable works of poetry, art and music.

The harem library held many books of intellectual distinction, access to which was often sought after by scholars of the realm and abroad—the emperor would sometimes grant entrance to learned men on a limited and carefully supervised basis.

The acquisition of wealth too was a harem occupation. Zanana women were often engaged in trade by ship and by cart with every part of the empire and with regions beyond. The lucrative business of transporting Haj pilgrims from the western ports of India to Mecca via the Arabian sea was a harem enterprise as well.

Khusro, as a boy in the zanana, was the little darling of all the women. When the prince was forced to leave at puberty as all the emperor's male children had to do, there were women so attached to him that they became despondent. None had forgotten his dark good looks or his magnetic personality. Now, that he had grown into a tall, confident man the attachment was even more intense. Unfortunately, he had only the younger, less influential women to wave his banner. But what they lacked in influence they made up for in devotion. It was they who gave Khusro the most encouragement and wailed the most at the news of his elephant's defeat

---

On the day of the banquet, even under the Begum's flinty gaze, the harem kitchen was chaos. Slaves and servants hurried back and forth, tending the giant fireplaces on each side of the room. Whole goats and lamb sputtered on slow turning spits, and huge caldrons bubbled with curries and vegetables. Bowls of fruit, golden candelabra, rolls of freshly laundered red damask, vases loaded with fresh cut flowers and musicians, actors, acrobats, and dancing girls passed in transit to the dining hall. But Ruqaiya drew the line when the emperor's gamekeepers began to take Akbar's hunting cheetahs through the kitchen.

"Stop!" she shouted, turning crimson, "By the Prophet, if you advance a step further, I will personally deprive you of your heads. I will not have my kitchen smelling like a zoo," she said grasping her cleaver. Wary of her famous temper the men stopped immediately, grinned sheepishly and turned the animals out of the kitchen.

Despite these distractions Ruqaiya strained to give attention to the minutest detail:

"Now I want the candles placed among the flowers, floated on palm leaves and lit the moment Akbar is sighted, " said Ruqaiya resting her hand on a servant's shoulder. Hundreds of red and yellow chrysanthemums were floating on the surface of the tank just outside the harem.

"The music must then begin," she announced to the company of slaves and servants that had gathered to take instruction.

"Make sure to synchronize it with the emperor's entrance, and I want the first of the food served the moment the Badshah takes his seat. We will start with the soup. Now listen carefully, for these must be presented in strict order: the fish xiacuti, followed by the pomegranate duck. Koftas of lamb in gravy, vegetable pulao, baked spiced bitter gourds, lamb kebobs. Serve all the other dishes in no particular order. Of course, there will be rice with dried fruits and pilaf, and piles of naan and chapatti. Then will come the desserts and an array of all the fruit in season. Akbar will want the white wine of Nashik and Maryam, the Madhu honey wine. See to it that their goblets are full at all times."

The feast the Begum had arranged consisted of over a hundred dishes rather than the 30 or 40 presented at ordinary meals. By the time the emperor had sampled these preparations and consumed the wine along with a pipe-full of good Malwar opium, she reckoned that he would be in a most pliant mood indeed.

To heighten the sense of occasion, the emperor had agreed to enter the harem through the lanes and bazaars of Agra Fort rather than his usual route via the marble halls of the palace.

The harem mahal was bounded by a wall of the fort where torches blazed at the ramparts. The path the emperor would take, from the male quarters through the lanes of the bazaar were lit with torches as well. White roses lay upon the streets and bellows blew vapors of heated perfume as the emperor maneuvered the paths in his gilded palanquin. Along the way were musicians in hidden niches and Nautch girls gracefully shimming in the torchlight to the beat of drums and clashing symbols.

Illness had kept the emperor away from the beds of his wives so there were coy smiles at the news that the still attractive Akbar would be once again be spending time in the harem.

For his part, the emperor was overjoyed at the invitation to the dinner. He needed the council of his women. The judgment he must make vexed him mightily. The burden of ruling the vast Mughal empire was wearing, and he wanted to be free of it. But there was one last decision of grave consequence—he must choose his successor.

The innermost circles of the court held that Akbar favored his grandson Khusro and he did lean somewhat in that direction. However, before he made up his mind entirely, he was anxious to get the opinions of the prominent ladies of the harem, particularly the views of his mother, Maryam Makani.

Since the time of Babur, in matters of propriety and policy, the Mughal emperors invariably turned to the real keepers of tradition and of the old wisdom: the Mughal women.

Finally, the emperor entered with trumpets sounding and all the chandeliers glowing with candles. He was wreathed with marigold as his palki glided into the immense hall. The women who greeted him dressed in the most excellent clothes and jewels and the air was fragrant with the smell of perfume and a fog of incense.

Through the cusped arches of the palace windows, blue clouds could be seen sidling by. Silhouetted against the darkening sky were the fort's chatrias where a flight of dark birds flew past their bell-like domes.

All stood as the emperor's palki glided into the great hall, proceeded by a troop of young eunuchs wrapped in elegant robes and glossy turbans.

A divan had been placed perpendicularly to the long files of silk mats where the ordinary women of the harem sat with crossed legs. It was the divan that received the emperor at its center, flanked on both sides with the most significant women of the harem. His mother to his immediate right. Ruqaiya Begum, and Salima Sultan, at his left hand.

"Assalaamu Alaikum," said Maryam Makani to her son. The emperor placed his right hand over his heart and gave it two little taps and bent his head in a tiny hello. He acknowledged Ruqaiya Sultan in the same casual way—the emperor's usual method of greeting his intimates.

"Ah, the loveliest women of the harem are at my side, I couldn't be happier," said the emperor as servants helped lower him between them.

"Nor could we," said his mother

And the feast began. Bare-chested slaves distributed chargers of elk and antelope and laughter and loud talk roiled the hall. When at last, all the instructions of the Begum had been followed and, the final huqqa of opium smoked, and the golden chalices were at rest, the main party, that is Akbar, Maryam Makani, Ruqaiya Sultan Begum and a few of the other leading ladies of the zanana retired to a side room.

The emperor smiled and appraised Ruqaiya Sultan with shrewd eyes.

"You have expended a great deal, so you must have a great deal to ask of me," Akbar said. The emperor was a shortish man with a handsome mogul face and a commanding manner.

"I suppose you know what we are about," said Ruqaiya returning the emperor's clever glance

Of course, but, it is I who should shoulder the expense; for it is I who seek your council."

"You are most welcome to do so, my son," said Maryam Makani with a wry smile.

"Then, let us consider the succession," said Akbar, " As is plain to see, the finger of old age has fallen upon me. My time has come, I can feel it in my bones. I must get this matter settled before long. Salim has been a sword at my throat, my enemy rather than a son. Yet, I cannot bring myself to hate him."

"It is rumored that you prefer Khusro," said Ruqaiya Sultan.

"Yes, I have considered him, but in truth I have always preferred Salim. Still, there is the problem of my son's waywardness."

Years earlier, Salim had had an affair with the emperor's favorite concubine, the nautch girl called Anarkali. When Akbar discovered this infidelity, he had had the dancing girl killed. Salim was so much in love with Anarkali that he never forgave his father. During his recent rebellion, in retaliation. he had arranged the murder of his father's close friend and biographer Abdul Fazl.

When the emperor mentioned Salim's "waywardness" he was referring not only to his sexual betrayal with Anarkali, but to his allegiances to both wine and opium. The emperor had lost two sons to wine, he was not going to place the weight of the empire on shoulders subject to the same vice and opium as well. But as Maryam Makani pointed out: "Khusro, would be a disaster, he is a head-strong child and many people consider him mad. Not suitable. Salim is really your best choice. He is not nearly as far gone in drink as were Daniyal and Murad. I vouchsafe, that he will be a dependable and effective ruler. But you do not have many options, do you?" Ruqaiya and the other women nodded in agreement, Akbar was also convinced of his mother's wisdom, and the emperor, relieved that the matter had been settled, whispered to Maryam Makani that Salim, inshallah, would be king, at the time of the emperor's death

---

Immediately after the dinner Maryam Makani set out to give her grandson the stupendous news. From Agra Fort, the queen-mother's palki raced along the Yamuna's dark shore to Salim's palace, where she found the prince alone in his study.

"Assalaamu 'Alaikum," said Maryam Mikani after she had been led into the room by a bare-chested servant.

"Alkium Salaam, mother," said Salim, "what is wrong?" alarmed at the arrival of his grandmother at such a late hour.

"Nothing is wrong, everything is right, you are to be emperor and the earth rejoices!" The room was dark, and Salim sat by the light of a solitary gee lamp. Maryam broke into a huge smile and clung to her grandson as he rose and danced around the room in circles taking her with him.

"Allah hu akbar," he shouted, "I will be king, it is true, I will be king," and broke into a smile as big as Maryam Mikani's. She had never seen Salim so happy. Suddenly he clapped his hands and a servant appeared.

"Rouse the palace," he said," and "make ready the audience room, your new emperor will celebrate. Brings us wine and afim and every wife that I have and slaves and concubines. Where are my musicians? Wake them and bid them play. And as for you my darling, don't I know that this is all your doing. I love you. Please take a glass of wine with me and a puff of this afim. We must celebrate!"

CHAPTER 2

SALIM WAS SITTING AMONG THE embroidered pillows of his palanquin. When his bearers brought it to a halt, he thrust aside its curtain and looked out at his son. Standing among his nobles, Khusro cut a regal figure. Tall and self-assured, he held his head high and gestured in the manner of a king or prophet. If his firstborn son hadn't presented such a dire threat to his future, Salim would have been most proud of this young warrior. Only seventeen and he had the bearing of a ruler. But as his son's expression made clear, even the loss of the elephant fight had not extinguished his ambition.

"Your time will come," Salim said, narrowing his eyes and leaning out of his palki to give his son's arm a hard squeeze, "but only when I have grown too old to rule. Until then, you must wait upon me and curb your presumption. My revered father supports this. I now have his assurance that I will succeed him. His army and mine will stand against any aggressor."

"And I have the assurance of mine own will that I—", Khusro said, standing firm with an angry face. He had stopped himself in midsentence as he saw the Rajah Man Singh approaching. The rajah radiated power. He represented ancient Rajastani royalty, and all Indians bowed before him. Man Singh's robes flew in the wind as he strode majestically to Khusro and put forth a brown hand to be kissed. Only afterward did he acknowledge Salim.

"Ah, sultan, Lord Shiva has blessed you today with a stunning victory," said the rajah with a condescending smile. He had just stepped from the garden of his riverfront mansion after having viewed the contest.

"Yes, Allah has been kind to his servant," said Salim, unwilling to acknowledge Shiva as his lord. "And my sages tell me that it is proof that heaven has decreed that I will rule. What do you think, Rajah Uncle?"

"If Akbar, too, acknowledges your angels, then I will most certainly bow in deference."

"I have my father's warrant," said Salim.

"Then today you are doubly blessed," said the rajah, giving a slight bow of his head so as to fulfill his promise.

After the emperor, Rajah Man Singh was the most powerful man in India. He was king of the vast Hindu principality of Rajastan and acknowledged as Akbar's ablest general. It was the Rajah's alliance with the Mughal conquerors that allowed Akbar to rule an empire whose majority population was Hindu. Under Akbar's rule, the Mughal elite had intermarried extensively with Rajastani royal women. Salim was himself the offspring of such a union. His mother also, like Khusro's, was a Rajput princess. Sharia law required *kafir* wives to embrace Islam, and of course, all children were reared under the guidance of the Qur'an.

It pained Salim that his son favored his mother's side, the Rajastani nobility. *"He thinks himself a Rajput prince even before he is a Mughal sultan. This is the cause of all his arrogance,"* thought Salim.

Salim knew that Man Singh was a flatterer. He had definite knowledge that he had assured Khusro that his claim to the throne was equal to Salim's. The Rajah had falsely intimated to Khusro that Akbar favored his grandson, that his seeming acceptance of Salim was only political gesturing. The young sultan had no idea that through him, his uncle would seek to rule. Salim thought it would be pointless to warn him, so much was the prince under his uncle's influence.

The wind had calmed, and the morning sun blazed with a foretaste of the burning heat that would come by midday. Salim was fatigued, and he longed for the comforts of his harem.

"Home, double pace," Salim ordered. Immediately his bearers shifted the poles on their shoulders and picked up speed. They darted past a pair of water buffalo ambling before a peasant's stick, then past a group of boys who, wet from swimming, bent to the mud in salaams under the impression that Salim's gilded palki was the emperor's. Other people strolling the bank salaamed as well. The prince exulted in the notion that this adulation would soon be legitimately his own.

Salim's palki slowed when it came upon the crematory *ghats.* It had interrupted a circle of Hindu mourners dressed in funereal white. A body wrapped in white cloth and honored with a marigold wreath was burning upon a sandalwood pyre. Above, vultures swooped in an ultramarine sky. A bare-chested priest chanted and rang golden bells at sudden intervals. At the far shore, a crocodile launched for something beneath the river's coruscating surface.

The Mughal prince was still in his thirties. He had a handsome face with a nose a trifle too long, the mark of a Rajput aristocrat. His wheatish complexion was Rajput as well, but his eyes were a Mongol's yellow. There was pride and imperiousness in those eyes, yet he seemed more a man of letters than a prince of the blood. He wore a plain white tunic, buttoned in front. His feet were bare but meticulously cared for. A turban of striped silk dignified his brow.

The palki resumed its steady pace. Salim drew on the snake of a huqqah. The smell of burning opium gathered in the compartment. After a time, his chin slumped to his chest as the drug took him to a place beyond the concerns of the body and where time passed in infinite moments.

Suddenly, a pair of black claws burst through Salim's curtain. A white ball of ruffling feathers squawked and flapped against the ceiling, then tumbled against the gilded walls and the chest of Salim himself. The prince looked up from his meditations and straightened in surprise. He followed the unexpected fellow with contracted pupils. Puzzled for a moment, he finally saw that his palanquin had captured a plump Cakravaka bird. He knew Cakravakas well. For a time, he had kept a pair at his aviary but soon dismissed them as being too common.

Salim smiled sleepily at the bird as if recognizing an old friend. Automatically, he pointed a finger, and the bird grasped it, shifting from claw to claw, settling its neck feathers. Salim, squinting at the bright sunshine, stuck his hand out into the air, and the bird joined a flight that was just then wheeling past the white face of Man Singh's palace. The flock then descended with arched and fluttering wings to resume strutting and pecking in the mire.

It added to Salim's sense of mastery that he could call the name of these birds and of most of the living beings inhabiting Agra's environs. He had trained in botany and could name a good portion of its leaved citizens as well. It struck his fancy that the next emperor would have an almost godlike knowledge of the life under his jurisdiction—human, animal, and vegetable.

As he was congratulating himself, Salim remembered that he still had cause for concern. He had gotten his father's blessings, but it had been a long fight with his brothers, Daniyal and Murad—both now dead from alcoholism—and soon, he noted, he would have to fight against his own son, Khusro. It was disquieting to think that Khusro might at any time overthrow Akbar's decree and strike at his father. And Salim knew that eventually he would. But at the present moment, by Allah's grace, there would be no war. He would be king when Akbar died.

The wind had come up again, and the palanquin's curtains blew out like silken wings. The prince lay back, luxuriating in opium's dreamy pleasures. Beneath him, he could feel the smooth rhythm of the bearer's gait as they trotted home over the mud and through the lapping water.

CHAPTER 3

WHEN HE CAME TO HIS father's palace, Salim brought gifts of gold and numerous elephants. As a token of submission, he had ordered his army to camp at the outskirts of Agra.

"Assalaamu 'Alaikum," said Salim as he prostrated himself before the emperor. Because of the heat, the court assembled in tents outside Akbar's private apartment.

"Alaikum salaam, my most auspicious child. The angels sing to see father and son united."

Akbar postured grandly like the proud father. The show was necessary to convince the nobles that a reconciliation had indeed occurred.

"Arise," said the emperor, presenting his hand. Instead, Salim bent and kissed his father's feet. The nobles voiced approval at this show of devotion with many "*Alhumdillahs*" and "*Supanallah's*." Then Salim rose and took the back of Akbar's hand to his lips. The amirs broke into applause. The uncertainties of the last few years were now resolved. Hindustan would be at peace and the nobles' prerogatives undisturbed.

"Let all men know that my most cherished son will rule the empire," Akbar announced in his orator's voice. While the court cheered, Akbar smiled benevolently. He took his son's hand into both of his and led him gently to his apartment.

Once they had entered the royal chamber, Akbar's expression changed abruptly. His face contorted in anger. With his left hand, he pinned Salim against the wall by his throat. With his right, he swung a hard slap to the cheek and then a backhand against the other.

"It was you who tried to poison me, wasn't it? Say it. It was, wasn't it?"

"I gave no approval, Father. It was done without my knowledge. I swear, Father. Allah is my witness."

"Then who would do such a thing without your knowledge?"

"Deo Singh was in my employ."

"You engaged that sniveler?"

"For the Deccan only. He has much influence there. His men in Agra saw an opportunity. They thought it would please him."

"Then it was he who killed Abdul Fazl as well. Admit it."

"That too was against my will."

"*Ya Allah*, it is one of the wonders of the age!" said Akbar, throwing is arms in the air. "A Mughal prince without a will! Tell me, by what agency does an emperor who has no will manage an empire?" he asked and slapped his son hard again. The king was still strong despite his illness, and Salim made no attempt to protect himself.

For the previous two years, Salim had plotted to take the empire by force. He had established a shadow capital and minted coins with his own image.

"Look at you! You have 70,000 horsemen, enough to win the empire, and you come here without an army. How can a fool like you pretend to defeat me, much less rule?" said Akbar. He was red in the face, and purple veins bulged at his neck. He pushed hi turban back from his brow. "Have you learned nothing from me?" he asked and smacked Salim once again.

Akbar released the grip on his son's throat, and the anger drained from him as quickly as it had come. "Compose yourself. Conduct yourself as a king," he said. He took a linen square from his sleeve and wiped the blood that trickled from Salim's mouth. He led Salim to the door where, outside, the court awaited. "And for God's sake, adjust your turban!" he said.

After having given himself a moment to straighten his own robes and fix his expression, Akbar strode out to greet his amirs with a smile. He was the consummate politician.

"All praise the future emperor," he chanted, indicating his son with a grand sweep of his arm. Salim's cheeks still glowed from the beating as he saluted the cheering amirs.

"God grant him the grace to rule wisely," said Akbar.

Many deep-voiced "Inshallahs" came in a chorus.

"And the love to rule justly," Akbar said, claiming more inshallahs. Then abruptly, Akbar announced,

"The prince and I will withdraw, *Khuda hafiz*," thus putting a quick and unceremonious end to the meeting. The nobles replied with their salaams and moved swiftly to the gates, anxious to spread the news of Salim's imminent accession.

CHAPTER 4

"Do you love death?" Akbar inquired. He was escorting Salim down a polished corridor that led to his private rooms.

Salim stopped short beneath a marble arch. "Death?" he asked.

He had always felt uncomfortable in his father's presence but now, even through his opium haze, Salim perceived real danger. Did his father want revenge? The emperor could decide in an instant whether a man lived or died. For all his good works, Akbar was capable of great evil.

"Some of our soldiers do love death, you know," said Akbar. Salim's brow contracted, and Akbar laughed as they entered the emperor's apartment.

"Be at ease. I have not brought you here to kill you," he said, "but there is something you must know."

Relief registered with Salim, but it was only in the abstract. The opium prevented him from being fully present at any of the events of his life. "You know the famous story of our victory at Panipat. Your great-grandfather won the whole of Hindustan in a battle lasting only five hours. Five hours, and India's destiny was sealed."

Inside the room, candles burned. The windows were curtained against the blaze of the afternoon sun. It was quiet. Only the faraway sounds of soldiers drilling on the maidan carried to the darkened space. A faint odor of incense hung in the air.

"Alhumdillah," Salim said perfunctorily. He and every noble, every Mughal, indeed every Indian knew the story. Why was his father mentioning this elementary knowledge now, he wondered?

"Our writers attribute the victory to Babur's introduction of the cannon of the Europeans."

"Yes, that is so," said Salim. Rather bored, he submitted to a fit of body scratching mandated by the opium.

"And certainly, there were cannon present at Panipat," said Akbar.

By the soft pulse of a s ghee lamp, Salim saw an old man in white robes enter the room. The man delivered a salutation to the emperor, then sat cross-legged on the thick blue carpet and began unrolling a scroll. When he had done so, the man looked up and smiled at Akbar.

"Sahib, please read for us," Salim heard his father say. The scholar stroked his white beard and, clearing his throat, read from the *Babur Nama*, the autobiography of the first Mughal emperor:

'But facing our men's arrows, the enemy fell back on his own center. His right and left wings were pressed so hard together that they could neither move forward against us nor push open an exit for their flight. When the incitement to battle had come, the sun was spear high. Until midday, fighting had been in full force. Noon passed. The foe was crushed in defeat, our men rejoicing and festive. By God's mercy and kindness, this difficult battle was made easy for us! In a single half day, that armed mass was laid flat upon the earth.'

"And that is true," Akbar said when the old man had finished. "But it is not the entire truth," he said and repeated, "By God's mercy and kindness, the difficult battle was made easy for us! For you see, when Babur's arrows ceased," Akbar continued, "his mounted archers parted, and the center was made open to the Brethren—God's real mercy and kindness."

Akbar paused for a moment and said, "Babur later revealed that earlier in the day, when the battle had gone against him and he had thought all was lost, he had visualized the sheikh of the order of Naqshbandi Sufis. Soon after, a man came dressed in white on a white horse, galloping at the head of a wild troop of white-robed dervishes. With just one furious charge, they pierced the enemy's defenses and vanquished Ibrahim Lodi's army. Afterward in camp, while the army drank and feasted, the sheikh rolled Lodi's head to Babur's feet and knelt before him with the name of Allah on his lips.

"Now, as you take up my sword, you must assume this knowledge: The Brethren are still at the center of our army and of our dominion over India," said Akbar.

Salim frowned. He had trained to be a soldier. He thought himself to be in possession of all the tricks of warfare.

The old emperor settled onto a divan and motioned to his son to sit opposite.

"As you know, we are Chatagai Turks, warriors by birth," Akbar said. "The Brethren are warriors as well but consecrated to God."

"Sufis?"

"Yes. They draw their inspiration from the wolf. They were founded by a captain in the Great Khan's cavalry. He had observed that wolves, when well fed, have all the attributes of men: cruel toward the weak, fawning before the strong, cunning, and jealous of their position in the wolfish hierarchy. But when the snow flies and food is scarce, they must go for extended periods without eating. They become surly, willing even to challenge their pack leader's authority. Such is their desperation that they will sometimes steal down from the mountain and attack herders, even those whom they have observed to be armed. But when the hungry days approach a fortnight, a change occurs. The officer went so far as to call it spiritual."

"With respect, Father, no one knows what animals think," said Salim. "How could an ordinary soldier presume to know a wolf's spirit?"

"Our captain was a mountain man a devotee of the Blue Sky, the nature religion of our ancestors. He observed that the wolves became much more at peace with themselves. At the same time, they were full of energy. They seemed to have ascended to a higher mode of consciousness. Single-minded and beyond fatigue, the wolves became much more effective and dangerous."

"And the Brethren took their lesson from the wolves and fasted?" Salim asked somewhat incredulously. He was in a dream state, trying to make sense of his father's revelations. His eyes closed, and he nodded sleepily. He ran an index finger along the base of his nostrils.

"Exactly. They found that their minds were clear and sharp, that they could execute the most intricate maneuvers with precision. They discovered that they had lost their fear of dying and thus were rarely defeated in battle. They became killers who would fight to the death. They were indefatigable. For them, retreat or surrender was unthinkable. Although dedicated to God, they were known as the Horsemen from Hell, Genghis Khan's elite cavalry."

"And they exist today in our army?" asked Salim.

"Have you not wondered about that group of horsemen who go into battle without helmets, without armor?"

"In truth, Father, I had suspected that those men might be dervishes. They never claim victory as theirs, are always humble, and disappear from the battlefield before spoils are distributed," said Salim.

"They are Sufis now, but they originate from the wolves whose spirit they have kept alive in their hearts. They are at the core of our success," Akbar said. "It is from their humility and lack of attachment that their power derives. Inshallah, you will speak to Sheikh Sirhindi, who will instruct you on how to use them in war."

"So that is why you tolerate Sirhindi, who opposes you at every turn," said Salim.

"Yes. He is difficult. He has no concept of politics or diplomacy. He works from the Sharia only," said Akbar.

"Many think him a saint."

"It may be that he is, but make no mistake, when dealing with Sirhindi, you must always let him know that you are king. Keep him at heel as I do my hunting cheetahs. Only then is he useful."

"But if it is fasting that has made the Brethren so effective, why has not this method been adopted by the entire army?" Salim asked.

"It was proposed in the time of the Great Khan, but it required discipline impossible to impose upon such a multitude of horsemen. In time, because of rivalry among the ranks, the method nearly died out but was revived only in the last century. Ever since, our armies have contained a cadre of the Brethren."

Talking to Salim had always exasperated Akbar. He was never sure it was worth the effort. Even this important information seemed to have no effect. For a few moments, his son seemed alert and interested, but then Salim's eyes closed involuntarily and after a long interval reopened. It was the effect of the opium, he knew, but still, Akbar could not control his irritation. Looking at Salim in the eye, he could see the dead, contracted pupils that made his son seem a blank wall. In the fury of a moment, he stormed out of the room.

"Lock him in!" Akbar ordered the guard standing at the door. "Give him what he wants in the way of food but allow no opium. Is that clear?"

"Yes, Majesty. No opium," said the guard, staring directly ahead. His body was at stiff attention within the straight line of his tunic and the drape of his cotton pantaloons.

Normally, the emperor would have asked after Deepak's wife and the health of his children, for he liked the cheerful upturn of the soldier's mustaches and the dark, compassionate eyes below the edge of his turban. But today his anger was such that he showed Deepak only the set of his teeth.

"And no wine!" Akbar cried.

The emperor was clothed in a jeweled tunic, and as he walked the corridor, he wheezed softly from his asthma.

The curtains had been set aside, and sunlight streamed into the room. Salim lay sweating with his face to the wall. For days, pain and nausea had tormented him. His head hurt, and his mind was foggy.

Salim was still trying to adjust to his new consciousness when the door swung open, bringing with it a cool breath of morning air. It was Akbar, preceded by a servant bearing an iced cantaloupe on a silver charger. Akbar held three balls of opium on a golden plate. Another servant followed, balancing a crystal flask of wine on a jeweled tray.

"Good morning!" said Akbar cheerfully. Salim turned slowly from the wall to gaze dully at his father. He could only find a smile when Akbar said, "Buck up. I have food and what you desire most." Akbar offered the golden dish.

Salim sat up and eagerly took the balls with a shaking hand. He swallowed all three, one after another, with successive gulps from the wine flask.

"Do not neglect the melon," said Akbar. "It is down from Kabul and even sweeter than the wine."

"I will need the *afim* first to take effect, Father," said Salim, trying to smooth out the wrinkles in his robes. He was haggard, and his beard overgrown. He hadn't bathed or shaved in four days.

After some time, when the opium had restored his equilibrium and the wine had settled his nerves, Salim stood up and said, "Why do you treat me so, Father?" He had begun pacing before Akbar.

"To show my displeasure with the path you have taken," Akbar said without hesitation. Akbar's servant sliced the cold melon and placed the slices on silver plates. The emperor speared a piece with his dagger and brought it to his lips.

"Delicious," Akbar said.

"And now you relent?" Salim said.

"I do, only because you must lead the empire. I have no time to reform you. You were born a warrior, and I have trained you to be hard and unyielding. But too much time have you spent in the zanana. You have become undisciplined and think more of the women and the opium than you do of warfare."

Salim had grown up in his father's harem, as had all the emperor's children. Only at the onset of puberty were the royal males separated from the women's caresses and made to live among the rugged men of the army. Salim had proved an apt soldier but in late adolescence had established his own harem, from which he had become inseparable.

"War is our life's blood, our reason for being," Akbar said. "We subjugate weaker nations, people who have gone flaccid under the sun. That is our business. We are successful because thanks to Allah, we are stronger. Babur despised India, the climate, the people, the way of life here. Now, *thoda*, *thoda*, we have become Indians ourselves, and as we submit to the sun, our grip weakens."

"In truth, Father, how could this have been avoided?" Salim asked.

Akbar rose to his feet. Angrily he waved Salim's words away. He shouted: "By bringing yourself up out of your weaknesses, by disciplining yourself like a true Mughal! Only in this way can we maintain our preeminence."

The rhetoric was inspiring, but Salim, laboring under the annihilating weight of the summer heat, could not believe that will alone could overcome the Indian climate. For three generations now, Mongol horsemen had refreshed the Mughal army. Annually, they rode in from the harsh Central

Asian steppe to seek their fortunes under the yak-tail standard. When that migration ceased, he knew that the empire would fall.

In having uttered these words, Akbar felt relieved that he had discharged his fatherly duty. He sat down again and spoke quietly.

"Before I take your leave, Hamid Beg will read a verse of our holy Qur'an," said Akbar, glancing at the scholar.

Hamid rose and, gathering his robes, bowed to the emperor. He left the room to do his ablutions at a courtyard fountain before touching the holy book. When he reentered, he reached to the highest niche in the marble wall for the Qur'an—the word of God must be kept high above all other words, written or spoken. He smiled with warm eyes at the emperor. He sat, crossed his legs, and set the Qur'an on a low stand. He read verse 17.23 aloud:

> And your lord has
> commanded that you
> shall not serve but
> Him, and show goodness
> to your parents. If either
> or both of them reach old
> age with you, say not to
> them so much as "Uff"
> nor chide them, and
> speak to them a generous
> word.

This was, of course, a rebuke to Salim for his rebellion and a sign that Akbar had become reconciled to the faith of his fathers. After having gone down so many different paths to God—including one that he had invented with himself at its center—Akbar was ready to face the day of judgment as a Muslim.

If the opium had not withheld his tears, Salim could have expressed his sorrow. As it was, he stared dully at his father and acknowledged the verse with a nod of his head and the blink of his heavy eyelids.

"May Allah be gracious to you," said Akbar. Sadness and disappointment settled on his features as he walked slowly out of the apartment.

"Khuda hafiz, Father," said Salim reverentially and made a resolution that he must take steps to clear his mental haze before his father should die. But, of course, he never could.

CHAPTER 5

In October of 1605, Salim stood in the throne room of the palace at Fatepur Sikri. His father lay dying upon a divan.

"You are my most capable son, Salim, and inshallah, you shall become emperor," Akbar said in a subdued voice.

"I shall make your memory proud," said Salim and sighed heavily. "Know that I love you as a son should," he said, expressing remorse at his rebellion.

"You despaired of my ever dying. You behaved as I would have," Akbar said.

Life was short. Salim had been in his early thirties, and Akbar at the time had shown no sign of weakening. It had appeared to Salim that his father might outlive him and deny him the grandeur of kingship.

"What is important now, Salim, is that you lead. Let what is past be past," Akbar said.

He had raised Salim to be emperor and knew that despite his addictions, he would be an effective king. At the age of thirteen, Akbar had taken over the empire from his regent and had guided it brilliantly. The empire was his masterpiece. He would not see it fall into Khusro's insufficient hands.

The grand vizier signaled, and a servant glided out of the shadows through long lances of sunlight piercing a high marble screen. He carried on a lavishly brocaded pillow, the sword of Salim's grandfather Humayun—what amounted to the scepter of Mughal rule.

Unsteady but still majestic, Akbar the Great arose from his divan, supported by servants. Salim keeled before him.

"*Subhanallah, Subhanallah, Subhanallah,*" Akbar intoned liturgically. The emperor seemed otherworldly standing amid a column of sunlight suffused with the smoke of incense. Shaking slightly and with a most solemn expression, he lifted the gold and purple turban from his own head and fitted it over Salim's smooth black hair. Like the crown of European kings, it was the paramount symbol of office.

"Subhanallah," Salim chanted in response. He too wore splendid robes. The emperor motioned. Salim took the jeweled weapon from its pillow and hung it at his side. And in that moment, it was done. The work of a lifetime passed on from father to son. Akbar recited aloud the first Surya of the Qur'an, the *Al-Fatihah*, the prayer for guidance, that Allah might guide the empire and bring it to even greater glory.

With this simple ceremony held before a small gathering of nobles, Akbar transferred the great Mughal Empire, the richest and most extensive on earth, to his son. All that remained was for the *khutbah* to be read at the mosque in Salim's name. This dedication, made before every Friday sermon thereafter, in every mosque in the empire, would announce to the world that Salim was ruler of the whole of Hindustan. It would claim for him the absolute obedience due a Mughal sovereign.

In the months following Akbar's death, Salim would put his own distinctive stamp on the country. Early on, he had established himself as a wise and generous ruler. His court was open and fair. He pardoned criminals, rewarded his supporters, and was lenient with his defeated adversaries. He even bestowed important posts on the best of them.

With the ladies of the zanana, he was most generous. He furnished the harem with silks and expensive perfumes and increased the allowances of its many residents.

Three times daily after prayers, morning, noon, and evening, the new emperor sat at a low window of his palace and answered the appeals of his people. He ignored no one; even the lowliest of his subjects could voice their concerns. No matter what the weather or condition of his health, Salim would appear at his window, a second Solomon from whom all justice flowed. He and the empire were a source of strength and stability from which his people could always draw comfort.

Salim also harbored a conceit that made the empire the axis of the geographic universe with himself as its center. It was from this delusion, fed by wine and opium, that he took for himself the outlandish title *Jahangir*—Seizer of the World. But, in truth, the new emperor was only an increasingly unhealthy man caught in the grip of addictions and suffering from a profound sense of inferiority to his illustrious father.

CHAPTER 6

SIXTY GOLDEN BELLS ON A golden chain hung from the parapets of Agra Fort and ran to an obelisk at the river. Jahangir had just awakened and was doing his ablutions when they rang melodiously but insistently outside his balcony. The sun had not yet risen.

"What is this?" cried the emperor to his general, Mahabat Khan.

"Your bells, sire . . . the bells of penance," he said and laughed.

"Ya Allah, I will stuff them with thy beard. Not penance, scoundrel—they are the bells of justice. Anyone with a grievance may sound them. As the Prophet has said, 'The cry of the victim of injustice, even if he be kafir, is never rejected by God,' Jahangir said. "Nor will they be rejected by me. Who rings them now?"

"I can make out an old woman, drunk, it would seem," Mahabat said over his shoulder as he strode out to the balcony.

"But what does she want? Mahabat, dear friend, see what she needs. My head still reels from last night's extravagances, and I have not yet had a moment even to light my afim. Rahanna, my pipe, please," Jahangir said to his servant. "Oh God! There are those bells again," he said, holding his head.

Mahabat shrugged. He took three quick steps to the marble rail, where he slid his arms wide and hung his head from his shoulders.

"Inshallah, I shall answer for the king," called Mahabat to the dark form below.

"Only the emperor will do, my lord. It is he who must answer. It is he who has cut my son's fingers."

Mahabat turned to consider the candlelit room. He watched Jahangir snarl and charge to the balcony.

"It is your son who has ruined my view!" shouted the emperor, leaning over the railing. "My champa trees are destroyed!" His cry echoed into the darkness.

"My son's hands are destroyed. Your Majesty has ruined them forever," she retorted and rang the bells again. Behind her, the Yamuna rippled with the moon tumbling on its crests.

"What do you want, crazy woman? The punishment was just," cried Jahangir.

"What is just? Son gave my only income. Majesty can grow new bushes, but son cannot grow new thumbs. Allah watches until the day of judgment. I shall ring and ring until Allah gives justice."

"And she will," said Mahabat under his breath. "I know mothers."

"She will give me no peace?"

"Not she, sire."

"What do you think, Mahabat? Shall I strangle her?" said the emperor half seriously in a low voice.

"That would bring pleasure, Majesty, but no peace," said Mahabat, shaking his head. "Give her some small money and send her on her way."

"Then in a short time she will fall in with the beggars who mill outside the mosque causing mischief. That is no good," Jahangir said and thought for a moment.

"I have another idea, Mahabat. I will assign a servant to her household, and he shall work at the palace as well. I have just the man."

"Have you an unmarried daughter at home, mother?" Jahangir called down.

"Yea, my Lord Conqueror. Zeena is still of age. Only Allah knows what will become of her."

"I think I have an answer. Do you fancy a husband for your child?"

"Why yes, Majesty!" she replied, taken aback at the question, but then she added suspiciously, "An upright Muslim only, sire, well settled."

"Mine own servant shall I provide for your daughter!" cried Jahangir.

"*Mashallah*!" she exclaimed, her eyes wide in astonishment.

"May Allah grant you long life," she said and cast her gaze up at the faint stars in the lightening sky. She smoothed her white-streaked hair into a semblance of order as an act of respect before God. "But when will this occur, most auspicious king? My child grows older by the moment," she said, coming back to earth again and not quite believing in this piece of luck.

The emperor turned to Mahabat Khan. "I *will* strangle her," he whispered.

"Give her a date, sire," said Mahabat, laughing.

"In two weeks' time. I pledge it, mother," Jahangir called sweetly.

"*Al hamdudillah*, I shall rush to give my daughter the happy news," said the woman joyfully. "May I take your leave just now, Highness?"

"Inshallah," said the king with relief.

"Praise be to Allah!" she hollered as she bowed and turned her bent frame toward home.

"Praise be to Allah!" said the emperor to himself in a low, exasperated voice. He was happy to be rid of her and pleased to have made what he thought to be a Solomonic decision.

Days later, in the heat of an afternoon, the bells rang again.

"Lord, it is my sister that you have buried," said the young Hindu standing humbly before the emperor's balcony. His head was bare beneath a ferocious sun.

In one of his drunken moods, the emperor had buried a servant up to her armpits, leaving her to broil in the summer heat.

"Judgment has been passed," Jahangir said. "She kissed a eunuch in the zanana. Two of my wives were witness to this outrage."

"Is this a grave crime, Majesty? A capital offense?" inquired the young man earnestly.

"Take this man away!" shouted the emperor, rousing the two guards who stood just behind the man, cooling their bare feet in the mud of the riverbank.

"The very sight of him is abhorrent. Give him one hundred strokes that he should learn how to speak to his king," the emperor said. In that, Jahangir, convinced himself that he was being lenient. Death, he mulled, would be the proper punishment.

He had given the same sentence to a woman who rang the bells to protest the death of her husband, a servant in the palace. For breaking a favorite Chinese vase, Jahangir had beaten him to death with his own hands. Jahangir's court slowly began to realize that human life meant nothing to the emperor, that he prized objects over men.

In time, the public evaluation of Jahangir's rule completely reversed, and only the very brave and the foolhardy had the courage to ring the golden bells.

CHAPTER 7

In the sixth year of his reign, Jahangir entered the Mina Bazaar during the annual New Year's festival.

A large space in the courtyard was covered over with luxurious awnings of Persian silk. A pavilion of silk and velvet rose over the emperor's throne. For the women of the harem and the wives of the nobles, a bazaar was erected with tents in myriad colors. The wives of tradesmen could also set up stands and buy, sell, or barter goods as in an ordinary street bazaar. Here in the Mina, women could circulate unveiled if they chose because no men other than the emperor and his eunuchs could enter. The emperor was privileged to gaze upon and flirt with the wives, concubines, and female slaves of his nobles without restriction. And it was here that he felt it politic to show the more benign side of his nature.

"Ah, Ammina, how much will you charge your king for that lovely string of pearls?" said Jahangir to the unveiled third wife of his examiner of petitions.

"Your Majesty's price is one thousand rupees only," she answered in a honeyed voice.

"A thousand? Surely you are trying to bankrupt the empire. Give me a just price, for heaven's sake!"

"My price stands." Her eyes sparkled.

"You have me by the throat. So heartless," said the smiling Jahangir. Because the proceeds of the goods sold by the harem went to charity, the prices were astronomically high and the bargaining good natured.

"Pirate! Swindler! Is there no justice in the world?" exclaimed the emperor, looking about him for an audience and enlarging his smile. "It is shocking to be treated so," he said to the crowd of ladies that had gathered. Then he sighed and paused for a moment.

"But a wise man knows when to submit," he said with a theatrical gesture of resignation. "Take the money, give me the pearls, and allow me to leave."

"It is my pleasure to serve you, Highness," said Ammina suggestively. She flirted shamelessly as she accepted the emperor's gold pieces. Women of every station considered it a great honor to make love to the emperor. Even if the woman were married, her husband would not object but would glory in her good fortune. Jahangir winked and smiled appreciatively but moved on through the perfumed lanes of the fantasy bazaar.

"Is Gujarat content these days? I'm told the rice crop is abundant and the oxen fat and healthy," Jahangir said. He was examining a bolt of chintz in the hands of a handsome tribeswoman. Pierced with a nose ring and wrapped in a red sari, she stood proud and tall. Gold bangles tinkled on her dark arms as she displayed the fabric. The bazaar was lively, attracting women from every point of the empire and every class of society. From the talk and attitudes of these women, the emperor could gauge the state of his nation.

"My village suffers from drought, and livestock are dying in great numbers. You are not told the truth, sire," the tribeswoman declared.

"Is that really so?" asked the emperor with genuine surprise.

"Upon my soul," she said and pressed her palm to her heart.

"What is your town?"

"Bansda, Highness"

"Near the Bika, isn't it?"

"Yes," said the woman. Her face lit up. She was astonished that the emperor would know her district's river, much less her town.

"Then we shall divert the river and bring you water. My engineers are capable of miracles. And grain shall be sent. No one shall go hungry, child; you may rely on that."

"Alhamdudillah! Bless you, Majesty!" said the woman. Jahangir nodded his head sympathetically.

"My gratitude for your honest words." Snapping his fingers, he ordered his chief eunuch to his side.

"The Exchequer will buy her entire stock of cloth. Feed and water this woman's animals and send a note to the governor of Gujarat. He is to be in Agra within the month."

There were tears in the woman's eyes as she fell to kiss the emperor's feet.

"May you live long and happily, Majesty!"

The emperor smiled graciously. "And you, child, may you prosper," said Jahangir. Then he moved regally on, sparkling in a blue *nadiri* set with emeralds and a chest pin glittering with diamonds.

Jahangir stopped before Ruqaiya Begum, his late father's chief wife, who was strolling through the bazaar. A woman who seemed familiar was at her side. Neither woman wore a veil.

"Assalaamu 'Alaikum, Mother," said Jahangir, "and Happy New Year. I trust the bazaar brings you joy."

"Oh, my Lord Jahangir, you know I'm happiest when shopping," said Ruqaiya, who had a razor-sharp mind but used the trick of frivolousness to put people off guard. Plain featured, past middle age, and overweight, she had maintained her ruling position in the harem in the face of competition from younger women through ruthlessness, her quick wit, and her unerring grasp of zanana politics. Of course, this was only possible because Akbar had valued her company and her intelligence above that of all his other wives.

"And your friend, who is she? I know you, don't I?" asked Jahangir, looking intently at the woman.

"Yes, Your Majesty. You and I have met. I am Mihrunnisa, your friend from the garden so many years ago," said the woman.

"Garden?"

"A bird in hand?"

"You!" he exclaimed. She smiled.

Years ago, young Salim had been walking beneath the sunlit palms of the palace garden. It was midafternoon, and the sweet-scented beds hummed with insect life. Fruit trees and flowers grew everywhere along his way. When he came upon a patch of Kashmiri irises, he felt an irresistible urge to pick a bouquet, but he had in each hand a dove that he was carrying to his aviary.

"Here," the prince commanded a passing girl. "Take these."

When he returned with the flowers, he found the girl holding only one bird. Salim's nose wrinkled with anger. "How on earth did that bird get away?"

"Like this!" said the girl, and she let the other pigeon fly from her hand. Somehow, perhaps by design, her veil slipped at that moment. The emperor-to-be was graced with a full view of this girl's exceptionally beautiful face: bright, serene, perfectly formed. The light of intelligence and mischief in her eyes, overwhelmed him. His anger faded. He tried to take her by the hand, but the impish girl bolted away quick as a doe. Laughing, she disappeared among the trees that overhung the garden path. For a long time afterward, the vision of her billowing blue scarf receding into the green depths of the garden lingered in Salim's imagination.

"And so, we meet again. I am still astonished by your beauty. Have you not married in all this time?"

"Oh yes, Majesty, I've married."

The emperor, crestfallen, smoothed his jacket.

"May I ask to whom?" he asked while thinking that any marriage could be undone.

"Sher Afghan, Majesty."

"Sher Afghan?" said Jahangir, relieved. "But he is dead."

"For nearly a year."

"And you have children, I suppose?"

"Only one. A girl, Ladli."

"Well then, you must come to court, and Ladli, she must come as well. You must promise me."

"Yes, sire."

"Tomorrow, then, after the noon prayer. You cannot ignore an emperor's request. It is cruel, and they tell me illegal," said Jahangir wryly.

"Inshallah, after *Zuhr*, Highness. I give you my word," said Mihrunnisa.

And so, the courtship began in the face of all the objections that could be made by the gossiping women of the harem: This Persian is thirty-four and already old, and she has a child. It was known that she had had many miscarriages. She cannot bear more children. She is a commoner, a climber, and wants only the wealth and position that the emperor could provide. She is not suitable for marriage. Why not take her into the harem as a concubine instead?

But Mihrunnisa would not accept concubinage; only marriage would suffice. She was in love with Jahangir. She had loved him all her life. Even as a girl playing at snakes 'n' ladders in the palace garden, she would see the young prince and nearly swoon.

Her father was then Akbar's master-of-works. In the bright heat of summer or during the monsoon season when the Yamuna clamored, she would beg to ride in her father's palanquin when it went along the riverbank to the palace. She thought that she would have braved the pit of hell to see the prince. It made her heartsick that until they met on that day in the garden, he had never, even for a moment, noticed her, and even then, she was too shy, too nervous, to allow the prince to grasp her hand. She had fled from the only man she had ever truly loved. How different her life would have been if she had had the courage to take Salim's hand. She thought about her life with Sher Afghan and shuddered.

Jahangir and she were married in May of 1611, two months after they had met at the Mina. She was his eighteenth wife and he her second husband. As the court astrologer had predicted, this was to be a happy and successful marriage and one that would transform the empire.

CHAPTER 8

May 25, 1611

At midnight, the sky filled with fireworks so bright they rivaled the light of day. The streets of Agra bloomed with roses. Everywhere in the city there was merriment. At Agra Fort, carpets were laid over the old blood of the executioner's stone. Banquet tents lined with cloth-of-gold were erected. The emperor's tent was bright with scented candles set in golden candelabra. Goblets, ewers, and sprinklers for rosewater all made of gold and set with gems glimmered among the feasting guests. Slaves in red livery served massive platters of roasted elk, wild boar, and antelope. Kormas and lamb curries were heaped on golden chargers. Peaches, cherries, and pomegranates from Kabul and choice local mangoes were piled on trays. Every flower in bloom glowed in golden vases, and incense perfumed the air. Golden cups brimmed with wine infused with rosewater, hashish, and fragrant spices. As the evening progressed, opium pipes burned as well. The emperor reclined on a gold-embroidered divan next to his new wife and lifted his cup in complete satisfaction.

"Rejoice," he said, turning to his wife. "I have a most auspicious name to bestow. Because you are known now as Nur Mahal, the Light of the Palace, and because the palace is much too small to contain the effulgence of your spirit, henceforth you shall be Nur Jahan, the Light of the World." Then, at the emperor's signal, musicians broke into the ecstatic beat of *qawwali* music. The queen rejoiced as she raised her goblet to her king. It was the realization of her fondest dream.

Earlier that day, the emperor had ridden out from his palace seated within a gilded *howdah.* Behind him, his most important amirs rode on plumed and be-skirted horses with manes plaited with sea-shells. The gilt, the mirrors set in cloth, the gleaming weapons of the emperor's personal guard, and the elephant's painted face and sparkling vestments made a dazzling parade as they rode along the road to Mihrunnisa's father's palace. A vast crowd surged in brilliant colors. They sang and danced at the emperor's approach, shouted salaams, and wished him good health, encouraged by the rollicking music and by state-provided wine.

At the manor, prayers sung out. A bearded cleric supervised the payment of the bride price and the signing of the marriage contract. A rain of gold and silver coins and trays of glittering gemstones, deluged the couple. Goblets of wine were uplifted, and salutations gorged the marble halls.

None could remember a marriage as joyously celebrated as this. It was as if people sensed that a great era in the history of the empire was about to begin.

CHAPTER 9

SHORTLY AFTER HER MARRIAGE, NUR Jahan was formally received into the harem. She was no stranger to the palace, but now she entered majestically as Jahangir's queen. She wore clothes of her own design: a white *shalwar* set with pearls and diamonds and spread tightly across her hips. A shawl of spun silk lay over a chemise of white satin. A pale turban set with pearls contrasted with her dark hair. When she walked, her clothing swept the air with an attar of roses that she herself had created.

Nur Jahan had been unnoticed, a fledgling under the wing of the Sultana Begum, a beautiful woman always, but hidden. Now she emerged from the shadows, brilliant, blinding in her beauty. There had never been a queen as gorgeous, as splendidly dressed, and as self-possessed as she who now glided through the mahal. From the moment a fanfare announced her entrance, she attracted every eye. Men and women bowed to her figure as if to the sight of a goddess. And as she went to Jahangir, sighs of admiration arose throughout the hall. Only Jagat Gosani, installed at the emperor's left, was silent. She was burning with anger and humiliation that Nur was about to take the emperor's right-hand side, the queen's position, the position of honor.

Jagat Gosani was the mother of Khurram, the third of the emperor's sons. She had been his most beloved wife. Witty and beautiful, she was, until the advent of Nur Jahan, queen and mistress of the harem.

Beneath a golden chandelier bright with candles, Nur Jahan brushed the emperor's cheek with hers as she sat. "My love, thy breath is as sweet as pomegranate," she said softly.

Jahangir had just begun to say, "Praise be to God," when Jagat squinted and remarked,

"Do you not think, my lord, that only a woman who has tasted the breath of many men could make such a comparison?"

Nur Jahan's response was immediate.

"Does that foolish Hindu think that only men breathe? It is she who thinks only of men."

"Enough!" Jahangir exploded. "This is a celebration, not a duel. You are both my wives. You must accept this."

"Yes, my lord," said Nur, smiling graciously, for it was Jagat who would have to swallow the bitter pill. Jagat Gosani glanced down at her plate with saddened eyes. It was now certain that she was no longer senior wife and mistress of the harem.

Jagat was a Rajput princess and would not disgrace herself by crying. As a devotee of the god Ganesha, she strove to look at life with the wisdom of full acceptance. She was confident that the Remover of Obstacles would push aside all her difficulties. She understood that her biggest obstacle was her own thinking, and she prayed that her mind would not ache with regret. Her time as queen had passed. Resistance was pointless. As the elephant-headed god filled her heart with his presence, she looked up from her plate and said, "Yes, this is a most auspicious occasion, my lord." And astonished the court by smiling beatifically.

She has capitulated, thought Nur Jahan. *I had expected a vigorous resistance, yet Jagat has given me almost none. Yes, these Hindus are most unpredictable—inscrutable, her father had said.* Nur wondered if this was subterfuge. Would Jagat strike at her in the harem once she had lowered her guard? The Indians were patient and devious. The Mughals had forced them to submit to their rule, but the Indian spirit was never conquered by it. They had embraced their Muslim rulers even as those rulers attacked their Hindu gods and destroyed their temples. She thought— *India, ever invaded but never vanquished.* She looked around her and saw how few pure Mughals were at court, how year by year the court had become darker and darker as countless Indian women had entered the harem. More Indian blood ran in royal veins than Mughal. Indeed, India had absorbed her conquerors. Nur had grown up in this country, but only now had she begun to grasp its subtleties.

And here was Prince Khurram, Jagat's son, strolling toward her, himself more Indian than Mughal, a vigorous young man in silken turban and coat, a figure as glamorous as she. He was a stranger to his mother but not to her. They both had lived at the sultana Begum's palace.

"Assalaamu 'Alaikum, Prince," said Nur with genuine affection, "how happy I am to see you."

"And I you, Mother," said the prince with sparkling eyes. He spun on his heel, and with his legs crossed at the ankles and arms outstretched, he bowed gracefully in an attitude of the classical dance.

"Such brilliance," he exclaimed, revolving his head to take in all the lights of the splendidly decorated room.

"Made all the more so by your presence, Sultan," said Nur.

"And what for this mother?" asked Jagat, indicating herself.

"To her I give my love and salaams," he said, perfunctorily. He bowed and brought her fingers to his lips.

"Seat yourself, my son of good omen," said Jahangir, raising his goblet. "Will you have a cup?"

"Oh, Father, indulge me. I have not yet acquired a taste for drink," said the prince.

"Quite right, my son. Would that I had never!" sighed the emperor. He then turned and made a sign to the musicians that sat at the wall behind him. Immediately, the orchestra struck up a raga with a singer whose voice crackled unpleasantly.

"Ya Allah!" groaned Jahangir, who had a sharp ear for music, "Stop that fellow!" he called to the musicians, and the music stopped immediately.

"Lord Khurram," said the emperor, turning to his son, "you must save me!"

"Really, Father, I am out of practice," said Khurram.

"Oh, but you must!" cried the emperor.

"Please, another time, Father."

"Now!" commanded the emperor with a fierce look.

"Very well, if you insist, Father, then inshallah, I will," Khurram said, "What would you have me sing? Can you bear another raga?"

"If it is my son who sings it," said Jahangir, beaming.

The handsome prince strode before his father and raised a bejeweled hand to the orchestra. The court hushed and, in a few moments, passed under the spell of the prince's supple improvisations and the sitar's importuning voice. Love was the theme, and the prince's song carried to every woman's heart. Even the nobles approved Khurram's beautiful phrasings.

"Oh, how you can sing, my son," Jagat rhapsodized, finally allowing herself a tear when he had finished,

"What purity of expression. You sing as if you have lost your heart," she said.

"But I have," Khurram replied.

"And to whom?" she asked.

"You know her name, Mother."

"Arjumand?" she asked, referring to his fiancée, the dazzling Persian.

Jagat was disappointed. She had hoped that he would mention the name of another. She had expected that his relationship with Nur Jahan's niece would have lost its luster. Princes of the blood were notoriously fickle, and Khurram had been betrothed to Arjumand since adolescence.

"You are not yet bored, Sultan?" asked Jagat.

"I am content, Mother," he said.

"But you are a prince, my son. What of the other women in your harem?"

"There are none that I love as much as she," he said.

"None?"

The emperor frowned. "Let us not trouble the boy, Jagat. He has spoken his mind."

"A mother has a right—"

"You have no right to badger!" Jahangir cried.

"There was a time when all I did or said was sacred," Jagat said bitterly under her breath but then realized that she was lapsing. *One must be constantly on guard*, she thought. She inhaled deeply and concentrated. Once again, the elephant-headed god came to mind. His many arms brandished the weapons of enlightenment: an ax to cut the ropes of attachment, an elephant prod to direct one to the noble path, a bowl of sweets to tempt one to righteousness. And as the god entered her consciousness riding on the back of his all-pervasive mouse, she inclined her head benignly.

"The emperor is right," she said and smiled. "I was wrong to intrude. I wish you and Arjumand happiness only."

Khurram smiled when he bent to touch her foot. "Mashallah," he said.

"Subhanallah, my handsome son," Jagat replied, using an Islamic term.

CHAPTER 10

As ALWAYS, THE ZANANA HALL was a chaos of bickering and petty maneuvering. The women went back and forth, trying to outdo one another with the latest clothing, the finest jewelry, the most cunning makeup. Their position in the harem, in fact everything in their lives, depended upon attracting the emperor's attention. The competition was shameless and the backbiting intense.

When Jahangir appeared in the harem that day, the feuding, the gossip, and the face-making stopped in an instant. Women who just a moment before had been haughty and disdainful lowered their eyes submissively and greeted him with a chorus of salaams. The sweetest voices of the harem sang of the emperor's prowess as a warrior and, indecently, as a lover.

The emperor did not stop but walked directly to the queen's private apartment past the leather-faced guards—Tartar women—who snapped to attention as he entered. Nur Jahan was resting on a divan.

The walls in the queen's apartments exhibited mirrors, tapestries, and costly paintings of Indian and European origin. Outside were the palace gardens and the luxurious bathing tanks reserved for the use of the queen and women of rank.

Silver pots of heating perfume spilled vapor that crept along the floor of the mahal like hunting cats. Jahangir strode with the mists climbing his legs and stopped before his queen.

"I don't have time for the niceties. You are well?" he inquired, looking unhappy.

"My lord, what has happened?"

"I have immediate need of the royal seal!"

"Yes, yes, by all means, but what has happened?"

"Suttee, that is what has happened!" Jahangir exclaimed.

"What do you mean?"

"I mean that it is an abomination."

"But you have always approved of suttee. You once told me that few among our Muslim women have ever shown such fidelity," said Nur Jahan.

"Yes, but today, for the first time, I have seen it performed upon a woman I know. Todar Singh has died today. It was his wife thrust upon the pyre. The poor woman screamed so that her mother fainted, and yet the burning continued. No one would rescue her. Indeed, her own brothers kept her in the fire by pushing her with long poles. "

"My God!" cried Nur Jahan, screwing up her face in horror, then relaxing it somewhat as another thought crossed her mind. "Yet I am told, my lord, that suttee women are dosed with large quantities of afim," she said.

"You justify these Hindu murderers? Her screaming still rings in my ears. Astaghfirullah, do you not fear the day of judgment?"

"My Lord, I only meant to say it is not so painful as one would imagine. I too hate this barbarity."

"It is madness!" Jahangir exclaimed loudly. "Their book says, 'Let these wives first step into the pyre, tearless without any affliction and well adorned.' That *is* madness, and it must stop! Bring me Hoshiyar to write. Give me the seal. I am sick to the heart." By long-established custom, the royal seal resided in the harem in the charge of the favorite wife. Jahangir paced impatiently while Nur Jahan called for the chief eunuch. When Hoshiyar Khan arrived, he sat cross-legged on a pillow before a silver desk. The king paced nearby and dictated a *farman*, which the eunuch transcribed with exquisite flourishes. When completed, it forbade, on pain of death, the practice of suttee anywhere within the boundaries of Hindustan.

Only after Hoshiyar Khan left and the document went to the palace scribes to be duplicated and distributed throughout the county, did the emperor finally relax. He sat on the divan next to his queen.

The courtyard of the palace was burning hot, but the mahal's windows were blocked from the sun by grass mats that were watered and flapped by slaves standing outside the harem. Female slaves also worked fans continuously within the room until it seemed as if cooled by the breezes of autumn.

"If we were Hindu, would you throw yourself on my burning pyre?" asked the emperor.

"I would do so regardless of my religion. I cannot live without you, my king," replied Nur Jahan.

"Nor can I live without you," said Jahangir, grasping her around the waist.

He inhaled the odor of her femaleness and ran his palm up the inside of her thigh, faintly embarrassed at the coarseness of his hand. She was, at the same time, excited by the roughness of his palm and the power that it implied. She convulsed when he drew his hand further up her thigh and then kissed him passionately on the mouth, receiving his tongue eagerly. When he entered her, she could not repress a sigh. With every motion, her excitement grew. She tried to control her rapture, but the voice of her passion filled the apartment and, for all she knew, the harem itself. But she was unconcerned. She was the queen, and Jahangir was her love.

When the passion subsided, she lay by the king's side feeling weak, cradled by the hard muscles of his arm with her head resting over the beats of his heart.

"My love increases day by day," said Nur Jahan softly. "This is what the sages mean by paradise."

They were lying naked in a secluded part of the apartment where they were not visible, but where the breeze of the fans could reach.

"Or is it only lust that increases?" asked Jahangir, leaning on his elbow and looking down at her with loving eyes.

"Oh yes, that too. The basest lust, my lord!"

"You lead me off the path of righteousness," said Jahangir.

"To paradise only," she said as if in a dream.

"Then let us journey there once again," he said. He covered her lips with his mouth and then glided his tongue to her breast, caressing her nipple with the light pressure of his teeth in the manner of her preference.

After the king had left her apartment, Nur Jahan went to the coolness of her bath to perform the *Ghusl*, the obligatory cleansing after sex enjoined upon Muslims. Her attendants had floated the marble tank with the petals of a hundred roses. She lounged with just her head above water and her black hair spread out among the red petals as she meditated on the beauty of her life and Allah's beneficence.

After the bath, she went to the chapel and stood behind her husband in the Maghreb prayer. Although her method of Shia worship differed somewhat from the emperor's Sunni orthodoxy, with each prostration, the royal couple drew closer and closer in spiritual union. Neither of them had ever felt more united to any other human being. This was a marriage truly blessed by heaven.

CHAPTER 11

THE LOSS OF THE ELEPHANT fight, taken by so many as an ill omen, had not quelled Khusro's thirst for power, nor had his father's accession. Immediately after his enthronement, the new emperor thought it wise to place Khusro, his eldest son, under house arrest.

Although the luxurious apartment in Agra Fort was hardly a prison, Khusro did not take to his new confinement easily. Even more bothersome: Khusro was compelled to attend court every day to be at his father's side, where the emperor could keep an eye on him.

"I would rather die than be treated like a disobedient child. I would sooner take my life," said Khusro. He was speaking to his wife, Rozana, as he paced before an arched window that overlooked the sparkling Yamuna.

"Astaghfirullah, there have been too many suicides. Your poor mother," said Rozana.

"Yes, yes," said Khusro, "my poor mother! Everyone knew of her depressions. Her moods went from the stars to the cellars. Such feelings run in families, but by Allah's grace, I am exempt."

"My lord, then we must be thankful."

"Thankful? For what must I be thankful? Losing the crown? It is *I* who should be king, as my grandfather intended," Khusro said. "I have told you many times that when father was caught with Anarkali, Akbar vowed that he would never succeed him."

"That is legend only," said Rozana.

"It is not legend. Your father has shown me the very room where Akbar entombed his little nautch girl. It is here in Agra Fort."

"Ya Allah, I know the story. They say that she was still alive when he sealed the room with brick," said Rozana. "Am I to believe that?"

"Believe? Your father witnessed it. You believe him, don't you?"

Rozana knew it was useless to argue with her husband, and she thought it somehow disloyal. She merely smiled and thought to herself how fortunate she was to be Khusro's bride. It was enough to gaze upon his handsome face. She thought that he would give her beautiful children.

The sun had begun to fade, and the polished walls of the apartment reflected the gentle light of the ghee lamps just lit. Massed candles burned in a chandelier of Venetian glass. Jahangir had not skimped on appointments. Thick rugs of Persian silk covered the marble floors. A magnificently carved desk set close to a window caught the evening light. The couple lounged on richly embroidered divans worked with pearls and gemstones. Khusro had only to clap his hands and servants would spread a red damask and lay golden plate. In an instant, a bath could be ordered, tobacco and opium pipes lit, or wine served in jade goblets. If Khusro chose, slave girls would cater to his whims. But Khusro never chose; he was happy in his marriage to Rozana.

"This is not a life; this is a death sentence. He will never free me. I cannot ask you to share my fate. You are free to go, Rozana."

"My lord, how can you say such a thing? My happiness is here with you."

"Please, for my sake, I cannot bear to see you imprisoned. Flee!"

"No."

"Go, for God's sake. Go!"

"No."

"Stubborn woman!" cried Khusro in exasperation. He walked away from her. Moments later he stopped and turned. An old idea had reoccurred. This time he meant to give it voice.

"Inshallah, then you shall free us both."

"Me? How can I?"

"Your father!"

"My father? He would never agree."

"To help his beloved daughter?"

"Yes, but I cannot ask that of him."

Rozana was Aziz Koka's favorite daughter. Petite, fair skinned with shinning black hair and sensual lips, she was as beautiful as Khusro was handsome. She was almost fanatical in her devotion to her husband.

"Either that or you must leave my presence. There is no other way."

Aziz Koka's mother had been wet nurse to Akbar. Among the Mughals, children suckled by the same mother had almost the same status as brothers or sisters. Aziz had used his influence with Akbar to arrange a marriage between his daughter Rozana and Khusro. It was Allah's blessing that the marriage, conceived as no more than an alliance, became a loving and enduring relationship.

After much wailing, Rozana successfully pleaded with her father to betray the emperor and free Khusro. It was Aziz Koka, along with Rajah Man Singh, who planned the escape.

1606

On an April night in the full heat of summer, Khusro called for his jailer.

"I will be leaving this evening to visit the tomb of my grandfather. My men are gathering now to assist me," he said. A company of horsemen had grouped in the courtyard below.

"With respect, Majesty, my orders are to keep you in the palace," said the jailer, a low-caste Hindu.

Khusro smirked. "If you take my advice, it would be better to keep your head on your shoulders than to keep me in the palace," said Khusro, in a rage that a person of such inferior rank dared to restrain him.

Acutely aware that Khusro's cavalry outnumbered his guards, the jailer bowed obsequiously.

"Majesty, your way is clear," said the still-bent jailer sweeping his arm before him.

"You have acted with wisdom. Mark my words; in future, we shall need men of your caliber," said Khusro as he walked past the jailer, patting him on the shoulder as he went.

The prince's armor shone in torchlight as he stepped into the darkened courtyard. Despite Jahangir's hypocritical edict forbidding alcohol, many of Khusro's men were drunk. They shouted when Khusro came among them and raised their swords and muskets in salute.

The humid night reeked of horse dung and human sweat combined with the rank smell of the river and the odor of burning sesame oil from the torches. A groom held an impatient black Arabian whose nostrils flared and whose hooves sparked as Khusro mounted and rode out from Agra Fort through the torchlit bazaar, and the salaams and zindabads of an admiring crowd.

The Rajah Man Singh stood alone facing the south wall of Akbar's tomb. Violet streaked the westerly sky. Shadows grew. From a high minaret, a muezzin's call pierced the hollow air, and as the blackness descended, the rajah heard once again the solemn music of the conqueror, the pious Islamic song that had overthrown his country. In the name of Lord Shiva, they would win it back. Man Singh had respected and admired Akbar's genius, but he would not countenance Rajastan under the thumb of Akbar's drunken son. His nephew would strike while Jahangir's rule was still unformed.

The marble face of the tomb's entrance shone in the light of the risen moon. The rajah turned to the road and, looking out at the night, saw Khusro and his horsemen coming on at full gallop. He smiled. His nephew had escaped!

Khusro dismounted recklessly as his horse still ran. He bolted through a cloud of silver dust to embrace the rajah.

"Uncle!" he shouted with arms held wide.

"Our adventure begins," the rajah said as he hugged his nephew and kissed him on both cheeks.

Khusro's small band was to swell to an army before they reached their destination at Lahore. Joining him along the way were nobles and their armies who had decided to gamble with the prince in taking the empire.

Khusro's horsemen made their way slowly, recruiting men as they went and sustaining themselves by looting farms and villages as they advanced through the Punjab.

Three weeks after Khusro had left Agra, he huddled with two men in a tent outside Lahore. They sat cross-legged on a carpet. A lamp's yellow light cast flickering shadows on the canvas ceiling.

"We have lost the advantage of surprise, my lord. Lahore Fort is teeming with soldiers," said General Hussein Beg. "The walls are unassailable." He put forth a hand over his enormous belly to pick at a dish of cashews.

"In honesty, Prince, we lack sufficient cannon, and our rag tags are no match for the imperial garrison," said Abdur Rahim.

"Let us come back with a real army well equipped. Then we will have a chance."

Khusro, filled with impatience, gestured with agitation.

"Don't speak nonsense, Abdur. We have no choice but to attack. We are fugitives from the emperor. Where would we go?" he said. "Let us be realistic. We cannot dismiss our men without paying them in money or in plunder. It would mean our heads."

"Foolhardy!" exclaimed Abdur Rahim. The stubble of his beard glinted in the lamplight like steel particles.

"No, Khusro is right. We have no alternative," said Hussein Beg. "Jahangir is approaching with an army. If we take Lahore, we will have a redoubt and at least a bargaining position."

"Let us go ahead, then," said Khusro. "Do you agree, Abdur?"

Abdur nodded, although reluctantly. He now realized how rash he had been. Because his father, had been Akbar's regent, Rahim had been favored at court. And Rahim himself had been Jahangir's tutor. In his heart, he chastised himself for his impulsiveness. In this sober moment, he knew their cause was lost, but feebly, he said,

"I agree, Prince."

They desperately set about preparing for the siege as reports of Jahangir's advance came into camp. Their army had more heart than skill, and the nobles put the men through a course of military training. They drilled in wheat fields trampled by elephants. Swords and lances were sharpened, matchlocks put in good order. What few cannon they possessed were greased and made ready.

———

From the very first, the siege went wrong. Khusro's advance was checked by guns booming from the fort's crenellated heights. The arching cannonballs disabled the rebels' cannon and scattered the infantry while the garrison's archers and musketeers picked off hundreds of Khusro's retreating soldiers.

After a few days, however, an equilibrium was achieved. Khusro's diminished army was tented down in a crescent around the eastern wall. The defenders were contained, and Hussein Beg, the old soldier, argued that if nothing else, the rebels could starve them out.

"But we have already lost, Beg," said Abdur Rahim. "When the imperial army arrives, it will be hopeless."

And it was hopeless. Severely weakened by a steady stream of deserters taking with them anything they could lay their hands on, the paralyzed rebels decided to abandon the siege and the war altogether. Abdur Rahim sent an emissary to Jahangir asking for a truce. But it was too late. Jahangir was already at Lahore. The emperor refused to negotiate and attacked instead.

Jahangir drove at Khusro's rear. Facing Khusro's regiments, the yellow flare of artillery belched from the smoking parapets. Cannon ball exploded the earth. Men were torn and bloody. A shouting torrent of cavalry broke through the eastern gate, and assaulted the retreating soldiers. Behind the horsemen came the infantry with their bows and lances and their muskets. The field clouded with cannon smoke. The dead and ruined were everywhere. Caught in a pincer, the surviving rebels dropped their arms and fled before the swords of a squadron riding in white robes without helmets or armor.

———

At dusk, from an embankment above the Chenab River, the captain of Khusro's personal guard, shouted down to a boatman,
"Assalaamu 'Alaikum! Prince Khusro will cross here. We go upriver. Make ready your boats." He shook a chamois bag presumably filled with gold.

"Excellency, boats are ready for sublime master," said the boatman. Three capacious vessels knocked against ramshackle piers. The boatman squinted into the setting sun, undid his headcloth, and wrapped its coarse fabric around his waist to show respect. He motioned to his men to do the same.

"Better to bring down horses and baggage before long, Captain sahib," said the boatman. The skirt of his ragged *kurta* flapped in the rising wind. "We sail against river, but breeze is with us now."

It took an hour to load the boats, but the wind still blew in their favor. Horses, whickering and stomping, were skillfully tied aft to prevent them from destroying the vessels in their fear. Baggage was stowed below decks. The cabins were reserved for noblemen; common soldiers bivouacked on the deck forward of the horses.

The captain stood on deck with his soldiers to watch the receding shore.

"Majesty," said the boatman, "I need ten rupees more." The bag of silver that the captain had passed on to the boatman was short of the initial payment agreed upon.

"Dear fellow, I cannot bother His Highness about such a trivial amount. He will add to the final payment. You can rely on that."

The boatman winced.

"It is out of my hands. Another thing: we will land further upstream at Riasi," Abdullah added.

"But that is twelve *kos* more, Majesty!" cried the boatman.

"Yes, yes, let us not quibble. You will be compensated."

"Please, Captain sahib," the boatman said, "I am a poor man." But confronted with the soldier's immovable face and his decks loaded with the prince's soldiers, the boatman had no choice but to bow and withdraw.

"Namaste," he said, turning away with a most bitter expression.

Prince Khusro's coffers were nearly empty. His baggage train had been looted by his retreating mercenaries, and the other objects of value and the camels and elephants had either been captured or abandoned during the retreat. Kabul, where his ally the shah had been notified of his coming, was his only hope.

———

During the night, all three boats, one after another, collided into an island sitting midstream. Awakened by the crashes, Khusro's men observed that the tillers on all three vessels had been lashed to port. The boatmen could not be found.

When dawn came, the sun bounced off the lance tips of Jahangir's horsemen picking their way over the stones of the riverbank. Soldiers, with matchlocks poised, stood among the neem trees on the mainland shore, emphasizing that resistance was pointless.

Khusro's boat jumped in the water at the impact of a cannon shot. A haze of blue smoke and the smell of gunpowder drifted across the face of the jungle. Khusro's soldiers had already deserted the boat when the prince rushed to Hussein Beg and Abdur Rahim on deck.

"In the name of Allah!" shouted Khusro.

"Sultan, we are undone! Look across the river," said Abdur Rahim, pointing straight at the shore.

"Our men offered no resistance," Hussein Beg said.

"What did you expect of pastry cooks and barbers?" asked Abdur Rahim.

"Ya Allah! I will not be slaughtered like a lamb," cried Khusro, drawing his sword.

"It's futile, Highness. Save yourself for the court of your father," Hussein Beg shouted, staying the prince's arm. "You may yet receive his mercy."

"It is not mercy I crave, Beg!" said Khusro, pushing his hand away with disgust.

"Save yourself to fight another day, then, Prince," said Abdur Rahim. "If not for yourself then for us."

Khusro's face fell as he realized the inevitability of defeat and the foolhardiness of resistance. He became suddenly meek and resigned to his fate. He flung his sword on the deck, bowed his head, and allowed the enemy to seize and bind his wrists as they swarmed over the vessel, taking all three men prisoner.

CHAPTER 12

It was morning in a sun-flecked garden. Jahangir sat beneath a striped awning flapping in a gentle breeze. The emperor's throne was a lofty gilt-on-wood affair brought from Agra on the back of an elephant.

Guards led the prisoners, who were dragging their chains. Khusro, Rahim, and Beg appeared before the emperor covered with dust and grimy faced from their stay in a cage inside the garden walls. It was the emperor's pleasure to sit with his two favorite hunting cheetahs at his sides when he convened his court. Their presence made the prisoners even more fearful of Jahangir's justice.

From his height, Jahangir looked down upon his son. His look was fierce, his cheetahs scowling.

"So, you thought to overthrow your own father. What have you to say?" asked Jahangir.

All the fight had gone out of Khusro. He stood trembling in his chains between the two nobles.

"What say you?!" roared the emperor. There was a gathering of vengeful noblemen standing behind the prisoners. The three heads hung in shame.

The harem had been silent. The women were always in attendance wherever Jahangir traveled, whether to hunt or to wage war. Mughal emperors could not live without the comfort of their women.

"Speak before I pass sentence," exclaimed the emperor. "Speak up!"

The prisoners shifted in their chains. It was only Khusro's fate that was being determined. The two other men had come to realize that they could not be excused. They were traitors and would be executed. Nothing they could say would save them. They remained silent.

It was true that Khusro wanted to speak, but when he tried, no words would come. His head was heavy with remorse, and he could not raise his eyes to meet his father's gaze. He gave no answer.

"Mercy, my lord!" cried a voice from behind the lattice screen.

Handsome and noble in spirit, Khusro had been a favorite in the harem, where he had lived amid the ministering hands of the emperor's wives. A hundred adoring mothers had he.

"In the name of Allah, forgive him," came another voice from the harem. Murmurings calling for death came from the male side, where his nobles stood.

"He is your son, Majesty!" cried someone else from behind the harem screen.

For many moments, the emperor was torn between conscience and duty, between the merciful heaven of the harem voices and the hellfire of the vindictive amirs.

"If there is no defense you will make," said the emperor, suddenly at peace with himself, "then I will pass sentence."

The following morning, the first part was carried out.

At dawn, the two nobles were brought to the slaughterhouse behind a palace nearly destroyed in the attack.

"Give me the fat one first," said palace butcher, who had barely escaped one of Khusro's cannonballs. "I have something special for him," he said.

Hussein Beg's hands were unchained, but his feet were left shackled. He shuffled over toward the butcher with his belly shaking. With the help of the jailer, Beg was hoisted onto a low platform. An ox's skin, freshly removed and still dripping with blood, was wrapped around his torso, and the butcher began stitching the already nauseous general into its folds. Hussein Beg's face was left uncovered, but the ox's head with its bloody muzzle and its horns intact was allowed to flop over his head. Flies swarming over the ox's skin made a maddening buzz around Beg's ears and tormented his bloody face unmercifully.

Rahim came next. He was sown into the fresh skin of an ass and his head placed so that his face showed through the animal's mouth. His blood-covered face also swarmed with black fly.

"Now for the transportation," announced the butcher gleefully. "We'll give these gentlemen a good ride into town, eh?" The jailer brought forth two asses and Beg and Rahim were each tied astride an ass with their bodies, facing the tail.

By now it was late morning, and the donkeys were led out of the courtyard into the sizzling heat to range the streets of Lahore. Each animal was guided by soldiers through the lanes and stinking alleys of the bazaar.

Oranges, pomegranates, peaches, and lemons, fruits and vegetables of every description stood in carefully arranged piles. Spices, tea, and garments brought in from every part of the vast empire filled the street stalls. Men sat at tables open to the weather and talked, sipping coffee, and puffing on huqqahs. Herds of sheep and goats filed through the twisting alleys, and single cows garlanded with marigold paced regally among the passersby.

As the sun rose higher and the day became hotter, the skins grew tighter around the prisoners.

Outside the carved pillars of a Vishnu temple, Hussein Beg's donkey stalled behind a cow that had raised its tail to flop its sacred manure.

"It is Hussein Beg of the army!" shouted a Hindu man draped in a ragged dhoti.

"The general?" cried another man.

"Yes, come see him," cried yet another

"Tell him that all our sons are gone. We have nothing left to give but dung."

"Is there any reason why dung should be withheld?"

"None whatsoever," cried someone else and spat at Beg. Then another spat at Beg as well. A volley of horse balls followed, and fusillades of rotten fruit bombarded him from the market.

"Enough! In the name of Allah, enough!" pleaded Hussein Beg. He was barely able to speak. The ox skin was drying rapidly and squelching his lungs. His breath came in small spasms, and soon words would no longer come. His face blued, and this general, this rich man, covered in filth and flies, begged the crowd of paupers for his life. But their contempt was so great that they allowed him to suffocate. His eyes rolled in horror as he gasped for breath. Two men pulled him down from his donkey and pressed his neck to the edge of a temple step. One of the soldiers, smiling benevolently, took the sword from his scabbard and presented it to a top-knotted man. And there, before Lord Vishnu's columns, with all the joy and passion of a religious celebration the man hacked off Hussein Beg's head.

Afterwards, they twisted the bloody head into a white cloth and placed it in a basket under the temple eves. Later, in the cool of the evening, the emperor's guard rode out from the fort and took the head and posted it on the city's gate.

For Abdur Rahim, it was different. His animal skin dried more slowly. In the past, he had distributed alms among the city's poor. As his mount wandered among the people in the bazaar, his fleece was constantly refreshed with basins of water splashed with cries of "*Bismillah!*" Although the shrinking skin nearly suffocated him, he survived the ordeal. And because Jahangir thought Rahim's survival to be an example of Allah's mercy, he restored him to his former office.

CHAPTER 13

THE HOWDAH CREAKED AS THE elephant swayed along the road to Lahore. A platoon of soldiers marched to the slow time of a military tattoo. Pipes played in a low register, and the elephant's ankle bells jingled more-or-less in time with the music.

Jahangir pressed his shoulder so close that Khusro could feel the dampness of his perspiration. Rows of stakes cast long shadows before them on both sides of the road. The emperor turned to Khusro with opium-lidded eyes and grasped his thigh in the vise of his hand.

"Son, behold the men in whom you have placed your trust," said the emperor. "Brilliant, are they not?"

Each of eight hundred stakes bore the impaled body of one of Khusro's supporters. The sharpened poles had been rammed through the anus and out through the mouth while the man was still alive. Some of the bodies still contracted in rigor mortis.

"Don't be coy, Khusro. These men have gathered to do you homage," said General Mahabat Khan, who was seated behind Khusro.

Although it was near the end of day, the heat bore down unrelentingly on the howdah. Mahabat's open tunic was soaked in sweat and sweat ran in rivulets down the bones of his chest and dripped from his brow. He had unwound his turban and hung it from his neck to absorb the moisture. A Marathi sword had once lain a stripe across his brow and cheekbone. The scar had endured white against his sunbaked face and his beard. His graying hair was cropped, and as he sat upright, smoking a huqqah, his eyes were fixed on the road ahead.

"Look," said Mahabat, laughing, referring to a tableau of impaled heads. "There is Jaleel and Ahmed . . . Muhammad." He took the names from his fancy, "All waiting to see the conqueror." The gilded howdah passed level with a monkey tribe jabbering in a banyan tree. "There is Dawood," said Mahabat, pointing to a head with blood leaking from its nose.

"And Bashir, your sergeant at arms, I think, all dressed up to greet you," he said, indicating a bearded head with staring eyes. A vulture hopped before their elephant and lifted toward a corpse slowly revolving on its stake.

The emperor offered his son wine from a crystal flask. "Drink," he ordered.

Khusro recoiled at the onslaught of his father's wine-sour breath. "No, Father, it is against the Qur'an," said the prince and wiped the sweat from his brow with his sleeve.

"Qur'an?" roared the emperor with a vehemence that fluttered the strung pearls of his turban. "What does the Qur'an say about duty to one's father? About treachery?" he asked, tightening his hand on his son's thigh.

In the dust of the road below, a group of emaciated Hindu peasants gathered to beg. Blind men, lepers, a thief punished by the cutting off of his nose and ears, a woman with starving children all stood limned with the red of the setting sun.

"I wanted the throne, Father, just as you had wanted it from *your* father," said Khusro, wincing from the pain.

"Drink," said Jahangir, unmoved. He forced the flask on his son.

A man with bulging eyes ran up to the emperor's elephant and was blocked by the shaft of a soldier's lance.

"Drink. It will make a man of you," said Mahabat. He prodded Khusro with the jeweled sheath of his dagger. Some of Mahabat's best men had been killed in the rebellion, and he was in no mood to be trifled with.

Khusro drank from the flask. He found that he relished the sweet taste and, as his stomach was empty, the quick lift it gave to his senses. He took another gulp and felt a warm sensation speed upward to his head.

"The throne is not susceptible to a weakling," said Jahangir contemptuously. He released the grip on his son's thigh and pushed Khusro away in disgust.

"Kill me, then," said Khusro, suddenly flushed with defiance.

The emperor laughed. "If you were anything more than a nuisance, I might," he said.

The emperor's words struck deep. Khusro looked inward and shook with shame and defeat. Then, abruptly, he broke into laughter, as if he had been told an amusing story. He took his gaze from the red lip of the horizon and focused it on his father. In the gathering shadows, Khusro looked at his father and thought he heard him murmur a cry of anguish. Khusro laughed again.

Jahangir bent over the rail of the howdah and tapped the driver on the shoulder with his crop. "Pick up the pace," he commanded. "Tell the sergeant to move. We must be back before evening prayers."

As Jahangir spoke, the Azan sung out from the minaret of a roadside mosque. Crows hurried over-head and light faded behind purple hills. Lepers, their bells made quiet, slipped wraithlike among the stakes to strip the corpses of their sandals and bloodstained robes.

CHAPTER 14

IT WAS TO KHUSRO, HIS firstborn son, that Jahangir had looked with the greatest expectation. Khusro's Rajput features, his hazel eyes—dangerous eyes touched with madness—had fascinated the zanana women from the prince's early childhood. He had grown to be tall and slim. His confident, charismatic manner had made him the choice of many of the nobles to be Akbar's successor. Now locked away in the dungeon of Agra Fort, Khusro howled with laughter. He was chained to a sandstone wall glistening with moisture. A torch flared above his head, and a brazier stood by his side with iron rods burning red on a charcoal fire.

The jailer pulled open the iron door to Khusro's cell and admitted the emperor, followed by a procession of his nobles costumed in silks and glittering jewels. But the emperor's clothing out shown them all. Jahangir's head was wrapped in a striped turban of Persian silk, stuck with a golden aigrette. A heron's feather, his personal emblem, showed there as well. He wore a light blue tunic studded with diamonds that glimmered in the torchlight. Dark purple trousers draped wide at his knees and clung tightly to his ankles. Shoes of golden satin with upturned toes cushioned his feet. His sword hilt was set with an uncut ruby of outlandish size and beauty.

Jahangir strolled majestically toward his enchained son. A fierce mustache drooped from his lip, and a pearl was at his ear. A servant had preceded him swinging a smoking censer to perfume the fetid air.

Jahangir had assembled his nobles to display for his son his personal glory and that of the empire. It was to be Khusro's last remembrance before the darkness descended upon him.

"Welcome, Father. Assalaamu 'Alaikum. So, kind of you to come," said Khusro, straining against his chains and laughing. "My friends, the serpent and the scorpion are not here just now," he continued. "They are shy. I greet you on their behalf. But beware the sociable rat, Father. He nips at the heel and would not scruple to gnaw on the royal toe." Tears of ironic laughter rolled down Khusro's cheeks.

Jahangir was very much in the grip of opium. When the drug periodically forced him to close his eyes, images would appear. The palms of Golconda, the face of a Portuguese Madonna, the army in spectacular battle dress melded one into another. This world of drifting images was his reality. To open his eyes on his gaunt, bare-chested son in this grimy dungeon shocked him with its raw truth.

Jahangir had half hoped that on seeing his son, he would allow himself to offer him clemency in exchange for his allegiance and be done with this interruption of his dream life. But Khusro's sarcasm was too much to ignore.

"What is in you, graceless boy? As always, you disappoint me. A king is born to be the shadow of God. He is not a fool," said Jahangir, "Now you shall find where foolishness brings you."

Jahangir motioned to the jailer, whose men held open Khusro's eyes. A man in a dark cloak stepped forward and plunged a red-hot filament deep into the struggling Khusro's left eye, then swiftly another into his right. Khusro's mad laugh transformed into cries of excruciating pain, which carried through windows set high in the vaulted room and across the courtyard into the palace.

The emperor closed his eyes in horror and went back to his pictures. Then he collected himself and cast a severe look at his amirs. Jahangir had wanted his nobles to see firsthand that there would be no leniency for treason, even if it came from his son.

The noble most conspicuously absent was the Amber Rajah, who had promised, however, to be present at the evening *darshan.*

CHAPTER 15

KHUSRO'S CRY PENETRATED THE ZANANA, and as the consciousness of its meaning spread, a woeful ululation arose from the harem. It continued through most of the night.

Jahangir had done the unthinkable. But what choice had he? Kill Khusro, his boy? No, as much as he had pondered it, he could not bring himself to do it, nor would the women of the harem have allowed him to do so. After much consideration, he had settled on the old Mughal solution in such matters: blinding. Right now, he could not stand himself or the lamentations of the harem that filled the palace corridors

The emperor, alone in the royal apartments, paced the cool marble floor in bare feet. He had unwound his turban and laid it in a strip atop a divan.

"Rahanna, my pipe," he said to a slave girl. "Let the evening begin."

With a clap of his hands, it seemed that the emperor could ignore if not dispel his demons. And while his servant was winding his head with the long cloth of a fresh turban, Jahangir's rooms came alive with the reassuring voices of his wives and amirs. Soon dancers, musicians, and poets arrived to make their presentations, although the emperor ignored them. For much of the evening, he sat upright, smoking his pipe, drinking wine, and talking with his nobles.

"Rajah Uncle, I have missed you these last few weeks," Jahangir said to the rajah Man Singh. He knew full well the degree of the rajah's involvement in the rebellion, but he chose to adopt an attitude of ignorance.

"Alas, I had been called to fix an important matter in Amber," said Man Singh.

"Pity you were not at court to fix the travail of your nephew."

"Just what was his offense, sire?"

"You have not heard?"

"I have heard rumors, but I believe nothing until it comes from the lips of the sovereign."

"Rebellion, Uncle, rebellion! Our Khusro sought to overthrow Allah's judgment."

"And place himself on the throne?" said Man Singh. "Feckless boy. They say he has been blinded."

"Would that I could ascertain his sponsors and apply the same," said Jahangir, hinting that he knew of the rajah's involvement.

"You have no mercy, then?"

"What mercy is due a traitor?"

"But your son, surely…"

"My anger has been appeased. I am assured of *your* loyalty, Uncle, am I not?" said Jahangir with a look of appraisal. It was, after all, no use to him to continue a war with the Amber Rajah.

"It is as if you were Akbar himself," said Man Singh, feeling nausea churn at the suggestion.

"Mashallah, dear uncle," he said, and all thoughts of war between the house of Kachwalah and the Mughal Dynasty were put to a final rest.

Whenever the opium closed Jahangir's eyes, images of Khusro appeared. The innocent boy. The charming adolescent. The charismatic young man so beloved of the harem. And the most difficult for him to accept: the madman who had attempted treason.

Khusro was his first son, born to Jodi Bai, his deeply loved Rajput queen. She had swallowed an overdose of opium pellets on the news of Khusro's rebellion. Jahangir thanked Allah that she was not alive to see what he had done to their child.

The emperor was well into drunkenness when he presented his jade cup to a slave girl and quoted Hafiz in a voice laden with sarcasm:

"Cupbearer! Brighten my cup with the light of wine;

Sing, minstrel, for the world has ordered itself as I desire."

Then he stumbled onto a divan, buried his head in his arms, and fell into a deep sleep.

Jahangir had taken more opium than usual, and his dreams were besieged with demons. Huge shapes appeared before him. Dark clouds that assumed the anguished face of Khusro swirled through the corridor. As the emperor ran from the apparitions, the corridor itself took on a distorted look, puffing and pushing in on him, then stretching to extraordinary heights. The cusps of the arches assumed the shape of gigantic teeth, twisting and snapping at him as he ran.

Outside, rain swept in torrents, slashing in under the open arches and flooding the marble floor.

The ululations of the harem tortured his ears. He ran to the women's quarters and found the harem dark. Not a light showed anywhere in the women's mahal, and yet the beating of palms against humming mouths continued.

"Silence!" he cried into the darkness. But even the emperor did not have the authority to stop the sounds of mourning. Only Allah could quiet the bereavement.

"Stop, I command it!" But the ululations went on. Nothing could contain their sorrow. For the women of the harem, it was as if Khusro had died. And Jahangir wailed disconsolately.

In the dark rain, he ran to the palace stables and ordered his mare saddled while thunder sounded overhead and drummed beyond the hills. He whipped his horse ferociously and drove through the gates as blue lightning snaked across the giant sky. The emperor awoke from this dream in horror, only to fall asleep and dream again.

CHAPTER 16

It was pitiable to see young Khusro deprived of sight. The emperor would weep when he saw him struggling to find his way along the palace corridors led by his sad-faced wife. Tortured with remorse, he would say feebly to his nobles, "My fatherly affection did not permit me to take his life."

When at last, he could take the sight of him no longer, Jahangir directed that Khusro be remanded to his apartment for the "safety of the empire," as he put it.

Jahangir drank heavily, six cups of double-distilled araq a day. Years earlier, his father's physician, a *Unani* doctor, had warned him of the threat his excessive drinking posed to his life. "There is little hope if you don't stop. Your people prefer to smoke this afim. Why don't you try?"

"Will I drink less?"

"Yes, but best is to kiss this wine goodbye altogether."

"I cannot quit, Doctor sahib. You know that. But inshallah, your afim I will try."

And Salim did try it, and it did reduce his drinking. But after the first year, the opium had as firm a hold on the prince as did his liquor. Twice daily, in the morning after the *Fajr* prayer and in the evening after the sun had set, the emperor's servants would prepare his huqqah with heavy doses of Malwa opium. In time, the sweet odor of the burning afim became a familiar smell during the morning audience, not only from Jahangir's pipe but also from the pipes of his amirs. Behind the marble *purdah* screen, pipes flamed with afim as well. The emperor had made opium smoking fashionable.

Jahangir's discontent was complete. He paced restlessly around the palace and drank much more heavily than usual. He shouted at his servants and bullied his amirs. Ostensibly to settle a backlog of sentences but actually to give himself a diversion, he scheduled public executions. They were held after the *khutbah* on the Friday after Khusro's blinding.

When the sermon was over, Jahangir and four of his nobles went out from the mosque to the fortress quadrangle. In the bright sunshine, a horse whinnied, a blacksmith struck his anvil, a camel dragging a lumber cart raised the dust off the courtyard floor. An elephant bedeviled by black fly swung his trunk ineffectually; another, shifting his weight lazily from foot to foot, brought a trunkful of straw to his mouth. A man loafing against the red fortress wall turned his head lackadaisically to watch the bejeweled emperor and his drunken amirs stagger across the quadrangle. The emperor had promised his lords a good show, and they were in fine spirits as they climbed to a room overlooking the courtyard.

Jamaal Udeen had been brought to the balcony's anteroom to be judged for his father's murder. The emperor assumed a cross-legged position on a low divan and looked fiercely at the defendant. His head hung in fear and deference. On each side of the emperor were two nobles. Four dark-skinned men in yellow turbans stood guard at the stone wall behind them.

The idea of avenging a patricide so possessed the drunken Jahangir that he thought it was not necessary for there to be any evidence to support the accusation. It was enough that Jamaal *looked* guilty. Jahangir settled his judgment quickly. Jamaal Udeen shook in his chains.

"There is no use denying it," said the emperor. "The imperial intuition is infallible, and even the astrologers have seen in the stars the murder that you have done upon your father."

"But Majesty!" the man pleaded. "Father's gun go off by himself. He was not knowing musket. First time he kill Eid goat, second he looked down barrel and kill himself. Everyone see." In the first instance, the barrel-heavy musket had pointed itself down to the floor and shot the tethered goat. In the second, the inexperienced old man had placed the butt of the loaded rifle down, and the weapon had fired, blowing off most of the old man's head.

"You have witnesses?" questioned the emperor, disappointed that his verdict might be overturned.

"Mother only," Jamaal said, crestfallen.

"There was no one else? There were no men?" asked Jahangir. The man shook his head sorrowfully. Jahangir was relieved. It was God's will that a crime so heinous be punished.

"Then how can I help you? You know what the law requires. There must be *two* women to bear witness. If only you had a male witness or another woman," said the emperor with false sympathy. He looked to his amirs for affirmation. Mutid Khan, his cousin, clanked his spurs drunkenly on the floor.

"Yes, that is Sharia, Majesty," drawled another amir.

"But Mother see," said the poor man, shaking violently at the thought of what was about to befall him.

"Please, Majesty, please!" the accused cried. He wet himself, creating a puddle on the floor.

The bemused emperor turned to his nobles.

"You see now why my revered father insisted the floors be made of marble?" he said, grinning. The amirs howled and stomped their boots.

Jahangir snapped his fingers. "Come, take the prisoner," he ordered.

The guards grasped Jamaal roughly by the arms and brought him to the doorway, where he braced himself against the arched frame and screamed over his shoulder,

"Please, I have done nothing! I swear to Allah!"

Mutid, suddenly incensed at the blasphemy, ran to the prisoner, and kicked him in the side. His brother Ahmed thwacked Jamaal hard on the back with his steel scabbard as the guards plucked him from the doorway and flung him headlong down the granite steps.

The nobles moved to the balcony to see a gray jumbo stroll toward them with undulating shoulders and a trunk that swung from side to side. His giant ears waved like flags, spotted pink at the bottoms.

Jamaal was dragged in leg irons beneath the blue sky and stood bent with a hand pressed where blood seeped through his checkered headcloth. He looked about suspiciously, trying to focus his eyes as the guards hooked his chains to the elephant's leg bands. Jahangir smiled at his lords and lowered his hand. The mahout dug in with his prod, and the elephant lurched forward. Jamaal's feet were pulled from under him. He landed on his buttocks with a surprised expression. The emperor guffawed, and the zanana women, at their own balcony, gave fluttering applause.

"Now you shall have your show!" Jahangir said.

"Poor devil," his cousin Mutid said, sober now and apologetic for having kicked Jamaal. He turned away from the courtyard.

"A man who has killed his father is a devil only. There is nothing to pity about him," the emperor said. "Even the harem women are pleased. Why do you go on so? Only Allah can know your mind, Mutid," he said with disgust and turned back to the pleasures of the courtyard. He took an especially long pull on his huqqah and cast his cousin out of his thoughts.

Tradesmen, servants, and low-caste Hindus stood quietly at the courtyard's edges. The elephant progressed with Jamaal bumping over the stones. As the elephant picked up speed, Jamaal's shalwar was stripped from his body, and his skin was scraped raw and bled. The more Jamaal screamed, the more the nobility cheered. When Jamaal could no longer tolerate riding on his bottom, he turned on his side and held his genitals. The women tittered decorously; many of them were drunk and smoking afim.

Jamaal Udeen's side was so abraded by the rough stones that his hipbone showed white under the torn red flesh. Screaming, he went unconscious. He rode, murmuring, on his back until he died. His lifeless head bounced on the pavement, making dull, meaty thuds as the elephant galloped on to the stables at the end of the huge quadrangle. The wild shouts and drunken applause of the nobles made emphatic the stunned silence of the ordinary people who stood at the courtyard's ends, shrinking from the horrific spectacle.

Jamaal's blood had not yet dried on the courtyard stones when two dignified men dressed in identical blue-striped robes and black turbans appeared. They walked across the quadrangle to bow beneath Jahangir's balcony and stand at a bloodstained block as old as Agra Fort itself. They were the executioners, and here they would do their work. By the emperor's decree, convicted murderers were subject to a spectacular form of execution: their heads were to be crushed beneath the foot of a royal elephant.

There were three men destined for killing. All three were members of the murderous sect of highway robbers and stranglers known as Thugs. For years they had terrorized the countryside. They had avoided capture by the simple expedient of murdering their prey. Miraculously, one of their victims had survived. He was a soldier in Jahangir's service who had been strangled by a party of marauding Thugs who had thrown him into a deep well and left him for dead. The shock of the cold water had revived him, and he had inched up the irregular stones of the well's wall and crawled to safety at his barracks at Agra Fort. In a matter of days, the murderers were put under arrest. After a speedy trial, handbills announcing their execution had been distributed throughout the countryside. A great crowd had gathered in the courtyard to watch the Thugs meet their end.

While the elephant that had dragged Jamaal Udeen rested in his stable, a fresh elephant went into service. This animal was more compactly built, and much more powerful in the legs. In its early adulthood, its tusks had been sawed off, shifting muscular development from the neck to the legs, where the weight of the elephant's head was now borne. It was a creature bred to its task: cracking the steel-hard shell of the human cranium.

The crowd swirled around this new elephant where it stood at the stone block under the control of a mahout who was adept at this form of execution. Three prisoners, single file and in chains, were escorted out from a slit in the fortress wall. As they were led to the block, a band began to play a raucous tune. The first of the three was a determined-looking man with walrus mustaches. His eyes burnt fiercely under the dark skin of his brow. The men in striped robes went to his chains and disengaged him from the file with a large iron key. They led the Thug to the stone block and together pushed his stomach to the ground. Then, with a smooth motion, they grasped his biceps, flung him forward, and held his head to the block. The elephant waited. The prisoner was bare-chested and barefooted. His only garment was a *longhi*, speckled with the dried blood of previous executions.

Above him, the mahout sat on the elephant's neck with one arm stretching into the air behind him for balance while he bent perilously over the elephant's head and peered down with great concentration. As his animal's foot rested on the screaming criminal's head, he whispered to his mount to give the slow, steady pressure necessary to crack its tough structure. Within a few moments, the head burst, and strands of shining, viscous red splattered the pavement. Lazily, the elephant's foot retracted, and his head and trunk lifted as if to look at the emperor. The men in striped robes picked up the body and threw it aside while the orchestra bellowed, and the emperor's window answered with applause and drunken shouting.

Then the next Thug, a young man, was dragged by his chains to the block. He, the most vicious of the lot, turned and spat on his executioners. An army man rushed to strike his head with a club, and the group of them pushed him to the granite. They held his head under the elephant's foot until it burst. And the band squawked a chorus as the third man went to the block.

CHAPTER 17

1612

A CANNON BOOMED OVER THE River Yamuna. Agra, a city bigger than London, was disgorging its population. More cannon fired. The city's governor had heard from the Europeans that the noise would disperse the rats, thought to be the source of the disease.

At first, they were not sure in Agra that it was the bubonic plague. This was the first attack the city had ever experienced. A week later, hundreds, then thousands of people fell ill with fever and diarrhea. Armpits and groins had swollen with buboes gorged with blood. Some people in a matter of hours were dead. It was now clear that this was, indeed, the plague, and panic spread.

The rats themselves had gone mad, running in circles and battering their heads against walls in their agonies. In every bazaar, hordes of diseased rats ran the narrow lanes. Entire neighborhoods had fled from the insane rodents and from the dying humans spitting blood.

Despite the chanting and lamentation, no attempt was made in the poor Hindu districts to burn the deceased. Only the white-robed and garlanded bodies of the wealthy were shouldered to the Yamuna's blazing pyres.

Muslim corpses were washed, wrapped in white sheets, and piled on bullock carts to be transported to graves on the outskirts, where they were buried in pine boxes. As fear increased, workers to perform these duties could no longer be found, nor could the governor find officials to direct them. Even the corpses of the rich were now left to putrefy on the city streets. The most afflicted parts of Agra were set afire in the mistaken belief that the flames would stop the spread of the disease.

Carts drawn by camels, bullocks, and horses and packed with the artifacts of thousands of families crowded the Great Trunk Road in a headlong escape from the deathly city.

The emperor and his queen were cooling themselves beside a fountain in their garden at Ajmer when news of the plague arrived. They had been preparing to leave for the capital.

"My Lord, Agra reels from contagion. Let us instead follow the army to the Deccan," said Nur Jahan.

"This report is staggering," said Jahangir, putting down the scroll, "People are perishing by the thousands, and medicine can do nothing. By all means, we shall avoid that dread city."

"The army will take us south."

"If we go, I will lead the army, not follow it," said Jahangir with irritation. Parviz's army had been thwarted in the Deccan and he had had to be recalled, for Jahangir was intent on conquering those southern lands.

"I had Sultan Khurram in mind to command," said Nur Jahan. "He is young but by nature a soldier; that is plain."

"But he is untried," Jahangir countered. "I will lead."

"You are now past 40, an age when an honored warrior retires and passes responsibility to his sons. Parviz has failed, but Khurram will not. What if you were killed? How would the empire fare without your auspicious presence?"

"A tragedy, but the earth will still turn," Jahangir said.

"What of me, then?" asked Nur Jahan. "When you are gone, blind Khusro will rule. I am not in his favor. You know of our differences. The question will then be will he kill or banish me?"

The image of the mad Khusro with his graying, waist-length beard sitting on the Mughal throne made Jahangir shudder. And the thought of Khusro harming his wife made him furious.

"Enough, enough!" cried the emperor, holding his palms to his temples, "Khurram will lead our armies to the Deccan." And the queen smiled demurely.

The sun had barely risen. On the outskirts of Ajmer, the nobles stood in a long rank beside their horses. The wind that blew down from the mountains set their animals shivering and shifting restlessly. They were waiting for the emperor. No noble dared sit on his saddle until the emperor had climbed into his carriage and signaled them to mount. Around them banners waved on newly planted poles. Caissons wheeled, infantry marched, and officers shouted orders as the gigantic machinery of a Mughal advance assembled.

Khurram's cavalry had left while it was still dark. They could proceed at a far faster rate than the movement of the emperor's ponderous entourage would allow. They would provide the advance guard until the next encampment.

Because the emperor was headed south, custom demanded that he travel in a carriage and that it be drawn by bullocks. If traveling east, he would have mounted an elephant with long tusks; if west, a horse; to the north, a palanquin. In this case, to pull Roe's magnificent carriage, Jahangir had instead substituted the bullocks with four fine horses. The coach, as Roe had promised, was attended by an Englishman in a gold and black costume very much like King James's livery—a theatrical touch that tickled the Mughal emperor. As soon as the emperor had entered his carriage, his nobles mounted their horses, and the entire cavalry mobilized. Trumpets sounded, and drums beat. The infantry raised their lances and marched, shouting their songs into the wind.

Before the king went mounted scouts and skirmishers, clearing the army's path. Then rolled the bronze cannon, then the camels and elephants. The strutting horse of the emperor's guard went next flying the white yak-tail standard. A line of drummers beating a dignified cadence marched before the commander-emperor in his English coach.

As the procession left Ajmer, both sides of the highway were crowded with the ragged poor wishing the emperor good health and beseeching him for alms. Jahangir shouted an order from the coach. "Keep from my sight defective people. I do not wish to encounter the leprous and the maimed. The blind and the sick also must not be seen." The order went out at once, and the parading infantrymen used their lance points to drive such people away from the roadside.

Immediately behind Jahangir went the cavalry. War elephants were next, dressed in chain mail, tusks fitted with enormous sabers. Hundreds of mounted archers followed, and behind them marched the rear guard of the infantry with their bright pennants raised to the sun.

At a half mile to the rear of the army went the royal harem in all its glory. Preceding it were mounted eunuchs and servants on foot carrying stout bamboo sticks to beat down any peasant or beggar who might straggle the road. Then came slaves suppressing the dust along the path with scented water flung from copper pots. Other slaves whisked away flies with bundles of peacock feathers. Others still, swung bronze censers of powerful incense against the stench of the road. Afterward came Nur Jahan sitting in a reproduction of Roe's coach with native coachmen in garments copied from the uniform of Jahangir's Englishman. Close by were mounted eunuchs in brilliant uniforms and armed female guards on horseback.

On and on it went. Hundreds of lower-status women journeyed upon palanquins hung between camels or small elephants. Women of rank enclosed in howdahs looked down haughtily at the dust and squalor of the roadside, where beggars in filthy rags gestured for food with bunched fingertips aimed at the mouth.

CHAPTER 18

TWO INDIAN SAILORS ON THE dock at Surat in Gujarat province: "It is the queen's ship!"

"How so?"

"See by the sail? They call it the grandest in the world. It returns from the *Haj* after so many years."

"The *Rahimi*?"

"Yes. It now returns."

The gigantic ship had just appeared across the bay. The *Rahimi* was now entering what were technically Portuguese waters. It had been gone for two years. On her decks and below were 1,500 pilgrims who had made the Haj to Mecca.

Bucking in a chop and with a giant puff of smoke, a Portuguese man-o'-war let loose a shot across the *Rahimi*'s bows. Another shot flashed from a shore battery hidden among the palms. A hole was rent in the *Rahimi*'s massive canvas. Astonishingly, the queen mother's ship was under attack from the Portuguese. In a few minutes, a white flag fluttered from the topmast of the unarmed ship. Heedless of the flag, another shot broke through the *Rahimi*'s hull, and a fire broke out below decks. Flames now lapped at the mizzen. A singing shot assailed the bow; another splintered the mainmast, which toppled like a felled tree. Pilgrims leaped one by one, and whole families jumped together, screaming, into the choppy sea. Then suddenly, like a passing squall, the assault was over.

It was now apparent that all the Indian ships in the harbor and along the river had been set afire. Flames flew from mast to mast, garnishing the riverside with a fiery necklace. Row upon row of the vessels bobbing at the Tapti shore crackled in flame under the Portuguese torch.

"Come, let us see what we can do," said one of the sailors. The two men scrambled in the shifting firelight, anxious not to miss an opportunity to loot.

CHAPTER 19

1613

THE QUEEN DARTED FROM THE stifling mahal into the dark night and sliced into the water of the bathing tank.

"Your Majesty!" cried her lady-in-waiting.

"Never you mind, Halima. Go about your business."

Nonetheless, in a few minutes, Halima and a half-dozen slave girls rushed from the brightly lit chamber into the dark garden carrying towels, robes, and articles of toilet. A rash of silver stars had spread across the sky, and the moon's crescent crinkled on the tank's surface. The queen swam on her back, parting the water with long, languid strokes.

"Really, you mustn't bother with me," said Nur Jahan to the servants, who were keeping pace with her, running alongside the pool. The queen dreaded that at the snap of Halima's fingers, the dark garden that was her sanctuary would blaze with a dozen torches.

The air was still and smelled of frangipani and lemon blossoms. A pair of sentinel torches hissed at the garden's outer gates, and tiny lanterns winked among the garden's boughs. A yellow monkey and a nightingale's silver could be made out among the black palms and mango trees. The night pulsed with the rasp of crickets.

"Madam, I've been looking for you everywhere." This was the voice of the head eunuch and could not be ignored. Hoshiyar Khan's elegant figure came into the garden, framed in the arch of light cast by the mahal chamber.

"Yes, Hoshiyar sahib," said Nur Jahan in a hopeless tone but continued swimming in a breast stroke in the direction of his voice. "What now?"

"The queen mother's ship has been burnt, Majesty," he said, rushing up to the tank and sighting her face to face.

"Burnt?"

"The Portuguese! Every Indian ship in the harbor at Surat has been torched. Please hurry."

Inside the harem, Jahangir lay on his divan. The bamboo tube in which the dispatch had arrived had been allowed to drop to the floor. He held the letter precariously between his thumb and forefinger.

"A runner has arrived with this," said Jahangir, waving the scroll. Nur Jahan stepped before him with a towel draped around her damp chemise. Another towel was wound on her head in a makeshift turban. Halima worked Her Majesty's shoulders with energetic fingers while Nur took the dispatch into her hands. The chief eunuch stood by with an expression of concern.

"One hundred nineteen of our ships up in smoke!" she said.

"Hundreds were drowned," added the emperor, lapsing into an opium swoon.

"How shall we answer this?" she demanded.

"How indeed? We have no navy," replied the emperor.

"The English!" she exclaimed with a sudden inspiration. Then, addressing Hoshiyar, she commanded, "Send for the Inglis Khan."

"Tonight?"

"I will speak with him now."

Two hours later, Sir Thomas Roe, the English ambassador, who had just arrived in Hindustan, stood in his buckled shoes before the emperor, making his reverences. Nur Jahan listened behind a purdah screen of filigreed marble. After Roe had finished his speech and swooped his feathered hat in a respectful flourish, Nur Jahan spoke from behind the screen.

"I will get right to the point. The Portuguese have burnt our ships at Surat. It is impossible not to respond."

"They have put my mother's ship to the torch as well. Hundreds of pilgrims were forced from her decks," said the emperor. "This is arrogance beyond endurance." Jahangir had already issued a farman condemning the Portuguese and forbidding commerce with them.

"Your vessels at Surat can help," Nur Jahan said.

"The English king has long wanted to be of use to the empire," Roe declared with a smile.

In any negotiation with a male, the law of purdah placed the queen at an advantage. Nur Jahan could see her interlocutor while at the same time he was not allowed to look upon the queen. She could see the look of anticipation on Roe's face. She knew she could get whatever she wanted from him.

"We shall require the assistance of the English fleet," said the queen.

"Upon my word, our vessels shall deliver you from the Portuguese. But there must be a *quid pro quo,* Majesty."

"Be moderate in what you propose. It is, after all, your presence at Surat that has inspired the Portuguese," said Nur Jahan, seeking the best bargaining position. It was clear to Nur Jahan that the Portuguese were fearful of the English initiatives in the Arabian Sea. They had sought to intimidate Jahangir into banning the English by burning Indian ships.

"Our requests are modest, Majesty: exclusive rights for the indigo and cotton trade, unrestricted use of the port at Surat, and a waiver of embargoes on English goods."

"Modest!" cried Nur Jahan, laughing ironically behind her purdah screen. But then she thought: *what harm could come from granting these requests? The emperor had already condemned the Portuguese and would no longer do business with them. England would fill the vacuum.*

"You are to protect our ships to Mecca," the queen said. Transporting pilgrims to Mecca was a hugely profitable business for both the queen and the queen mother.

"Accepted," said Roe.

"And the Portuguese right of Cadiz must end."

"Accepted, madam."

Ships sailing the Indian Ocean were compelled to call at a Portuguese port, describe their destination, and pay duty on their cargo. In return they received a *Cadiz*, literally a card, which insured their safe passage through Portuguese waters. The Cadiz, stamped with a representation of Jesus and the Virgin Mary, was disturbing to Muslims, and only resentfully did they accept it. If a ship was found not to have the Cadiz, it was seized and burned by the Portuguese authorities. In the case of the *Rahimi* and the other ships in the Bay of Cambay, false accusations concerning the absence of the Cadiz were used to justify the attacks.

The queen's last stipulation amounted to allowing the English the freedom of the Arabian Sea and denying the Portuguese their ports at Goa, Gujarat and Kerala. It was a call for an offensive against Portugal. How else could the right of Cadiz be revoked? For the time being, the English forces were not strong enough to challenge the Portuguese fortresses at their home port of Goa. However, Roe was confident that English supremacy on the high seas would soon be demonstrated.

Jahangir had requested "a comely personage," and King James had sent him Sir Thomas Roe. The previous two ambassadors, Hawkins and Best, were rough sea captains with semiofficial status. Roe was both fully credentialed and a gentleman of noble birth. He was an official of the East India Company as well.

An ambassadorship to India was looked upon in England both as a grand adventure and a posting of dire hardship. Roe was just the man to fill the job. He had a few years earlier sailed the perilous coast of South America in a trading scheme that had failed but had given him a taste for both commerce and foreign adventure.

He was an elegant man, nephew to London's lord mayor. He had been esquire to the body of Queen Elizabeth and personified the English notion of the perfect courtier, a notion lost on the Mughal court, which had no idea of the quality of the English court or of England's high stature among its European peers. The Mughal conception of Europe and Europeans had been formed mainly by their contact with the bristly Portuguese, who had taken control of most of the ports of the west coast of the subcontinent.

Roe had landed at Surat in 1616 under the scrutiny of the resident governor, who insisted that all incoming cargo, including personal belongings, be searched. "This is an affront to the English crown," Roe had exclaimed, standing on the foredeck of the *Lion.* "I will allow no such thing."

"We are in stalemate, then, sahib. No *farangi* goods can be unloaded without searching," said the customs official through an interpreter. He was a short man with a dark, scowling face, who kept his distance. He was disgusted by the doughy-faced Europeans and their foul odor. He looked at Roe's white skin, mindful of the Indian notion that it indicated leprosy. He was relieved that the English had made a to-do about the searching. He could depart without further contact.

"Then I must take my leave, sahib. No progress is to be made here."

"Fare thee well," said Roe, turning up his nose. He felt no love for the Indians, whom he considered savages.

"Khuda hafiz," said the customs agent as his two men started down the starboard ladder. A lone oarsman aboard the customs tender paddled to keep it steady with the incoming tide. One by one, they dropped catlike from the rope ladder and thumped with naked feet onto the little boat that was rising and lowering on the swells. Only a small breeze was blowing, and the sun was extreme. Roe, on his foredeck, was wilting in his English clothes.

The *Lion* had dropped anchor thirty hours ago and floated in a line with three other English ships at the estuary of the Tapti River. The six mouths of the *Lion*'s cannon gaped at the town, along with the cannon of the other English ships. It was this artillery that prevented the port authorities from arbitrarily seizing the convoy's cargo. Except in the case of the Portuguese, this was usually done with incoming ships under a foreign flag. Goods confiscated could only be redeemed by payment of bribes to the port's governor.

Roe, sweating in ruff collar and heavy doublet, was conferring with the ship's captain. The Indian customs officials were being rowed back to shore, riding with the tide.

"This is a beastly place, Keeling," said Roe, looking at the shore and wiping his brow with a white handkerchief.

"Aye, Sir Thomas. I've half a mind to let go with the cannon," said the captain, William Keeling. He waved a stiff scrap of canvas to cool his drink-mottled face.

"I pray God that you could, Captain," said Roe as he considered the wooden walls of the customs shed and the customs vessel heaving on the wave. "Damn you," he cried, and in case the retreating heathens hadn't heard him, he shouted, "Damn you again!"

He leaned against the smooth skin of the mainmast in utter perplexity. He had come halfway around the world—eight months at sea—only to be treated like the down-at-the-heels citizen of some puissant nation. In their arrogance, they had refused even to accept his bona fides as King James's representative.

Sweat ran down Roe's face. His once starched and pleated collar lay in a limp ring about his shoulders. His breeches were wet with perspiration, and his narrow boots had become purgatories for his swollen feet. He had kept his broad-brimmed hat shading his head, but now flung it down to the deck with a furious "damn it all!" as he watched the customs boat tie up at the jetty.

———

A day later, when Roe had regained his composure, he sent off a letter to the port's governor demanding due deference. He was, after all, Sir Thomas wrote, "the official representative of an important European power." Could not the governor see how the English navy would counter the Portuguese? And the emperor himself had encouraged his embassy, he emphasized. After a week of petitioning, the governor relented, and the English were allowed to land their goods and baggage unmolested.

There was much Sir Thomas had to do in Surat. Paramount, was the opening of the city's first East India Company factory, a warehouse where goods would be kept for transshipment to and from India. He had also the task of establishing himself as the true chief company official in India. He had found that there was a rival claimant who had to be suppressed by force.

When all this was done, Roe took a deep breath and was ready to press on to meet the emperor. His chief business in India, his mandate from the company, was to gain exclusive trading rights from "the Great Mogor."

"Assalaamu 'Alaikum," said Abdur Rahim, Jahangir's chief vizier. He greeted Roe in Bhurhanpur at a bend in the River Tapti. Beneath the pier where Rahim stood, the river flowed in a sluggish brown stream. The baking heat of summer had come, and the vizier was shaded under an embroidered parasol held by a slave. High on a hill above him, the fortress ramparts curved, and a white palace shimmered in its garden of fruit trees and glossy palms.

Roe and fifty of his men had journeyed up the river from Surat on hired barges. The trip had taken nearly two weeks, and Roe was anxious to meet the king.

"Alas, sahib, the emperor now resides in Ajmer," said the vizier. He spoke in Persian, which Roe knew well. Roe's barges had been tied to the dock. In the shade of Rahim's umbrellas, servants brought Roe and his chaplain red lacquer chairs to sit upon and silver goblets of sherbet to slake their thirst.

Still hot and tired after he had assumed his seat but poised with his legs elegantly crossed, Roe could only smile at the futility of his visit. His long face with its aristocratic nose terminated in a manicured goatee. His wide, intelligent eyes contemplated the vizier. Abdur Rahim was an old, brown, handsome man almost as tall as Roe. He wore a purple turban and a simple white robe made distinctive by a ruby pin at his heart.

Abdur Rahim wondered at the English and why they endured the burden of clothing designed for a different clime. *Foolish and vain*, he wrote in his mental notes.

"When will His Majesty return?" Roe asked. He put a spoonful of the ice into his month. He had never tasted anything quite like this rose-flavored sherbet, and he spooned it as greedily as dignity would allow. He licked his lips when he finished.

"After Ajmer, the emperor goes to Mandu. But do not despair, sahib. I welcome you on behalf of Prince Parviz, the emperor's second son."

"I have heard much of the prince and his magnificent court," Roe lied, still smiling.

"Tomorrow you will appear at the court, but you will come now to the hammam."

For a moment, Roe thought that the vizier had meant harem, and he smiled. "Hamman? I'm afraid, sir, I don't know..."

"A bath, sahib, then the Akbari Sarai for the night." Again, he was confused. Did the vizier mean seraglio? Roe startled his chaplain, John Hall, when he translated this thought. Roe looked quizzically at the grand vizier.

"You will see," said Abdur.

Everything had been arranged. Sir Thomas and the chaplain were hauled up the hill and sheltered from the sun, each in his own curtained palki. Preceding them was the vizier's own palanquin.

The caravan wound up a twisting road through brown grass and stunted bushes scorching under the summer sky. Following them came the troop of English soldiers covered in dust, clumsily hiking the rocky path and roasting in the thick red wool of their uniforms.

At the summit of the hill, the procession stopped before an impressive building. Roe thought it might be the palace and was astonished when informed that it was only the Akbari Sarai of which he had been told—a way station built by Akbar for travelers. The gateway was made of red brick inlaid with marble in the style of the tombs he had seen back in Agra. Passing through its portal were a line of camels laden with goods. Then a work elephant under a red painted howdah struggled to get by. Men in multicolored turbans and a variety of tribal robes went unceasingly through on foot, on donkeys covered with dust, and on horses whose flanks glistened with sweat. At both sides of the gateway, a farmer's bazaar of lean-to tents rested against the Sarai's brick wall.

The vizier swung out nimbly from his palki and walked over to Roe. "We are here, sahib. My servants will take you within. Inshallah, I will see you this evening," shouted the vizier above the din of vendors, clattering hooves, and beggars competing for alms.

"My deepest thanks. Until then, my dear Abdur," said Roe, who had risen from his litter and was bowing in his incongruous garments while the dust of the road swirled around him. Hall too, in his dark singlet, black breeches, and high-heeled shoes, rose, bowed, and swung his buckled cleric's hat in an arc before him. The ambling crowd of men in longhis and shalwar chemise halted and looked with surprise and curiosity. Women in saris and even those in the black robes and veils of deepest purdah gathered to gape at the spectacle of the pallid Europeans and their odd clothing.

The hammam was a large domed room inscribed with geometric patterns in scarlet and gold. The ceiling's dome was pierced with a half-dozen naked holes the size of barrel heads. Shafts of sunlight struck through, flushing the bath with golden light and candles flickered in brass fixtures hung from the smooth marble arches. The bath itself was long and wide with the capability of accommodating one hundred people, although now Roe and his chaplain were alone. The English soldiers were splashing, pale and naked, in a mountain stream at the back of the Sarai.

"Ah, the opulent East," said Roe, taking in the marble room. It was his first encounter with luxury in India, and he accepted it enthusiastically. Two slave women approached with towels and signaled for the white men's clothing. Hall blushed.

"Hall, when in Rome," said Roe with great sangfroid, gathering his face into a smile and stripping down with dignity.

"Sir Thomas!"

"Really, you must overcome your bashfulness. These women mean your soul no harm," said Roe, the sophisticated veteran of King James's bawdy court.

"I refuse to disrobe before women no matter what their intention."

"Then I must order you to do so. I will not jeopardize this entire mission because of your obdurate priggishness."

"Then God will be your judge!" cried Hall.

"He is in all things. Off!" Roe ordered.

Deeply embarrassed, Hall had no recourse but to comply. He turned with his back to the women and began to strip. Removing each particle of clothing as if he were pulling a hair from his head. When he had taken off the final linen, he faced the slaves and reached, red-faced and knock-kneed, for a Turkish towel. He wrapped his lower self and jumped impetuously into the pool.

"Well done, sir. You do England proud!" shouted Sir Thomas. His uproarious laughter and the tinkling giggle of the female slaves mingled and echoed in the huge hall.

Now, made defiant by the jocularity, Hall let go of his towel and started to splash around in the bath like a great blond bear. This brought still more laughter from the women. A cocked eyebrow and an imperious look from Sir Thomas was enough to silence them and send them on their way, hiding their smiles behind their hands.

"Hall?" inquired Sir Thomas with a smile.

"Almighty God has preserved me from infamy," the chaplain said, now in possession once again of his dignity and skimming along the surface with neat, deft strokes.

"Yes, praise the Lord, the crown jewels have gone unremarked," said Roe, laughing.

Hall buried his face beneath the water and swam to the furthest end of the bath. He surfaced, shaking his tow head, and said, "And I will not be undone by thee or the heathen. I am a Christian." But in a moment, he turned his thick-muscled frame over and floated on the surface, spouting like a whale. When he heard Roe's roaring laughter, he too laughed, gurgling and spitting water.

"Methinks you've found a home here, Christian," cried Roe.

"Not here, sir. Never here. But when will we eat?" Hall shouted, his laugh echoing in the empty hall.

And eat they did. A banquet was spread on a thick cloth in the grand hall of the Sarai. Thirty dishes were laid. Meats roasted and stewed. Curries of vegetables and river fish. Waterfowl and wild fowl from the forest, all washed down with the tart wine of the countryside. Afterward there were mangoes (which the Englishmen had never tasted and marveled at), peaches, apricots, plums, and fragrant melons. Dates and spiced tea were brought. Presently, the air became sweet with burning opium and hashish. In honor of the farangi, the pipes were loaded with tobacco as well, although Jahangir had banned this substance only months earlier. Rahim presented dancing girls, who filled the hall with perfume and trailing veils, and suddenly the room resounded with thudding tabla and the clashing of cymbals.

"The grand vizier has thought of everything," said Roe. "Even women."

"Women especially must you desire after your long voyage, Sir Thomas. They are at your service . . . and you also, Father Hall, sahib," said Rahim, using the form of address that he had learned from the Jesuits. Hall's eyes were red with hashish, which Roe had tricked him into smoking, calling it a form of tobacco that would be impolite to refuse. Hall grinned stupidly at the vizier. He drew deeply on the snake of his huqqah. Then, as if licensed by the vizier's hospitality, the chaplain rose to take the hand of a whirling nautch girl whose dark eyes had flashed at him from behind the wisp of her veil.

Sir Thomas's private suite at the Akbari Sarai was sumptuous: a long, open room with a smaller room on each side furnished with comfortable divans. The apartment stood in a corner just above the battlements. The window, arched and cusped, framed a view of the moonlit Tapti flickering beneath the black leaves of the forest. The apartment smelled of incense mingled with the subtle odor of roses.

Hall came into the rooms humming a North Country air. A red striped turban covered his head. The circle of his ruff collar still bloomed over his tunic, but Hall's dancing girl had enlivened it with a bridegroom's wreath of hyacinth. Hall sang as he removed his collar and singlet and let the fragrant necklace lie over the curled blond hairs of his chest. Hall's woman bowed to bring her brow to the back of his hand and to touch his feet with her delicate fingers. She lit incense in a silver censer and cast her kohl-lined eyes upward.

When Hall bent and swept her up, she cried out joyfully in her sweet voice, and her sari swooshed to perfume the air. What the future would bring, Hall could not imagine, but he knew that for the first time in his life, he was tasting happiness.

At dawn, the Englishmen arose to the sound of bugles. Hall's lady had left for home an hour earlier.

Outside the Sarai, the English soldiers stood in the dust beside an elephant sent to take Roe to the palace. Roe and Hall took their places in the howdah and looked down. It was the first time either man had been upon an elephant or had ridden so high above the ground.

"I believe I shall never leave this country, my lord," said Hall, glancing at his superior.

"Me, I shall be only too happy to leave," said Roe. "But you surprise me, my friend. I have never seen a more rapid conversion. What has happened? Are you no longer a Christian?"

Hall smiled but did not answer.

"Ah, it is that woman. You are smitten. But surely you know that such encounters are not to be taken seriously."

"Forgive me, Sir Thomas. I am wise enough to know what matters and what does not."

"Then you are in love?"

"Let us say that I have crossed a threshold."

"And let me say, my dear Hall, that I find this rocking highly disagreeable," said Roe diplomatically changing the subject. He looked up the dusty road over the mahout's shoulder. Past his marching soldiers, he could see the tulip domes of Parviz's white palace.

"Yonder lies our destination. Thank goodness," said Roe, pointing. "Much more of this ride and I should be sick."

Parviz met Roe and Hall in the hall of private audience while the morning was still cool, and he was relatively sober. The space was open to the air and the morning songs of the birds in the surrounding garden. It was a colonnaded marble extension to the palace, open on three sides. At the fourth, which was the wall of the palace itself, the prince sat at his throne and received the ambassador. Mahabat Khan, on leave from the emperor and curious to meet the farangi, stood at his side.

Parviz's Persian was fluent. He said, "Welcome," after the Englishman had bowed in the European manner.

"I'm honored to meet the voyager from . . . where is it?'" Parviz said to rob the English diplomat of his self-importance. A turban of gold Gujarati cloth set with diamonds crowned Parviz's head. His tunic matched his throne in the number of glistening jewels.

"England, sire," said Roe with suppressed anger.

Sensing his irritation, the prince pressed on and said, "Ah yes, but I see that you are unwilling to make the customary obeisance's to the court."

"Not even before God does an Englishman prostrate himself," said Roe haughtily, expanding his chest. Hall distended his as well and grimaced.

"The English, then, must be an important people," declared Mahabat, amused at the Englishmen's self-assurance. "What makes them so?"

After thinking a while, Roe cried, "Whiskey!" with a great blustering laugh. He had been informed of the prince's drinking, and he wished to take the edge off the conversation.

"And what might this 'whiskey' be?" Parviz asked, enjoying himself. He had of course known of whiskey and especially had indulged in the distilled spirits of the Portuguese and the rough-edged *arrack* of his own country.

"I have some bottles here for His Majesty," Roe replied, gesturing toward the four cases his men had piled on the marble floor.

"Then step forward, wily Englishmen. You know of my affection for bottles," said Parviz, chuckling. He was beginning to like this farangi.

"A disposition I myself cannot help but share," said Roe affably. Two of the prince's servants were dispatched to take up a case to the throne. The prince clapped hands for cups, and the Englishmen were motioned forward to the prince.

"Interesting bouquet," said Parviz, sniffing at the scotch he swirled in his jade goblet. Mahabat considered his goblet suspiciously and made a face.

"Before you sip, may I suggest just a bit of water? It brings out the flavor," said Roe. But Parviz did not listen and took a big gulp. Mahabat did as well.

"Ya Allah! I have never tasted anything so harsh," croaked Parviz, sputtering and spitting out the whiskey. Mahabat's face was a mask of displeasure, but he bore up stoically.

"I must again aver, most mighty prince, that water will improve it," said Roe, a bit disconcerted. "Allow me the privilege of preparing His Majesty's beverage." Roe motioned respectfully for the prince's and the general's goblets.

"A touch of water only," said Parviz. The corners of the prince's mouth were downturned. His nostrils quivered; his head shook disapprovingly. Roe was rightly concerned that this despot might turn vengeful.

"A touch is what is required," said Roe and floated a thimbleful of water on the clear gold of the highland whiskey. "Now, sip slowly, Prince, to get the effect. General, allow me," said Roe and dripped a bit of water into Mahabat's cup as well.

"Smoother, but still it tastes like medicine," said Parviz, turning up his nose.

"Drink it down, then, my lord. It gets better with the drinking."

After the prince had drunk his cup of malt, he called for another to continue the experiment. "Improving," said the prince as the whiskey burnt a path to his stomach. He liked that this drink could accomplish in one cup the euphoria wrought by an entire bottle of wine without the harshness of arrack or the cloying perfume of Portuguese brandy. Mahabat was not at all impressed with the taste of the whiskey but approved the giddiness it had induced.

By the fourth drink, the prince had become acclimated, by the fifth he became an aficionado, and with the sixth a partisan.

"Now let us praise England and drink to the health of our King James," Parviz said, clicking his cup to Roe's and to Hall's and Mahabat's. "And to you, my dear ambassador, my deepest thanks."

In an hour, they had finished two bottles.

"Whatever you wish, if it is in my power, you shall receive," said Parviz, clambering off his throne. "My dear Mahabat," commanded Parviz. His eyes rolled in his head, showing the whites, and tragicomically, he stumbled and nearly fell, knocking his turban askew. "I shall hold you responsible for serving the noble ambassador," Parviz drawled thickly in Persian. His servants took his arms and dragged him to his palanquin.

Roe had reached that stage of drunkenness where thinking becomes crystal clear. Parviz had moved well beyond this for he had done most of the drinking and now needed to be loaded into a palanquin and carried to his apartment for a nap.

"Trade concessions for the English, Your Majesty!" Roe shouted with his hand cupped vulgarly around his mouth as four young eunuchs, whose bare feet slapped the marble pavement like empty gloves, carted the prince away.

"As you wish, Sir Thomas," said Parviz, waving feebly from his palki. Then with a sudden burst of drunken energy, he looked forcefully at his grand vizier and wagged a finger. "Abdur, take note!" before collapsing into his pillows.

After Roe had departed, Nur Jahan remained behind the purdah screen. She would use the English, but she had second thoughts about granting them trade rights. That would be an infringement of imperial prerogatives. In any case, of what importance was this nation of penny-pinching merchants who presented the emperor such insignificant gifts? The Portuguese called the English king a fisherman! The English were constantly asking for concessions, but what goods had they? Although Nur Jahan had imported English novelties on her own ships and had made important profits, few of the English goods were of any general use. English cloth was too heavy for the Indian climate, and most of the English manufactures were produced here at home at a cheaper price. Only English luxury items had any value to Indians, and those were coveted mainly by the rich zanana women and the women of the aristocracy.

Nur would allow these Christians to harass one another. That would bring about a balance along the west coast without troubling the empire, she mused. She smiled as she thought of her sagacity and walked around the screen to Jahangir's divan.

"The English will be useful," she said.

"I am not fond of the sea," said Jahangir, his eyelids drooping.

"My lord, do not forget my trade with Mecca."

"Yes, yes, I will not, and I do not forget the hats," said the emperor, smiling lightly. "I am aware that your ladies admire those farangi hunting bonnets."

"And Roe has given you an English coach, which much pleases me," said Nur Jahan. "That I *do* admire."

"At last, a suitable gift from that insignificant king," said Jahangir. "He has given me an English coachman as well." An idea crossed Jahangir's mind. "Shall I build you a copy? Would you like that?" he asked.

"Then my coach would follow yours in every procession. Yes, Alhumdillah, a majestic spectacle," said the queen, smiling. She saluted him by raising her goblet of spirits.

The court musicians gathered in an anteroom to preserve them from a view of the zanana. As they began to play, the emperor called for more alcohol. Nur Jahan filled his jade goblet; then the empress attended her own with a motion of the jeweled ewer. After each musical piece, though, Jahangir's body slumped. He commanded that his jade be filled with arrack.

His queen poured for him again but expressed a concern. "My lord, let us not celebrate to extinction."

"What do you mean?" asked the emperor testily.

"Only that it is wise to measure each drop."

"There will be time enough to measure when I am dead. Tonight, I follow the Greek philosopher: eat, drink and be merry! Eh! Fill my cup!" the emperor commanded.

"My lord, I do not think so."

"Then your lord shall help himself." Jahangir was far drunker than usual. He grabbed the ewer away from his queen and began to pour. Outraged, she pulled it from his hands.

"Damned woman, I said I will drink!" he shouted and slapped her sharply across the face. Shocked, she ran from him, spilling liquor as she went. For a moment, the emperor's old agility returned, and he sprang and brought her down. The ewer flew out of the queen's hands and landed on its side, spinning out its contents. The two monarchs struggled furiously, rolling on the marble floor, cursing, and groaning. They bit and scratched like cats, shocking the servants and the few noblewomen who were in attendance. No one had the presence of mind or felt they had the authority to stop them.

Then, from the purdah room adjoining, the musicians who could hear the ruckus made a commotion of their own, weeping, sighing, thumping arrhythmically on the tabla, making the sitar sound like a forlorn animal. Soon the royal couple forgot their own struggle and rushed next door to see what was the matter. When they realized that the outburst was staged to distract them, Jahangir, and Nur Jahan, with a scarf shielding her face, broke out laughing. The emperor, now in a good humor, threw a handful of silver rupees at the smiling musicians.

"I demand an apology!" said Nur Jahan when they were alone in the queen's apartment. "By our covenant, you were to have six cups and no more. I will not allow you to defy me," said the queen.

"I will do as I please."

Nur Jahan had turned away from the king and stood with her hands on her hips, facing the wall and tapping her foot. Jahangir could not bear her not facing him.

"Turn to me!" ordered the king.

"You know you have been naughty," she said, still with her back to him.

"My dear!"

"I will give no ground," said the queen.

"A compromise, then. I will allow my shadow to cross yours in the garden, nothing more," said Jahangir, talking to her back. He slouched onto the divan. He was too drunk to stand.

"Yes, yes, you bad boy," whispered Nur Jahan affectionately as she turned to Jahangir and stepped to the divan to pinch his cheek. She had gained a tiny concession. She would always try for the maximum and settle for the least if she had to. That was her method. But it is with these small triumphs piled one upon the other that she had taken control of Jahangir and, over the years, the empire.

"You are worn out, Your Majesty," said Nur Jahan.

"Yes."

"And ready for bed?"

"You fight like a tiger, my love," said Jahangir, yawning.

Nur Jahan clapped her hands. In a short while, four female slaves appeared. "Undress His Majesty," commanded the queen.

"One last cup," the emperor pleaded.

"Only one," the queen allowed indulgently.

The emperor's health had declined in recent months, and his hand had become so unsteady that he could not hold a cup without spilling it. While the slaves removed Jahangir's slippers, the queen held a cup to his lips as if she were feeding a child. She slung her other arm around his shoulders and hugged him.

"Drink, my beloved king. You are my life."

"And you mine, blessed woman."

When he was completely undressed, the queen smoothed her palm from his chest to the bulge of his belly. She concluded by giving his genitals a motherly pat and commanded the slaves to dress him in nightclothes and put him to bed.

CHAPTER 20

"*Allah hu akbar! Allah hu akbar!* (God is great! God is great!") called the muezzin. Twice more he repeated this praise from his tower. Then two times in a carrying voice he cried, "*Ash-hadu an la ilaha ili-Allah* (There is no God but God.") Then, "*Ash-hadu anna Muhammad-ar-rasoolullah* (And Muhammad is his prophet.") And "*Hayya'alas-Salah* (Come to prayer") twice. And "*Hayya'alal-falah* (Come to success") also twice.

"Allah hu Akbar," twice recited, completed the call to prayer as the sun declined behind Jahangir's scarlet tent. Inside, Jahangir and Nur Jahan had prostrated themselves in the evening prayer. Jahangir prayed alone and she behind, bending shoulder to shoulder with four other wives of the harem. After the prayer, Jahangir called for dinner to be served to just the two of them.

"My Lord, Mandu at this time of year is pleasant and close to the battlefield should you need to instruct Khurram in tactics," said Nur Jahan as she grasped the fried okra on her plate with a small piece of naan. "And there the plague has yet to penetrate."

"Yes, of course, Mandu."

"I find you most unenthusiastic," she said.

"At the moment, I wish to hunt."

"The world is in turmoil, my lord Jahangir!"

"All the more reason to hunt. It distracts the mind. Will you come?" asked Jahangir. "It is not unreasonable to expect lion in these precincts."

"You exasperate me. The topic is Mandu."

"Hunt with me."

"Mandu!"

"Mandu after the hunt, my dear," said the emperor.

"I will not bargain!" said she.

"Then I shall go alone, but I shall miss you," said Jahangir.

"Oh, for heaven's sake, I will come. But Mandu after a month."

"Inshallah!" exclaimed the smiling emperor, happy that he had gotten his way and that his queen would be there to keep him company.

Nur Jahan was not wrong in allotting a month to prepare for the hunt. She had participated in many and knew what preparations had to be made. The memory of Akbar's grand hunt years earlier still lingered. For a month, Akbar had employed 50,000 beaters over an immense circumference to herd wild animals of every description into an area of a square mile where the hunt would be conducted. Then falcons, the emperor's hunting cheetahs, and the indispensable hounds were marshaled. In addition, troops of foot soldiers and cavalry were ordered to patrol. When the hunt finally began, very little pursuit was involved. It amounted to no more than a slaughter of animals driven among the emperor's nobles.

It took nearly two weeks to locate a lion's den.

"So, where are we?" asked Jahangir of his head gamekeeper.

"Your Majesty, my men have circled lion with nets and will be beating to drive him."

"To?"

"An ass tied to a stake, and then we will kill, sire."

"Ah, yes, kill," said Jahangir. "But sometimes I think it must be wrong to kill a beast as lordly as the lion," the emperor added. He longed to have a lion in his zoo.

"Have you ever tried to tame one?" asked the emperor.

"Oh yes, my lord. I can capture."

"How would you manage that?" asked Jahangir, intrigued.

"Afim, sire. We put much afim in his water."

"How would the lion locate this water?"

"No, sire. Ass's water only. Lion eats and becomes sleepy. Then the nets," said the gamekeeper, making an enveloping gesture with his arms "Ingenious! Inshallah, we shall try your method!" said Jahangir, patting the man on the back.

Three days later, the emperor and empress swept into tall grass, bouncing in a gilded howdah. Ahead in a clearing, the master of the hunt and several amirs, also mounted on elephants, were confronting a lion. A day before, the lion had killed and eaten the drugged bait but did not behave as expected. The moment was tense and dangerous. The growling, full-maned beast sat coiled on its haunches. Soldiers on horseback surrounded the lion, who pawed at their inclined spears.

When the king and queen arrived, the men broke ranks to give them access. At Jahangir's command, his mahout maneuvered in close to the lion. Both monarchs aimed their muskets and waited.

"My lord, your experiment has failed. What a pity!" said Nur Jahan.

"So, it seems. Will you take the first shot?"

The king and queen had their weapons angled downward on the howdah's golden sill. And then the lion sprang at the royal elephant's swaying trunk, passing in line with the emperor's musket. Jahangir let go an echoing shot. Sulfurous smoke filled the back-slanting howdah as the elephant raised his trunk and trumpeted. The lion stopped in midair and shook his mane wildly.

A cry of "*Padshah zindabad!*" rose from the emperor's men as the lion fell. The petite queen also shouted cries of victory. She jumped, grasping Jahangir's forearm in excitement and jubilation. The gamekeepers rushed in with their nets. The soldiers cautiously held back their straining horses and lowered their pikes for action.

"Yes, he is dead!" cried the chief gamekeeper, kneeling beside the lion. Another louder "Padshah zindabad!" was shouted and another and another until the men were hoarse with the cheering. The slaying of a lion was a propitious foretoken, a wink from heaven for an army about to risk their lives in battle.

"I could not allow the opportunity to pass," said Jahangir, his eyes red from the musket smoke.

"It is a triumph and a blessed augury," said the queen. She laid her head on Jahangir's shoulder.

"Yes, our war will be successful. There is no doubt now."

CHAPTER 21

IT WAS RAINING, AND THE wind struck Parviz's tent forcefully.

"Father has sent you to depose me, I take it," said Sultan Parviz.

"Nothing like that," said Khurram. "Your victory has been taken to heart at court, and he wishes to honor you."

Parviz had defeated the forces of the Abyssinian ex-slave Malik Ambar. However, the victory was incomplete, and Malik continued to harass imperial forces with guerrilla attacks.

Parviz was drunk. He rose from his pillow with the help of a servant and paced to an open window to watch the rain.

Everything inside the tent was a shade of red. Even the tent posts were sheathed in red cloth worked with golden thread. Windows in the shape of cusped arches were cut into the walls of embroidered cloth. Except for two on the lee side of the storm, the windows were blocked outside with hanging carpets, which shook in the wind.

"Your presence here can mean only one thing. Father is displeased," said Parviz, looking away from the window for a moment, "Yes, yes, I drink. Everyone knows that. But I have won a great victory. I won. Shouldn't that satisfy him? How many times need that be said?"

"You are my elder," said Khurram. "I won't presume to give you advice. I can only tell you that my orders are to relieve you of command."

"And If I refuse?"

"You won't refuse."

"Yes, you are right. I won't refuse," said Parviz, reeling, holding onto the cloth of a tent post.

"How can I? I may be the elder, but surely, brother, you are the better." Parviz screwed his face into a bitter grimace and turned again to look out of the window.

"Really, Parviz, self-pity does not become you. I have no idea what father's motives are," said Khurram with calm arrogance, sniffing at a rose blossom.

"Shall we ask Abdur Rahim? Yes, let us inquire. He will have an answer," said Parviz.

Parviz's eyes were following Abdur Rahim as he happened to be crossing before the tent under the cold lash of the rain. Parviz stuck his head out of the window and called to his vizier, who was walking with his head bent beneath an oilskin.

"Abdur, come here! Settle this dispute!" he shouted.

Abdur, startled out of a reverie, glanced at the tent and nodded. He stepped gingerly among the rivulets, stone to stone, the short distance to Parviz's pavilion. He walked inside the tent and took the oilskin from his shoulders.

"I shall need some tea," said Abdur to the servant, who rushed to take his wet garment.

"And you may bring my special tea as well," said Parviz. "And you, brother . . . something to warm your bones?"

"Many thanks, but no."

"Forgive me. I had forgotten that you drink only water from the Ganges," Parviz said savagely. Turning to Rahim he said, "The emperor has seen fit to recall me. What do you make of this, Abdur? Am I to be covered in glory?"

"It is the emperor's wish to honor you, Prince," replied the vizier, still shivering from the cold. "In the interim, Sultan Khurram will carry the colors in the Deccan."

"Let us be honest, Rahim; it is your victory as well as mine," said Parviz.

"I had little to do with it," said Abdur Rahim, rubbing his hands together. "You give me too much credit, Prince."

"But it is so. Will you accompany me to Mandu? You deserve the emperor's praise as well."

"Not while Malik Ambar remains at large," said Abdur Rahim.

"Thus Khurram?" asked Parviz, whose mind was so clouded with drink that only now had he grasped the real reason for his recall.

"I'm afraid so, my lord prince," said Abdur Rahim in a moment of candor.

"Where the devil is that tea?" asked Parviz, casting his glance to the rug. His hand shook as he pulled the bell cord for his servant.

With difficulty, Parviz brought his eyes up to his younger brother and smiled grotesquely. "I suppose I should wish you well," said Parviz, reaching shakily for Khurram's shoulder. "And for the sake of the empire, I do. Godspeed!"

CHAPTER 22

1617

"BEAUTIFUL, IS IT NOT?" ASKED Khurram of the young prince. Khurram had subdued his grandfather, the proud Rana of Mewar, the last of the Rajput kings who had resisted Mughal dominion. This wild mountain boy, the heir presumptive, had been sent as proxy to surrender before the Mughal king.

To reach Mandu, they would have to pass through the Mughal tents that spread before the city as bright and as lucent as ships sailing under the sun. Both men were on horseback. The young rana cantered his restless mount and took in the vast windblown metropolis sitting on the cliff above.

"It is like a city of clouds, the home of angels," said the rana in wonder.

"Angels hardly! We are known as the scourge of God, Rana," Khurram declared, laughing heartily.

"Astaghfirullah!" cried the young rana with mock fear.

"Do you not know of my famous ancestor?

"The one called the Great Khan?"

"Yes," said Khurram. "He has written, 'The greatest pleasure is to vanquish your enemies and chase them before you, to rob them of their wealth and see those dear to them bathed in tears, to ride their horses and clasp to your bosom their wives and daughters.' These are your angels, Rana!" cried Khurram.

Then the rana gave Khurram a wild look.

"To hell with you, Mughal!" he shouted at the top of his lungs. He grasped his Arabian by the mane and, laughing, bent him into the wind. After him came Khurram, mad with laughter, galloping on a chestnut mare. Then together they raced, raising dust and cutting a thunderous path through the vacant land and up to the plateau, charging before the wind.

Khurram and the rana rode up above the desert floor to the Mughal camp.

"Here is your abode of angels," said Khurram, turning to the prince. "But mind the camel dung!"

The princes entered a broad thoroughfare. On either side were the low A-shaped tents that housed the infantry.

"This road cuts the city in half. It is twenty kos 'round. Do you see those flags flying over the pavilions? The saffron indicates the dwellings of officers of high rank, the blue of administrators and important merchants. And look, the yellow flag flies above the bazaar where tin-ware is sold. The green shows where there are vegetables and fruit, and so on through the colors."

"It is most orderly," said the rana.

"And complete. Everything to be found in an established metropolis can be found in our ephemeral city. Akbar designed it so," said Khurram, arcing his arm before him to encompass the city. "And he held the entire blueprint within his head. Nothing was taken down on paper."

"Impossible!"

"No, it is so. Akbar had learned the memory method of the Jesuits."

"But the camp seems as large as the capital itself," declared the rana, removing a scarf from his face that had been wound to filter the dust of the desert below.

"Larger," said Khurram. "Nevertheless, Grandfather kept every detail in his head."

"Mashallah!" The rana looked at Khurram in astonishment.

"And so thoroughly did he learn from those Italian priests that even though he was illiterate, he could recite long passages from the Qur'an as well."

As they passed through a district of luxurious pavilions, Khurram said, "These are the dwellings of His Majesty's amirs"

"All white, are they?"

"Yes, that is the color for nobles. They are forbidden the imperial red."

Here and there scattered among the nobles' pavilions were low A-tents where servants slept. A platoon of soldiers marched briskly down the road. A curtained palanquin bearing a Hindu merchant crossed before their trotting horses. Camels crouched at the roadside, and an elephant stood wagging his trunk lazily beside a white pavilion. Some soldiers lounged beneath a canopy where food was being served. Others cooked on open fires. Racing toward the princes on the other side of the road were two galloping Brahma bulls pulling a two-wheeled carriage. Within was a Mughal amir, grossly obese with rings on his thumbs and a greasy turban over his forehead. He sneered as a group of Hindu workers who ran to get out of his way

Directly in the princes' path, men threw dice under the branches of a banyan tree while a procession of women in saris, water jugs balanced on their heads, passed single file along the roadside.

"Those, my friend, are the emperor's tents and the tents of his women. My dear father won't move even a *guz* without the comforts of the zanana," said Khurram, pointing down the road at the distant center of the encampment where the emperor's pavilions glowed in crimson silk. "And, young rana, look over the tent tops," said Khurram. "Can you see yonder tower where a lamp shows at its summit?"

"Ah yes, but I know what that is. It is called the light of the universe, the Akadsia lamp that burns night and day at the center of the world, the fire that every man can see," said the rana, reciting from memory what he had once read in a Mughal proclamation.

"Well said but remember that it is also the all-seeing eye that searches the land ceaselessly, for nothing escapes Mughal surveillance!" said Khurram. "And tonight, under the Akadsia's watchful eye, I shall move my treasure to my father's tents."

Prince Khurram, seated upon his prancing horse, and the rana just behind him led a long train of camels and elephants that bore the captured wealth up from the plain. They had entered via the same avenue as before. The sun had already set by the time they reached the plateau. The road was torchlit, lined with cheering soldiers and their women and children, all dressed in the unique finery of the various tribes that made up the army. Camp followers in their saris, artisans of every kind, and peasants in white longhis raised their voices in praise.

Smiling every bit of the way, Khurram waved to the crowd like true royalty. Behind him came the rana, then the drums, the fifes, and the long laden train. The crowd knew that once the booty was tallied, the emperor would distribute alms, and they shouted joyfully as the rich columns passed before them.

The emperor's encampment blazed with torchlight. The yellow and orange of the flames blending with the red of the taller imperial tents gave the impression of a gigantic fire at the center of the campus.

The two princes dismounted before Jahangir's magnificent *durbar* pavilion. Grooms rushed to take hold of their horses. Huge pots of burning ghee that flamed against the black sky stood on enormous teakwood elephants at the pavilion entrance. Leaving the rana behind, Khurram entered as guards in magnificent livery ushered him through the brightly lit tent amid the cheering of nobles. The emperor sat on a jeweled throne. Nur Jahan, her brother, and her father were standing next to him. All were brilliant in jeweled clothing glittering in the light of a hundred torches.

"Welcome, my son of good fortune. Henceforth you shall sit at my side," said the emperor as Khurram approached. Jahangir indicated a chair on his left.

Khurram's eyes were wet with tears as he bent to kiss his father's feet. It was unprecedented that even a prince of the blood be allowed to sit in the emperor's presence at court.

"Majesty, you honor me beyond my wildest expectation," said Khurram with uncharacteristic humility.

"Nonsense, my son. You have triumphed . . . a major victory," said Jahangir, waving away his son's comments.

"You have made me proud," said Jahangir as he placed his hand firmly on Khurram's shoulder. "And now I anoint you Shah Jahan, King of the World." The air rang with shouts of praise.

"My lord, you overwhelm me!" said Shah Jahan, bowing.

"In addition, you will receive a *mansab* of 30,000 personal and 20,000 horse," said Jahangir, overflowing with fatherly pride. "Step forward," ordered the emperor.

Jahangir placed a golden robe of honor over Shah Jahan's shoulders. The garment was stitched with pearls worth thousands of rupees. Jahangir wrapped a diamonded belt around his son's waist and attached a jeweled sword and dagger. The emperor made a sign, and servants came forward with trays of jewels and gold coins, which he poured over Shah Jahan's head with great joy and affection. The audience broke out with good-natured laughter and shouts of "Shah Jahan, zindabad!"

Shah Jahan bowed again and brought his brow to the back of his father's outstretched hand.

King of the World—that suited him. Shah Jahan thought that no title could have better described him. Extremely handsome, graceful from the study of dance, and hardened from a lifetime of military training and experience in war, he was the very picture of a king. He had conquered the Deccan. The Indian southland that had successfully resisted his Mughal predecessors had fallen to him. He was convinced that no living human was his equal.

"My dear, you have won a great victory. The map of Hindustan is now complete," said Nur Jahan. "The last rebellious part of Rajastan joins the empire!"

Nur Jahan and her brother Asaf Khan had welcomed the prince into her luxurious quarters at Mandu Fort. Throughout Mandu, there was celebration. Nur Jahan had given her victorious stepson a magnificent party. Fireworks broke in myriad colors above the palace. Music echoed in the great hall, and nautch girls swirled before an audience of drunken, clamoring nobles who had fought in the war.

"We could not be happier," said Asaf Khan at Nur Jahan's side. "You have come of age. You do our family honor."

Asaf Khan was speaking of himself, his sister, and his father, Iti-mad-ud-daula, the empire's minister of finance. It was these three along with Shah Jahan who had become the real rulers of the empire in the face of Jahangir's de facto abdication.

Shah Jahan's relationship with Ghaya Beg's family had been made concrete by his marriage to Arjumand Banu. She was Asaf Khan's daughter, Nur Jahan's niece, Iti-mad's granddaughter, and now Shah Jahan's wife. Shah Jahan was indeed a member of the family.

CHAPTER 23

NUR JAHAN, AS EMPRESS OF Hindustan, received the prince Karan. She was beautiful. Her skin glistened with perfumed unguents. She wore striped silk pajamas. Strings of pearls encircled her throat and crisscrossed her breasts, shielded only by a tissue of translucent silk. Pearls also bordered her turban, and the royal heron's feather stood upright from its crown. Garlands of hyacinth and yellow marigold hung from her neck. An uncut ruby inscribed by Jahangir depended from a golden necklace. Golden bangles banded her upper arms and wrists. In her left hand she held a red rose, which she lifted to her nostrils as her whim directed.

Nur Jahan had arranged a mirror so that if the young man considered it, he could see her and do her homage without breaking the laws of purdah, which forbade a direct view. It was a stratagem devised by a European artist so that her portrait could be painted. The prince, so much the country bumpkin, was flabbergasted. Dressed in his clumsy robes, he bowed to her image.

"Namaste, most gracious queen," said Prince Karan

"Assalaamu 'Alaikum," said Nur Jahan. As the representative of the empire, it was she who would receive the capitulation of the rana. It was essential that the proud young Rajput not feel slighted by the absence of the emperor. By way of compensation, she dressed in a manner that would be unforgettable to the young man and perhaps even encourage a personal bond.

"This is the most auspicious of occasions. Welcome to the empire! Welcome to prosperity!"

"On behalf of my father, the Maharana of Mewar, I submit to Your Highness." Karan threw himself at the floor before her image in the mirror. At a sign from the empress, Prince Karan rose but kept his head bowed in respect.

"The emperor looks forward to a fruitful partnership with your illustrious house," said the queen. Her servants had placed a pot of smoking incense beneath her figure. She appeared to the young prince as a goddess speaking directly to him through the clouds of heaven. "I have prepared for you a robe of honor and the Sword of the Empire." Two female slaves appeared at Prince Karan's side, one with an embroidered robe studded with emeralds, which she placed upon Karan's shoulders and another with a jeweled sword. "This sword confirms you as amir in the empire's roster of nobles. In the palace stables are an Iraqi stallion and one of my favorite elephants, which I bestow as personal gifts. Khuda hafiz, Prince. The empire holds you in its esteem." With that, a servant removed the mirror, and the queen was gone.

Shah Jahan, who had been standing behind the prince, moved up and hugged his shoulders. "Now, Prince, you are with us," he said. He felt a connection to this guileless mountain boy and had relaxed his normal hauteur.

"That vision is your mother?" exclaimed Prince Karan, overawed. "I have never seen a woman more beautiful!"

"She is not my mother. She is my father's favorite wife, a Persian. I am by birth mostly Rajput. Did you know that?" said Shah Jahan.

Prince Karan's face screwed up with puzzlement.

"My mother is Jagat Gosani, daughter of the rajah of Jodhpur, and my grandmother is the daughter of Rajah Mal of Amber," Shah Jahan explained cordially. Prince Karan smiled and embraced the shah.

"Ah, a Ranawat prince. We are Sisoda. Sometimes we are enemies," said the rana.

Shah Jahan raised an eyebrow. "And now?" he asked.

"We are joined," said Prince Karan with real warmth. "Let us look at that Iraqi, shall we, Khurram brother?"

CHAPTER 24

"No, he made no demands," said Nur Jahan. "He is either crafty beyond his years or he plans an audience with Jahangir."

"The Sisodas are preoccupied with Chittor. He will ask for that. Are you prepared?" said her father. "Chittor represents their honor, more important to a Rajput than money."

"I will not give him Chittor." The queen drew her face into a scowl.

"Then the sore will continue to fester, and we will have no peace. Make him a present of it before he asks," said Iti-mad-ud-daula. He glanced at his daughter with shrewd eyes. "Then he will eat out of your hand. You will own him for a pile of broken stone."

"They will restore their fort and cause mischief!" said Nur Jahan but then stopped to say, "But why is this accursed place so important, Father?"

"Ah, I knew you would ask eventually, Beta. You see, long before you were born, the emperor delivered a crushing defeat upon the Sisodas at Chittor Fort."

"But that should not—"

"Please allow me to continue. Faced with inevitable defeat, the noble Rajastani women, rather than submit to the embraces of the conquerors, chose to perform *Jauhar.* Do you know what that means, Beta? They chose to burn themselves alive. Thousands of them made a bonfire of themselves. And the men, also in their thousands, mounted their ponies completely naked. Riding bareback, they attacked Akbar's 60,000-man line with only their lances. Of course, all the Rajput men and women had eaten large doses of afim to fortify themselves. And while the women burned, the men were cut to pieces by Akbar's men as a scythe mows grass. It was the greatest act of valor that Rajastan has ever seen."

"By God, there was poetry in that, Father."

"Doubtless, that is how a Sisoda would see it."

"I don't understand. What should they have done, cowered in the crevices of their fortress waiting for Akbar's men to defile them? That is not the way of the warrior, nor is it my way."

"Then you will understand that, foolhardy or not, the Battle of Chittor is part of the Rajput identity, and they want the fort returned. It is a token of their fearlessness."

"I suppose. But again, you have gotten me to agree with you without my wanting to," said Nur Jahan, frowning, disappointed at herself for not having seen it as another of her wily father's gambits.

"Do not be dismayed, Maa. In time you will learn this art. Are you not my daughter?" said the Iti-mad-ud-daula chuckling. Nur Jahan nodded. There was a hint of the little girl about her.

They were sitting cross-legged on carpets around a charcoal brazier. The old Persian, wizened and gray, sat with dignity. A warm Kashmir shawl was draped over his upright shoulders. They were in the deserted public audience hall of Mandu Palace. The hall was open to the air, and through the files of arches they could see the hills beyond the palace. The monsoon rains had ended, and the surrounding countryside was fresh and green under an early morning sun.

"Now the question is, what will you ask for in exchange?" asked Nur Jahan's father.

"Nothing more than fealty."

"And the garrisoning of troops?" said Asaf Khan.

"My husband wants only safe passage for our army to Gujarat. Shah Jahan has already made him that suggestion, and he has in principle agreed."

"Speaking of the prince, I don't think he can be fully trusted. Since his triumph, he has become even more arrogant, if such a thing is possible," said the old Persian,

"Tell me, will he agree to marry Ladli?"

"He says he loves Arjumand," said Nur Jahan.

"And my daughter loves him! said Asaf Khan with sudden ferocity, he wanted no competitor for Shah Jahan's affections, "You, think only of your own advantage."

"To secure the future of our family only!" cried Nur Jahan, narrowing her eyes.

"While Shah Jahan secures his future with our disunity," said the Iti-mad. "Let us not argue."

"Sister, Khusro might be suitable for Ladli," Asaf Khan offered as a token of peace.

"He too loves his wife!" said Nur Jahan.

"They both suffer in prison," said Asaf Khan.

"Ah, yes," said the old man. "Look into this, daughter. An offer of freedom. Who can tell?"

CHAPTER 25

THE INTERIOR OF THE PRISON at Agra Fort was dark and, even in dry weather, damp. Its porous stone sucked moisture from the sands of the Yamuna. Khusro's cell was a far cry from his former accommodation in the fort. It was small, and only a barred vertical slit in the thick wall admitted light. The smell of cooking hung for hours in the airless room. Rozana did her best to keep it tidy, but dust always managed to filter in and lie over the meager furnishings. Nor could she do much against the cobwebs that grew continually at the room's corners.

"The empress calls!" a deep voice announced from beyond the thick wooden door after a loud thumping. The jailer admitted the chief eunuch, holding a lantern with Nur Jahan trailing. The queen greeted the couple from behind a diaphanous veil, which allowed only the sparkle of her eyes to escape.

"Assalaamu 'Alaikum, dear hearts," said the queen. She brought the sweet odor of perfume into the stale room. "I am so sorry to see you in these circumstances," she said with genuine feeling.

"Alaikum salaam, Majesty," said Rozana. Khusro, in a muffled voice, said the same, running over her words. Adversity had drawn Khusro and his wife even closer. They were very much a couple. This dank cell was their home.

Rozana stepped forward into the stripe of dusty light cast by the narrow window and bent to touch Nur Jahan's feet. Khusro, wraithlike, kept to the shadows, wary of the queen and confused by her presence.

"My dear Khusro, why haven't you responded to my letter?" said the queen, addressing the shadows. "If only you would do the sensible thing, this dreariness would end. Ladli is noble in heart and mind and beautiful. Why do you resist? Allah has given you the opportunity of many wives. Surely you would not deprive him of the means of freedom?" asked the queen, turning toward Rozana.

"Majesty, it is..." said Rozana. She broke out crying, lowering her wet cheek to Nur Jahan's feet.

The queen pulled her up to her face and embraced her.

"Sweet, sweet, my sweet darling," said the queen, wiping the tears from Rozana's eyes with the thumbs of both hands.

"It is I who will not allow it!" interrupted Khusro violently.

Rozana turned to face him. He held out his hand for Rozana to guide him closer to the queen. The reports that he was self-sufficient had been exaggerated. He could see only dimly through his improved eye and then only in bright light. Rozana brought her husband into the light to stare abstractly at the queen. His robe was tattered, and his gray beard hung to his waist, where it was indifferently tucked into his cummerbund. His head was bare. He had long ago given up the affectation of a turban. His face, once so handsome and full of life and intelligence, was now a mask of anger.

"We are bound souls. I will do nothing to disturb this!" Khusro said.

"But my daughter would complement you both. In freedom—"

"I will not have her!" he thundered with the vehemence of a desert prophet. "I will not!" His entire body shook with anger.

"Insanity has overtaken you!" cried the queen, turning on her heel. She ran to the door, where she rapped with the base of the jeweled chalice she had brought as a gift. The chief eunuch hovered protectively at her back.

"Jailer! Jailer!" she shouted. "Take me from this madhouse!"

CHAPTER 26

"This Ambar has again reared his ugly head," said Jahangir. "Is there no end to him?"

The emperor and Shah Jahan were alone in the royal apartment. Jahangir reclined on a divan. His son sat across from him with crossed legs. Both men were bareheaded and wore simple cotton tunics.

"He now munches on Bijapur and has his teeth set for Golconda, Father. His strength grows day by day," said Shah Jahan, rising to his feet and striding gracefully to and fro before his father.

"I will need you in the Deccan once more. Are you up to it?" said the emperor with a worried look.

"I am, Father, but I am wary of departing Agra."

"Wary?"

"Since the betrothal," said Shah Jahan.

"But Ladli and Prince Shahryar pose no threat."

"How do I phrase this?" Shah Jahan said, stroking his chin. "Your health—"

"Ya Allah, stop! If I die, then Khusro, not Shahryar, will succeed me," said Jahangir.

"My point precisely. Khusro is in Asaf Khan's custody. I cannot leave my future in the air."

"What *is* your point? That you don't trust my wife?" asked Jahangir.

"The queen loves you, Father. She is under no obligation to love your sons. You have led me to believe that I will be your successor."

"Inshallah!"

"Then give me the support necessary. What if something were to happen to Khusro? He is blind and not able to take care of himself. He is vulnerable. It wouldn't take much to finish him off. Ladli is to marry Shahryar. Would it be prudent for me to leave when Shahryar might be made king in my absence?"

Jahangir was amused. When Nur Jahan had proposed Ladli's marriage to Shahryar, there was an air of desperation about her. He knew that after his death, his wife, so beloved of power, would have none. Shahryar was in line after Shah Jahan but was not fit to be king. Shallow, lazy, many thought an imbecile, Shahryar had earned the nickname *Nash udani*—Good-for-nothing. Nur Jahan had vowed that she would make up his deficiencies, that through her son-in-law, she would reign.

"That is unlikely. But what support do you want?"

"Give me my brother!"

"To take with you to the Deccan? Absurd!"

"He and his wife will be well protected; you have my word. Khusro will not be affected by the war; I swear it."

"Impossible!"

"Then I cannot go. It would be folly to leave."

"The empress. . ."

"Father, she would never grant permission," said Shah Jahan, knowing full well that the plan was Nur Jahan's brainchild in the first place. Asaf Khan also favored the move, as did Iti-mad-ud-daula.

"Permission resides solely with me!" cried the emperor, enraged to be seen without authority. "But I know that the queen favors your plan," he said more calmly.

"You have spoken with her?"

"It is I who resisted."

"Then?

"You will go to the Deccan with Khusro. But mind you, take diligent care of your brother," said Jahangir. The Deccan was too important to allow even the well-being of his firstborn to get in the way.

It was Khusro's refusal to marry Ladli that had turned the queen against him. And as Ladli was to marry Shahryar, she no longer needed Khusro to further her imperial ambitions. She would have descendants at the Mughal court without him. With Khusro and Shah Jahan in the Deccan, the two most powerful contenders for the throne would be away from the center of action in the capital. Who could tell what the outcome would be when her husband died?

Shah Jahan also wanted to keep Khusro, so popular with the people, away from Agra. Should his father die, Khusro, the next in the royal line, would ascend to the Mughal throne. Shah Jahan would then have his work cut out for him. But even then, nothing would keep him from realizing his destiny. He would be king. About that he had no doubt. And the astrologers agreed.

Shah Jahan left the winter court in Lahore, riding an elephant presented to him by his stepmother. His father lavished upon him, many presents and a huge army. Garlanded and gliding through the cheering streets, Shah Jahan saluted Jahangir, who stood at a palace balcony. It was the last time he would see his father.

In Ahmadnagar, Shah Jahan met with swift success. Bijapur and Golconda fell to the Mughal onslaught as well, and tribute from all three jurisdictions went into the imperial coffers. The Mughal hold on the principal cities of the Deccan, however, was not complete. Malik Ambar, the Ethiopian slave turned conqueror, was still at large, but for now, the Deccan was pacified. Shah Jahan's army erected their tents at Bhurhanpur.

CHAPTER 27

SHAH JAHAN WAS EXAMINING A rough diamond brought to him from the mines in Golconda. "How much?" he asked, hefting the stone in his hand.

"For a stone of this quality, 80,000 rupees only, Majesty," replied the Baniya merchant, Amrit Lal Gupta.

"Amrit, sahib, I am much too busy for such jokes," said Shah Jahan, laughing lightly and handing the stone back to Gupta.

"My profit is thin, sire. To sell for less I will lose money." Gupta's price was greatly inflated. This was his first dealing with the prince, and Gupta did not know the deep knowledge that Shah Jahan had of gemstones nor of his sharp business sense.

"Forty thousand rupees would be a fair price," said Shah Jahan. At that moment, Abdur Rahim signaled from the other end of the bustling hall that an important message had arrived. Shah Jahan acknowledged him with a nod of the head and motioned that Rahim move forward with the letter.

"That is my final offer, sahib. Speak with my *diwan* if you want to do business," said the prince perfunctorily, offering his hand to be kissed.

"But Majesty, please," said the crestfallen Gupta.

"Enough!" said Shah Jahan, looking down at the merchant with stern eyes. He motioned to guards to escort Gupta out of the hall, but as they approached, Gupta made his own way out of the crowd after bowing obsequiously to the prince.

Shah Jahan's face tightened as he read the message just placed in his hands.

"My lord, the news is not good?" asked Abdur Rahim.

"My father is seriously ill." Shah Jahan stroked his chin. "I am at a disadvantage, stuck in this hinterland."

"You have not forgotten why you brought Khusro?" said Abdur.

"Of course not. Tell him nothing of this message. Oh yes—find Raza Bahadur and bring him to me."

"I pray that he is not drunk."

"That may not be a bad thing. Tell your men to find him."

———

A week later, while Shah Jahan went north following his beaters, Raza Bahadur slipped away from his tent and joined two other men in the outer ring of the encampment. Fires burned, and men sat playing at cards, drinking arrack, and singing obscene songs. The high flute and ringing tambourine made music for the dancing girls, whose fire-flung shadows scurried on the panels of the low tents. It was payday after a long period of paylessness, and drunken soldiers sat flipping copper paisa at their darting forms. Prostitutes in brilliant saris and painted faces paraded outside their tents. There were nearly as many prostitutes as customers, and their competitions made their gestures forced and vulgar.

The moon was full, and the men walked in silence, with Raza limping. Swords swayed at their sides. They went to where a soldier held camels. A chi pot was boiling on the red embers of his campfire. The soldier gave his salaams and, with his stick, made the camels kneel to receive them. The men mounted and immediately rode out, kicking up small clouds of silver dust. They rode in an arc around the camp and after twenty minutes came to a door in the citadel's wall where a solitary torch burned overhead.

"The sky is red," said Raza, reciting the password. The door creaked open, and the men entered. They were led across a dark quadrangle to the light of a palace entrance and then down a deserted corridor. Their guide was a military man of middle rank, tall and severe, with a black turban and drooping mustaches. He stopped before a teak door. He crossed his lips with an upright forefinger and then withdrew, stepping quietly away along the tiled floor.

"Assalaamu 'Alaikum, Sultan!" said Raza Bahadur, jovially addressing the door. He was drunk and happily contemplated his reward for Khusro's murder. He was a man of medium height, dark faced with dark eyes that burned with contempt, an assassin by trade and inclination. Raza had been born with a defective leg, and when he walked, his good leg snapped forward as his other delayed behind him. It gave the impression of his having been vehemently pushed back and then forward.

"Open, dear prince. I bring tidings from our king."

"Who calls?" asked Khusro.

"An emissary from our gracious king, your father, sire."

"Who?" .

"A robe is for you, Sultan. The emperor requests that you accompany him on his pilgrimage to Ajmer."

"Go away!"

"An Urs, sire, at the Chisti tomb. The emperor requests his son's presence. You cannot refuse."

"Yet I refuse. I want no robe or salutation. Who are you? Go away!"

"Open your door, most happy prince, and speak. Words are soft and do not strike through heavy timber."

"I can hear. Go away!" said Khusro.

We will take down your door, sire, so that we can speak face to face. We know you cannot see, sire. That is why the door must come down—so that you can feel the garment. It is set with rubies and diamonds, Sultan. Gold . . . it shines with gold. If only you could see. A few moments more, bear with me. I will bring down the door." Raza's men worked frantically to remove the door from its hinges.

"I want the door let alone."

"Only a few more minutes, if you please, sire . . . just a few."

"I command you, leave it."

"Sire, it is only a matter of minutes." Raza stood with his *rumal* taut between his hands and a wolfish grin on his face. His two men pushed the hinge pins with the tips of their daggers. Simultaneously, the pins slid up from their hinges.

"The door will soon be down, sire, and then we can speak. I cannot hear you properly. What do you say?"

"Leave me alone!"

"Oh, we shall be alone, sire, quite alone." The men pushed the door upward and off the hinges. Raza snapped forward in his strange walk with a face full of malice. The blind prince stepped backward. His wife was away visiting her father, and the servants had been bribed.

"Now you can hear me, can't you, Prince? Can't you?"

"Who are you?" Khusro lurched forward as he sensed Raza's men stealthily advancing on his flanks. He pulled a dagger from his cummerbund and pivoted from one side to another, searching the air for his assailants. The light, a dim lantern brought by the intruders, was invisible to him.

"I come from your brother, the Shah Jahan. Can you guess why?" Raza Bahadur laughed. He was in his glory. He snapped again forward with his strangling cloth stretched tight.

"Leave me or you shall pay a price," said Khusro. His eyes fluttered, and he rolled them from side to side as if he could see. Raza's two henchmen sprang and grasped for Khusro's arms. Khusro swung his dagger in the dim light and caught the man on his left with its tip.

"Oh yes!" cried Raza as he saw the knife puncture skin. "Yes, yes, Sultan, you have gained a point," he said, laughing. His eyes glazed with pleasure as he saw in the faint glow of the lantern the blood dripping from his confederate's arm.

Both of Khusro's arms were caught tight by Raza's men, and when he could no longer struggle, Khusro turned toward Raza's voice and straightened his jaw. "I am not afraid. I am a king!"

Raza laughed, slipped the scarf over Khusro's neck, and pulled it loosely.

"Can you feel it, King? My towel? Now are you afraid?" Raza tightened the rumal. "Are you afraid now, King? I will strangle the life out of you. Just like killing a chicken. You are nothing to me, King!"

"And you are worthless before almighty God. Pull your rag. I am not afraid."

"Nothing!" cried Raza, howling like a beast. His forearms bulged as he tightened the cloth. As Raza strained, Khusro's hands broke away and went to his neck. He gasped as the scarf winched tighter. Raza stared with fixed eyes, extracting every bit of pleasure from Khusro's desperation.

When the prince went limp, the men quickly placed his body on the divan, smoothed the bedclothes over him, and ran to the entrance door to replace the hinges.

The following morning, the corridors filled with sunlight. Khusro's door stood ajar when Rozana entered the apartment in the brightest of moods.

"Dear, I have had the most delightful time with Father," she called into the bedroom. "He says that our ordeal may soon come to an end!" She froze when she saw the coagulated blood on the yellow tile floor. "My lord Khusro! What has happened?" she cried. She went to where Khusro lay and saw that he was dead. She ran out into the hallway screaming. In moments, the corridor and Khusro's room filled with guards and nobles. Later, a hakim came with an earthen jar and gave her a sedative.

CHAPTER 28

"FOR THE FIRST TIME, FATHER, I fear for him. He struggles for breath even while he rests," she said, looking up from her embroidery. Nur Jahan was sitting in a quiet room of her father's mansion. Her father sat opposite.

"What do the doctors say?"

"Doctors! They say what you want them to say. If they suspect that you wish him dead, they will say that a scarlet cheek is the first sign of fever. If you hope for his life, they will smile and say his complexion is rosy, so indicative of health. But I know that my king declines. The afim haunts him, and wine has taken his soul. Astaghfirullah, I can do nothing," said Nur Jahan and sent her father a look of great sorrow. "My world breaks into pieces," she said. "You know, Father, Asaf has begun to drift. I can see it in his face. I sense that his allegiance now shifts from me to Shah Jahan," the queen continued.

"Should it surprise you that he sees his future with his son-in-law?"

"When Khurram's mother died, he turned to Asaf and to Arjumand, of course. But he did not seek me out, although I loved him as a mother."

"A prince has many mothers. The pendulum swings. You must acknowledge it."

"What do you counsel, Father?"

"You want Shahryar king, but let us see what will happen in the Deccan. No one can predict the course of war."

That night the queen was too disturbed to stay at her father's house as he had suggested. She longed to see her husband. The Iti-mad's mansion was just downriver from Agra Fort, a short trip along the dark shore. Instead, she elected to return to the palace through Agra town and the cheering lights of the bazaar.

It was as if the townspeople knew the mind of their queen. Along the road, they greeted her palki with warmth and patted their chests as they uttered salaams. She was beloved of the people. Through her devotion and generosity, she had many times shown her love. Now it was returned as her name was reverently chanted. The love came back, wave after wave, as men jostled to help shoulder her palanquin and women swarmed to kiss the hem of its glittering curtain.

The queen had given in charity to all who suffered. At Eid, at every Urs she had lit the fires and fed the poor with her own hand. She had given support to every destitute girl. For every female orphan who asked, she had made a marriage. Tears rolled down her beautiful face as the love flowed in upon her.

Along the way, in the streets and crowded lanes, votive lights lit pictures of the Christian Madonna and Shakti, the Divine Mother. Under the blazing light of torches was Kali's terrifying image, necklaced with human skulls and red with the blood of her victims. In the minds of Muslims, Nur Jahan was Khadija, Prophet Muhammad's wife. To the Hindu masses, she became Parvati and Jahangir her Lord Shiva. To all her people, she was a goddess.

Spontaneously, a procession of hundreds formed, singing her name, and guiding her home with lighted candles.

Above the immense geometry of the fortress walls, the white palace floated like a mirage. Moonlit domes sat on cusped arches. Gems set in the palace walls took the moonlight and sparkled like stars in a marble firmament. Latticed windows glowed with lamp-light.

At the entrance, two guards in their brilliant yellow turbans and scarlet cummerbunds stood beneath the blaze of torches. Nur Jahan's palki was borne through the gates and brought to her private apartment.

She called for a bath. But before she slid into the warmth of the marble tank, the queen lit a huqqah filled with hashish. Normally she kept a clear head, but tonight she was so unsettled that she allowed herself a comforting smoke. By the time she had finished the bath and her servants had dried, perfumed, and dressed her, her mind flooded with reminiscences.

She remembered the tales her mother had told her of the hard journey from Persia, to Akbar's court in Fatehpur Sikri. On the way, while still in Persia, bandits attacked their caravan, and everything they owned was taken. They were left penniless. Somehow, they managed to travel to Afghanistan, where she was born at Kandahar. Her parents had named her Mihrunnisa, the Sun of Women. Later, in a moment of utter despair, her parents, unable to feed her, had left her at the roadside. Relenting, her father returned to find an enormous black snake coiled around his infant. Frantic, he drove the cobra into a hollow tree with a stick and rescued his daughter. That, at least, was the legend.

The queen smiled when she recalled this tale. How improbable, she thought, that Ghiyas would abandon her. It was unthinkable that her mother would. Still, she liked the story. It added to her mythic stature. Someday she must ask her mother what was the real truth.

She knew how her father had risen in the imperial ranks. She envisioned the moment he had been led into court to meet the emperor. She could see him standing humbly before the emperor in threadbare clothing and Akbar instantly warming to his elegant Persian manners and extraordinary intelligence. His decency and perceived honesty had won him an immediate posting to Kabul as treasurer. She recalled her father then and those sunlit years spent at Kabul when she was a little girl. His rise from then on was unbroken. Under Jahangir, her father received the title Iti-mad-ud-daula, "pillar of the government," and he and his family were forever bound to the fate of the empire.

Then the queen's thoughts ran to the story her father told of the prelude to her first marriage. All week long, he had said, she had been acting strangely.

She had taken to her bed on Monday and had not come down for days. Ghyas Beg was sure that it was just a simple fever. But Asmat was beside herself with worry. She had prayed that it was not Rat Fever or, heaven forbid, the sweating sickness that had taken her cousin just weeks before. She had shuddered at the thought of how the poor man had suffered.

By Thursday morning, both parents were so alarmed that they summoned the court physician. In the dark before dawn, the hakim had cut through the river mists in a bouncing palki. The physician had not had time even to wind a turban. His Small Boy sitting cross-legged in the palanquin hurriedly wrapped a long blue cloth around his head. He was acutely aware that should Ghyas's daughter die, he would be out of a job or, worse, given the emperor's temperament and the esteem and affection he held for his chief minister. *Ah, but I must not allow myself to think of the worst consequence*, the hakim thought.

Yellow cooking fires were burgeoning along the riverbank, and early boatmen sliced their narrow craft into the water. In a few moments, the palace of Iti-mad-ud-daula took shape, and the doctor's palanquin rode into its darkened courtyard. He was about to bark orders to a bareheaded figure standing alone when he realized that it was, Astaghfirullah, the chief minister himself.

"Assalaamu 'Alaikum, Excellency," said the hakim while thanking Allah that he had avoided making a disastrous error.

"Alaikum Salaam," Ghyas Beg said anxiously as the hakim alighted from his litter. "Upstairs," said Ghyas impatiently, indicating a lamp flickering at a first-story window. "She has not been down for days, not taken a morsel." Beg was wringing his hands. "Her mother is herself on the verge of collapse," he said.

"I will prepare a sedative for them both. May I ask the age of the young lady, Excellency?" the doctor said as he strode with Ghyas toward the palace. His barefoot Small Boy followed the hakim's fluid robe, bearing a tray with a reassuring collection of medicaments in silver and gold containers. Some were set with rubies and emeralds, others swathed in shimmering cloths.

"She is to be eighteen next winter, but see her, sahib. Put my mind at ease," said the old Persian, urging the doctor in with a low sweep of his hand.

"Ah, a sensitive age. She has been in good health until now?"

"The best of health. Hurry."

The physician bowed his head deferentially as he filed behind the minister through the portal.

As they ascended the marble steps, the men saw Asmat standing outside the girl's room, nervously fingering the circle of her Tasbih beads. Tears came to her eyes as she saw her husband. She took a quick step forward as he reached the landing.

"She has taken poison," Asmat said.

"God forbid," said the doctor, taking the last step on the stairway.

"You know this? How?" asked Ghyas.

"From herself," said Asmat. "She said she didn't want to leave us."

"Therefore, she takes poison?" said Ghyas, shaking his head. He felt dizzy and steadied himself against the wall.

Asmat's tears now came in a torrent. She put her head on her husband's shoulder.

"Good God, why?" asked Ghyas.

"You know perfectly well why," said Asmat, lifting her head from his shoulder with a look of scorn. The tears slowed as she stood erect, sniffling into a handkerchief.

"With your permission," said the doctor, making for the room without waiting for an answer. A servant girl rushed to shut the curtains surrounding Mihrunnisa's bed as the doctor entered.

"Assalaamu 'Alaikum, dear one," said the hakim to the closed curtain. "I'm Dr. Abdul Aziz. You must know me from the palace. I'm the handsome one with the gray beard," he joked.

Silently, Mihrunnisa's parents crept into the room and stood behind the doctor in a daze. They stared with intent at the purdah curtain as if they could find an answer to their daughter's malaise among the floral patterns of the fabric.

"Yes, I *do* remember you, Doctor sahib. Alaikum salaam."

"What has befallen you, dear one? Your mother shakes with apprehension. She tells me you have taken poison. That cannot be true. Astaghfirullah, I would have to bleed you."

"Ugh! Where is Mother now?"

"On my instruction, she awaits the good news just outside," said the hakim, turning to her parents with a silencing finger to his lips.

"And Father too?"

"Yes, he too."

"Then I can tell you, no, I have not taken poison, but I am miserable nonetheless. I cannot eat, and all night I lie awake considering my fate." Asmat breathed a nearly audible sigh of relief and grasped her husband's hand.

"What troubles you, sweet child?"

"My parents have told you."

"No, no, I am innocent."

"They have not mentioned that they intend marrying me off to a soldier?"

"A soldier?"

"Yea, it is all the doing of the tyrant Akbar!"

"Shush, child, some sentiments are better left unuttered!" said the hakim, looking around the room for informers.

"Ha, what do I care for death? My days are a living death."

"You will revive. Give me your wrist so that I can recommend a potion."

"I am indifferent," said Mihrunnisa, but immediately let her arm fall through a slit in the curtain.

As the doctor felt her pulse with his spidery fingers, Ghyas slipped out into the hall and spoke in hushed tones to a servant. When the servant returned with a pitcher of fresh buffalo milk and a plate of plump dates, the doctor had stepped out to his tray of medicines. Ghyas silently requested his wife to leave the room. Then he went to the bed and pulled back the curtain.

"Father!" Mihrunnisa shouted in shock. Her cheek was flushed, her eyes shone, and her black hair had taken a delicate curl. Ghyas thought that she had never looked more beautiful than now, under the pink gloss of fever. The old man sat down on a pillow by her bed and crossed his legs. He ordered the food placed near her and pointed the servants out the door.

"Forgive me, Beta, but why am I surprised when my child acts like one?"

"I am not a child!"

Ghyas raised his eyebrows. "Not a child? Then simply an ingrate?" he said.

Mihrunnisa began to cry. She tried to sit up in bed, but she was too weak. Ghyas put a supporting hand under her elbow, and she rose, folding her legs beneath her. She didn't even look at the food.

"Oh, Father, I can't marry that terrible man."

"But he is handsome, wealthy, and a Persian. What is so terrible?"

"He frightens me," she said.

"You *are* a child," said Ghyas with a look of disgust.

"Why does the emperor want this so badly? There are other women."

"A reward."

"But I warrant no reward."

"Not you, him. You know that Sher Afghan saved Salim's life."

"I was not aware. Saved him how?"

"It is a complicated story."

"Am I not entitled to hear it?"

"Yes, I suppose you are," said Ghyas with a sigh. "To put it succinctly, Salim fondled a tiger cub in the wild. The mother attacked the unarmed prince. Ali Quli Beg, in the nick of time, ran the beast through with his sword and saved Salim's life, thus earning the sobriquet Sher Afghan: Tiger Killer. And of course, the emperor's undying gratitude. When the emperor told Afghan that he would reward him with whatever was in his power, he chose you."

"Me? Oh my God!" she shouted. "Am I to be a gift, a trifle one gives away on a whim, a prize at a raffle?!" Then she broke out in piteous wailing. "I will not be that tyrant's gift, Father."

"Ya Allah, I had hoped for so much more for you, but what can I do?" said Ghyas, spreading his hands. "Akbar is no tyrant. We owe everything we are to him," he said without looking up. "We must do as he wishes. It is our duty."

"We? It is only I who must sacrifice."

"For our family" said Ghyas, finally looking at her with tears beginning to form in his eyes.

At this point, Asmat Begum, who had been listening at the door, rushed to her daughter. She ran to the side of the bed opposite her husband and began to cry.

"You must do as the emperor wishes," she said, "or we are done for. No one can disobey the emperor."

"Oh, Mother!" Mihrunnisa said and began crying again. "Must I? What would he do?"

"Remove your father from his position. Banishment. Worse, even!"

"He would execute his chief minister?"

"One who disobeyed him? Of course."

"That is Akbar's way, Astaghfirullah," said Ghyas, shaking his head wearily.

And the two women wailed, for they knew that Mihrunnisa's future could not be altered.

She could still see him on their wedding night, true to her expectations, drunk and taking her with such bestiality that she, from that day on, harbored a simmering hatred. He had fathered her daughter, yes, but never again was there any thought of love. She considered herself fortunate that he was a soldier and not much at home.

The night of his death had haunted her, and she had thought she would never regain her sanity.

She had seen Sher Afghan run his sword through the belly of Khubu, Jahangir's foster brother, who had come to arrest him. Then the retaliation. She could still see, etched in her memory, the flying ends of a black turban, a dark man turning upon a dark horse, the arch of the scimitar gleaming in the silver moonlight, the toppled head, her husband staring with static eyes as his head fell.

To see a head severed from its body, that was a sight that even now, in memory, made her shudder. Blood spurted out of his headless torso to make a red fountain saturating the humid air with its sweet odor. His body staggered and fell as his heart pumped blood into the soil to mingle with Khubu's blood already there. She retched and retched and then fainted away into the soaking ground.

Haidar Malik, one of Jahangir's amirs at the scene, had carried her indoors, where her servants washed away the blood and put her to bed. After she had come through that ghastly night, she felt such gratitude to Haidar Malik that she ran to him and caressed him when he came the next day to check on her condition. A gross violation of Islamic protocol, she knew, but she could not help herself. In return, Haidar hugged her in such a sensual way that she had to separate herself from him, a cause for their mutual embarrassment and for her to denounce her beauty as a curse. However, the truth was that she was greatly attracted to this handsome man and under different circumstances might have responded to his advances. She never saw him again until after Jahangir's death, but she always wondered what would have been the outcome had she succumbed.

Events now moved rapidly. She was taken back to Agra, first to her parents' home and then to the bosom of Raqqua Begum, Akbar's beloved wife. Under the tender mercies of the queen mother, she mended and, not incidentally, learned the byzantine politics of the harem. Raqqua was the queen of politicians and Mihrunnisa her most avid pupil. When she graduated from Raqqua's school, she was not only fit to run the squalling harem but also to rule an empire. Oh, how she missed Raqqua!

It was getting late. She had to see the emperor before retiring. He would never stand for her not saying goodnight. Nor would her heart allow her not to.

The lamps were low when the queen entered the king's private quarters. Jahangir sat quietly by himself, listening to the poetry of Hafiz recited in the sonorous voice of the court poet. Above him was a painting of a Portuguese Madonna and Child. A gilt nimbus set off each head. Since childhood, he had found this picture particularly soothing. To him it represented the ideal of nurturing motherhood.

"I had nearly given you up," said Jahangir.

"I was deep in conversation with Father. It grew late without my knowing."

"But you seem melancholy," said Jahangir.

The poet, with his scrolls of poetry, slipped hastily into the anteroom without looking at the empress. Nur Jahan strode over to Jahangir and kissed his cheek. She sat down next to him and wrapped an arm around his shoulders.

"I worry about your health," said Nur Jahan, "and the future of the kingdom."

I have just the poem to comfort you," said Jahangir. "Hussein, recite once again 'Your Mother Is My Mother.'"

The poet, hidden behind the purdah screen, looked through his manuscripts for Hafiz's poem. He had recited it less than an hour ago. In a short while, he found it and read:

"Fear occupies the cheapest room at the Inn,
And I would like to see you living better.
For your mother is my mother.
Isn't that so?

"The Innkeeper lives in
our end of the universe.
Get some sleep tonight
And see me tomorrow.
Together we will speak to Him.

"I won't give assurances,
Just know that if you pray,
Somewhere in His world,
Something good will happen.

"Our Friend wants to see a
Twinkle in your eye,
Laughter in your soul.
Love is how he finds it.

"You and I tickled one another
In the Beloved's womb.
Our hearts are one.
We are old friends."

The queen began to cry again and fell into Jahangir's arms. "Very old friends," she said.

CHAPTER 29

"MY DEAR SIDDHICADRA, HOW PLEASANT to see you," said Jahangir. He and Nur Jahan were dining in the harem among some of his other wives, concubines, and female relatives.

"Namaste, most gracious Highness," said the monk. He pressed his hands together and bowed his shaved head.

"Your attendance pleases me as well," said Nur Jahan. "Please take food with us."

"Your Majesties will forgive me if I sip water only?"

"Yes, forgive him, my dear. Siddhicadra is averse to meat," said Jahangir, turning to his wife. "And he will not allow wine to pass his lips. You have chosen a hard path, my son."

It was because of his asceticism that Jahangir allowed the young monk free access to the harem. He came usually to study the works of literature and poetry contained in the harem library. Sometimes at the invitation of the emperor, he would deliver a sermon or enter into a philosophical discussion.

"And, I am told, he is averse to women also," said Nur Jahan, smiling. "But I daresay, women are not averse to him." Siddhicadra grinned self-consciously and adjusted the folds of his white robe. He was an extraordinarily good-looking young man of twenty-five.

"The question is, why do you do it?" Jahangir asked. "You are at the time of life when you are in most need of a wife. You are too young to be celibate." This was an old argument of Jahangir's. The king had in the past gone so far as to command the monk to marry a woman he had found for him. When he refused, Siddhicadra was, for a brief time, banished to the forest.

"But it is my youth that compels me, sire," Siddhicadra explained, "The turn of the wheel of time now brings spiritual decline. It is the young who must uphold the *dharma*."

Nonsense," interrupted the queen. "By your own system you are in error. In the ancient wisdom of Hindustan, when a man has had his fill of the pleasures of the senses, only then does he withdraw from the world."

"That is the way of the sanyasi, not of the Jain monk, Majesty. We avoid pleasures always and do not kill any of the earth's creatures," said Siddhicadra.

"But that is preposterous. Allah has created all the world for us to use. The animals are our food. In the way of the Prophet, the person living the ordinary life of a householder may enter the spiritual path. That is the true way," said Nur Jahan.

"Forgive me, Majesty. Truth is one; paths are many."

"This is an impossible argument," cried Jahangir. "Like my revered father, I encourage all religions to flourish in my domain. Is that not just? Does my queen not think so?"

"Yes, my lord. I am enthusiastic, as you already know," said the queen. She was well aware that the atmosphere of religious tolerance benefited her family and the many other Persian Shia at Jahangir's court.

"And you, Siddhicadra?"

"Only then can the truth be seen," said the monk.

"Then let this bickering cease," said Jahangir, putting forward his hand to be kissed. "I am intrigued by your philosophy, young man. You must come again to wait upon me."

"Yes, Majesty. I will reveal to you our Jain philosophy. It is summed up in one word: Ahimsa," said Siddhicadra, giving the emperor something to grapple with in his absence.

"Ahimsa?"

"Yes, nonviolence. From this, all else follows," said Siddhicadra, clutching his white robe to his chest and bowing while stepping backwards out of the chamber. "Namaste," said the monk.

The emperor dreamed that night that the handsome monk had entered his private rooms. He grasped the young man and began wrestling with him until the monk agreed to renounce his vow of celibacy. Siddhicadra cried loudly in pain. Jahangir struggled to awaken. In the early morning light, he realized that the sound he had heard was an elephant trumpeting beneath his window. He realized also that he had fallen asleep in his *jharokha* room and that he had missed this morning's darshan.

"Why in the name of Allah was I not awakened?" demanded the emperor of two servants, who cringed before him. "Why not?" He was already positioned to backhand the one closest, who was trembling with fear. Such incompetence in the past had moved Jahangir to beat the offender even to death. But before he willed himself to strike, the emperor recalled the conversation of the evening before and said to the servants gently, "I had fallen asleep here without your knowledge, is that so?" Jahangir lowered his hand and smiled.

Both servants smiled back gratefully. They would live another day.

"Yes, Majesty, the queen ordered us to find you. We had just come into the room when you awakened," said the servant who had been threatened.

"Alhamdulillah, I am blessed with a loving wife. Now, dear children, you must take me to the window. Brush me off first and dampen my face with water," said Jahangir. "If my audience has not already gone, I will allow darshan."

The emperor was not as late as he thought, and a crowd still awaited the sight of his figure at the window. The shouts of welcome lifted his spirits. Even before he had the first draw on his huqqah, he smiled broadly and waved to his people.

Already Siddhicadra has done his work, thought Jahangir as he stood before the crowd. *I will see much more of this young saint.*

Beneath Jahangir's balcony, the daily life of the empire unfolded. The blue Yamuna sparkled in the morning sun, and river craft began to fill its stream. Two elephants stood among the marsh grasses, playfully spraying each other with river water under the watchful eyes of their mahouts. On the far side of the water, the smoke of cooking fires curled into a cloudless sky. The emperor could see the forms of sleepers arising from rope beds before the walls of the imperial gardens.

A caravan had arrived trailing the line of the river. Camels laden with produce nibbled the sparse grasses along the shore. Jahangir could see the gestures of the caravaneer haggling with boatmen to fix a price to cross over into Agra.

Jahangir was filled with the knowledge that he was lord of every living creature, of every particle of earth that lay before him. Here was the vast land of Hindustan, won by blood and violence and bequeathed to him by his fathers. Like his fathers, he was a soldier, and a soldier's business was to shed blood and conquer. But Siddhicadra had set Jahangir thinking about the worthiness of it all as he stepped away from the window and went to the chapel for morning prayers. However, he could not concentrate on God. Images of bloodletting ran through Jahangir's mind. In his failed rebellion against Akbar, he had ordered Abdul Fazl killed in revenge for the murder of Anarkali Fazl was his father's biographer and close friend. The killing had alienated Akbar and caused him enormous pain. The guilt had never left Jahangir. He let the pictures of his past cruelties continue to run through his mind until the thought of ahimsa gave him relief.

Part of the attraction of Siddhicarda's Jain philosophy, Jahangir had to admit, was the youthful monk's good looks and graceful demeanor. The emperor enjoyed the physical sight of him as much as his ideas. It was a special occasion when the monk came to call.

"With respect, Majesty, we do not believe in a god who does or does not answer prayers," said Siddhicadra in response to Jahangir's question.

"Then God has no place in your thinking?"

"We believe that we attract good and evil by our actions and by our thoughts. Only by pure thought and action is the soul liberated." Siddhicadra was nearing the end of the time allotted for his audience, and he stood humbly by as Jahangir absorbed this last thought.

"Then I am doomed!" cried the emperor.

"Oh no, Majesty. You wipe the soul clean when you attract new karma through your actions. Every moment is new!"

Jahangir thought deeply about this Jain idea. Of course, this was not Islam, nor was it the Hinduism of his mother. But its truth resounded. Still, nothing could save his life, he was quite sure. Everything had its limits. His soul was beyond redemption. He thought that he no longer belonged on earth. Opium and alcohol had taken his physical being. He was already a traveler on the road to extinction. With the idea of eternity before him, Jahangir began to roar with ironic laughter.

"My lord king!" cried Siddhicadra.

"Dear boy, do not be offended," said Jahangir, halting his laughter. "It's just that your wisdom comes too late."

"But, my lord, it is never too late."

"Never for you, perhaps, but for your king. . ."

"Majesty, you are a scientist, as everyone knows. Take the vow of ahimsa and see what it brings."

Jahangir searched the monk's eyes for signs of duplicity but saw only earnestness. In the space of an instant, he decided. "I *will* take your oath," he said. "What shall I do?"

"Vow never to shoot with a gun or harm any living thing with your hand," said Siddhicadra.

"I do so vow," said the emperor with energy.

"In time, peace will descend upon you, Majesty."

"Even me?"

"Most especially you, sire. Because your burden is heavy, your relief will be great."

"I feel the peace even now as you speak," said Jahangir, his voice trailing off. He was drunk and fell asleep, slumping on his throne.

The queen lay awake in the royal chambers when the sleeping king was borne in on his palanquin. The chief eunuch, tall and imperious, was supervising.

"Wake him up!" the empress commanded as four young eunuchs placed the emperor's palanquin close to the bed where she awaited. They were four brown, supple boys freshly brought from Bengal. They were clumsy without proper training, and they were grim. All the humor of youth had been taken from them along with their maleness.

"Majesty!" said the chief eunuch.

"Wake him!" Her eyes flashed with anger. "I won't have him thrown next to me like a sack!"

The emperor rose slowly and rubbed his bloodshot eyes. "Quite right! I am not an article to be flung about!" he said playfully, although he did resemble a precious item. His tunic glimmered with rubies and emeralds and tilted down on his forehead was his turban of Persian silk stuck with a heron's feather. The toes of his satin slippers pointed upward at the palanquin's silken top like curled elephant's trunks.

"I want to speak to you," said Nur Jahan and made a sign dismissing the bare-chested eunuchs. In this early stage of their emasculation, they often became suicidal and could behave unpredictably, even toward the emperor. Hoshiyar Khan, the chief eunuch, school-marmishly extended his arms and gave a theatrical push that ordered them to leave the empress's private suite.

"Oh, how I hate you when you are in one of your foolish moods," said the queen after the boys had gone.

"I have a crushing headache. Can we not speak tomorrow?" the emperor lied, pushing his turban back from his forehead.

"Now! Now only! Don't you understand? I have serious business to discuss."

"What is it, then?" cried the emperor impatiently.

"I am nervous about Shah Jahan!" the empress declared.

"My dear, you are always nervous about something."

"His activities in the Deccan are not consistent with those of a loyal son."

"Your spies tell you this?"

"The news writers, as always. Patience, my king. I'm attempting to be delicate."

"What is it, then?" asked Jahangir, suddenly concerned.

"Khusro is dead," she whispered.

"Oh my God! How . . . how can this be?"

"My lord, he was in Shah Jahan's keeping," said the queen as if that were an explanation.

Jahangir rose fully from the palanquin and began pacing before his queen's divan. His mind was purged of alcohol. The opium still clung but allowed him to think clearly. He had his hand on the hilt of his dagger.

"Yes, yes, what are the details?" demanded Jahangir. "You must not spare me. Where is Shah Jahan?"

"It is Shah Jahan who has sent word. I have the letter wherein he states that Sultan Khusro has died of colic. Here, read for yourself."

"I cannot read now," cried Jahangir. His eyes clouded with tears. "Colic? Is that so?"

"It is what the letter states."

"When? What date? When did he die?"

"Shah Jahan says it occurred two weeks ago. The letter was signed by Abdur Rahim as well, to attest the cause."

The emperor laughed bitterly. "Not to arouse my suspicions, I suppose," he said. "And where is Jagat Gosaini's son now?"

"He writes from Bhurhanpur," said Nur Jahan. "There is a second letter, my lord."

"Oh?"

"From Nuruddin Quli, whose letter arrived from the same place. He puts Khusro's death in November, two months ago." She placed the letter coyly before the king.

"Read it! Read it aloud!" he said. "I have no patience now for reading."

She unrolled the scroll and began, "Most invincible, most mighty king, the divine rays of the almighty—"

"For God's sake, spare me the flowers! What does this devil want of me?"

"Quli is loyal to you, sire."

"Upon my soul! Out with it!"

"He tells you of his suspicions, nay of the facts of Khusro's death. That an assassin strangled him on Shah Jahan's orders. While the prince was away hunting, the deed was done."

"Is Quli to be believed?" asked Jahangir, examining his queen with sharp eyes.

"He has my trust."

"Then Shah Jahan must come to court. Where is Khusro buried? Does the letter say?"

"Shah Jahan does not say, but Quli discloses that Khusro lies in a garden close to the palace."

"I will have his body taken to Agra. You must make the arrangements."

"I will, sire. It is my duty."

"The summons to my son must come directly from me." The emperor paced resolutely, full of fury. With his shoulders held back, for a moment he was again the warrior king.

"The Persian king is threatening Kandahar," said Nur Jahan out of the blue.

"Why do you bring this up now?" Jahangir demanded. "I cannot deal with everything at once."

"Because the garrison is weak, sire, and there are idle soldiers in the Deccan," said the queen.

"Ah, I see. Then Shah Jahan can be called up north," said Jahangir.

". . . without making obvious the issue of Khusro," said Nur Jahan. "Call him to defend Kandahar. It is true we need him there now. I have word from Aziz Khan. Without the prince, Kandahar will fall. Aziz sends out sorties daily, but it is not enough to slow the Persian advance."

"Send word to Aziz that I will ask the governor of Multan to assist him with rice and ghee and such troops as he can muster until my son arrives."

That night, runners were dispatched to Multan, to Kandahar on the Persian border, and to the Deccan. By relay, messages could reach the ends of the empire in a matter of days.

CHAPTER 30

THE LAST RUNNER IN THE chain from Agra ran breathlessly into Shah Jahan's tent and pressed his head and chest to the carpet. He placed Jahangir's summons at the feet of Abdur Rahim. The grand vizier took a coin from his purse, flipped it at the prostrate runner, and motioned him to leave. A servant sprang to lift the bamboo cylinder and hand it to Abdur. "It is from your father," he said, unrolling the scroll.

"Give it to me," said Shah Jahan. "He orders my return to Agra," he said, holding the unfurled scroll in both hands.

"No mention of Khusro?"

"None. He says Kandahar needs defending and orders me to come."

"Persia attacks once again?" asked Abdur Rahim.

"Of course. Shah Abbas is ever eager to cause trouble. He praises my father on the one hand, and with the other he strikes like a cobra when his guard is down."

"You know the Persians; they resent our strength and our wealth. Not to say that we drain off their best men to work in our service."

"There are Persians among us I wish I had never seen," said Shah Jahan ruefully.

"The Iti-mad-ud-daula is one, I dare say," said Rahim, laughing. "And his daughter?"

"She will be my undoing," said the shah with a scowling laugh. "This summons reeks of her perfume. Eh, Abdur, is that not so?" Shah Jahan sat winding the scroll.

"Your father has abdicated in favor of an ambitious woman. But what is to be done?" said Abdur, shrugging his shoulders.

"I can say what won't be done," Shah Jahan said.

"Yes?"

"I will stay put."

"And in so doing admit to murder? You place the throne outside your reach, my lord. Your father is ill. Stay here and Nur Jahan will crown her daughter's husband the moment death strikes the emperor."

"My father-in-law is a Persian who loves me. He will block her."

"His own sister?"

"To advance his daughter? I think he will."

"Better to tell your father that we will proceed to Mandu and wait out the rains before coming to court, and then ask for full command of the army of the Punjab as a condition."

"My stepmother will never agree. Gradually she forces me away from the center of power. She looks after herself. When Jahangir dies, she will retain power only if my imbecile brother Shahryar is crowned."

"Yet Kandahar will fall if we are not there to save it, and Kabul will be next."

"This is the dilemma that diabolical woman places me in," said Shah Jahan.

"If you stay, you will be denounced as a traitor," said Abdur Rahim, "and the imperial vengeance will rain upon you."

"If I go, I lose my base in the Deccan and all the work I have done to secure it," said Shah Jahan. "And if I am off in Kandahar and my father dies, I chance missing the throne. I am completely in the hands of that *Shaitan*."

"I urge you, send word that you will spend the monsoon in Mandu. Your father will agree. He will not want your army in Agra, soaked and unruly. This will buy us time and give the appearance of compliance. Even Nur Jahan will not have grounds for complaint."

CHAPTER 31

THE RAVI RUSHED IN A gray torrent, swelling its banks. All river traffic had ceased, but in Lahore, the streets throbbed with humanity. Men in longhis, women in saris and naked little children danced joyfully in the cool rain, praising Allah's mercy in quenching the blazing inferno of summer.

A dark curtain of rain swept against the palace. Awnings sheltered windows and entrances. At every doorway, little groups of servants gathered to see the rain and watch the palms bend to scrape the palace walls. The rain was so heavy and the sky so dark that it seemed to be night while the sun had risen just hours before. Inside the palace, ghee lamps flickered before the currents of damp air that scurried through every opening.

"He begs to spend the season in Mandu while Kandahar falls," Jahangir exclaimed irritably, putting down the message that had just arrived at the jharokha door. Nur Jahan stood at his side. The daily darshan had been canceled for the duration of the monsoon, and so had the elephant fights. The royal couple stood before the window to feel the skimming wind and to watch the river race beneath them. On the other side of the water, villagers crouched under awnings hung from garden walls and in doorways to watch the rain slide in sheets into the foaming river.

The empress had received word from the south that Shah Jahan had attacked her prince. She had been waiting for the proper moment to tell Jahangir, a time when it would produce the most outrage.

"My lord, Shah Jahan now presumes to control lands that you have most graciously bestowed upon my son-in-law," said Nur Jahan.

"Of what do you speak?"

"What you had given in *jagir* to my prince, Shah Jahan now claims as his own and makes war on him."

"War?"

"Much blood has been shed."

"My most favored son! He is the cause of all my sorrow. He is unworthy of all the favors and cherishing I have given him. He brings me shame upon shame. I shall find the cause of this boldness, rest assured!"

An abrupt change in the course of the wind brought a blast of cold rain through the unglazed window, soaking Nur Jahan and making her gasp. Two servants rushed at her with thick towels, then led her to the brazier that warmed the marble room. Other servants ran to close the shutters. Still others went on their hands and knees to dry the floor with large irregular sponges.

"Are you well?" asked Jahangir, walking over to where Nur Jahan leaned against a pillar with dripping hair and wet, disheveled clothing.

"I must change into dry clothes. Meditate on a course of action. Not only does he refuse his duty in Kandahar, but he does ill in Shahryar's rightful territories. This is sedition!"

Nur Jahan brushed aside the offered help of her servants. She walked briskly out of the jharokha room and went down the corridor to her apartments. There, she was greeted by her chief female servant, who bowed low and asked, "Madam?"

"I shall not bathe again. Just prepare dry clothes, the ensemble we considered earlier . . . the red bodice, the shalwar. . . You know the one."

"Yes, Majesty," said the servant. With the help of a slave, she had already begun to undress the queen. Other female slaves rubbed her naked parts with towels.

The chill had caused Nur Jahan's nipples to harden and her skin to tighten. Warmed aromatic oils were rubbed onto her body as she stood naked beside a brazier glowing with red coals. A slave held before her a gilt looking glass that Roe had brought from England. The queen looked first at her face. In the mottled silver of the glass, she could see the perfect line of her nose, the glint of her eyes, and the high arch of her eyebrows. She blinked at her image and smiled. She then ordered the slave to place the mirror before her chest. The sight of her upright breasts pleased her. She held a hand under one to appraise the wide crimson circle of its aureole and did the same with the other.

She ordered the mirror lowered so that she could view her pubis. In accordance with the *sunnah* of the Prophet, each morning it was shaved and rubbed with pumice so that its smooth skin glistened. She could see the lines of the delicate place below, so cherished by her husband. She smiled when she thought of an intimate moment. But this location was more than a seat of pleasure, she reflected. In the philosophy of the Hindus, it was the center of power and had the same name—Shakti—the site most loved and feared by men.

The mirror looked below her thighs. She ordered her kneecaps smoothed with pumice. Every part of her body was rubbed vigorously with perfumed oil, and she shone in the mirror like the statue of a goddess.

Yes, the queen is beautiful, she thought. *More than that, the queen is wise in the ways of the world and smarter than the world would ever guess.* The empire was now in her hands, and she would make of it a prosperous and decent place for all its citizens. This was her calling and, Alhamdulillah, her duty. Jahangir had lain the burden of empire at her feet, and she had taken it up. She had designed government policy, constructed extraordinary buildings, created rest stations along the highways, and built gardens across the empire. Her father's tomb was a masterpiece designed by her and cherished by her subjects. Her ships crossed the Arabian Sea, bringing pilgrims to Mecca and goods to the empire's markets. She sent caravans into the interior to fetch produce, spices, and medicinal herbs. Agra had become the vital center of the empire's commerce, and its markets overflowed with Hindustan's abundance. And yet the nobles considered her rule a presumption, that Jahangir was a weakling from whom she had wrested the empire. She had gone so far, they said, that she had persuaded him to mint coins with her image: "Whosoever wields the sword, coins are stamped in his name" was a slogan often quoted. All that remained was to have the sermon at Friday prayers recited in her name and the realm would be slave to her Shakti!

Nur Jahan knew what they said: a man submissive to a woman was weaker than a woman. This was not true, she reflected ruefully. Her husband had incapacitated himself with drugs and drinking, and if the truth were known, there would be no empire were it not for his spirit and intelligence. Her husband was a strong man who had stumbled. She and her brilliant Persian family had taken up the load, and the empire had benefited greatly. *That* was the truth.

To be a queen, one must be absolutely fastidious in dress and in every other particular, she thought. *And I will be queen. My king needs me. The empire demands it. How long will my beloved last? He is very near the end. And Shah Jahan? He is a puzzle that must be solved.*

"Yes, Ammina, the white garments, but I will wear only the amber beads and the diamond strand. The emerald broach I shall leave for another time. I think my veil should be white." said the empress.

"Oh yes, Majesty, white only." The servants finished the job of dressing her and brought back the mirror.

"Yes, yes," she said, looking at her bare midriff. "Fit the Bengali ruby into my navel and we shall be done."

"Sedition is the word," said Jahangir, remembering the conversation in the jharokha room earlier. They were sitting in the main chamber of the palace. Musicians were accompanying dancers, a score of them moving with classical Indian form. Jahangir had taken an opium pill. With the help of a female servant who held a jade goblet to his lips, he was sipping yellow wine. He sat presiding over a gathering of Hindustan's most powerful nobles and generals.

"I will give command of the Kandahar forces over to my fortunate son, my Shahryar," said Jahangir.

"Alhamdulillah," murmured the queen, who sat listening behind the purdah screen.

"But, Your Majesty, hadn't you better reconsider?" said Mahabat Khan. "With all due respect, Shahryar is hardly suited to the task."

"What do you suggest?" asked the emperor. His hands opened in an inquisitive gesture.

"Shah Jahan is by far—"

"No, no, do not mention my infamous son," Jahangir quickly interrupted. "The wretch refuses my orders and is in a state of rebellion. In fact, I have already taken measures to bring him to heel. Henceforth I shall finance the Kandahar expedition out of Shah Jahan's northern jagirs. That should give him pause for thought."

CHAPTER 32

"THERE ARE TWO REPORTS THAT require your attention," said Abdur Rahim. "First is the dire news that Kandahar has fallen. The other is that Jahangir is moving the treasury from Agra to Lahore. Both items come from Asaf Khan."

"Ah, my father fears that I move on Agra."

"Asaf says that the news of Kandahar's fall has not yet reached Jahangir's ears; thus, he moves the treasury to be used in its defense. Jahangir plans to send our good Abdullah Khan to guard the citadel!"

"Ha! And my father calls *me* unfortunate!" said Shah Jahan, laughing, and then more seriously, "It is only a matter of time before he discovers the true situation. Send to Abdullah Khan. He is to turn his thoughts toward the treasury. Strike camp, my dear Abdur. We move immediately!"

CHAPTER 33

"MY HANDS SHAKE SO, MY darling, that I can no longer hold a pen. I have had to ask a scribe to help complete my memoirs. I fall in and out of delirium." The emperor was propped upright on pillows arranged against the wall. He sat on his divan, puffing his bubbling hookah. The queen had draped him with a warm pashmina shawl. His face was drawn, and he stared hollow-eyed beneath his turban. The room was sunny. Outside, the torrents of dark rain that had assailed the harem walls had ceased days ago. The monsoon was over, and the palace garden was alive with the extravagant green of spring.

Aside from the female guard who stood stoically at the entrance, the royal couple was alone.

"Kandahar is as near death as I am," said Jahangir, still unaware that the city had fallen.

"You mustn't speak that way!" said Nur Jahan. A blue vein throbbed at her temple. Her eyes were awash with tears. "This will pass. Both you and Kandahar will survive," said the queen, who sat cross-legged before Jahangir.

"We are at the edge of civil war. This is where my son has brought us. I name him, now, Bidaulat—Wretch—you must also call him the same. Not Prince, not Sultan. Bidaulat is his title. Because he now moves on Agra, the momentous affair of Kandahar must be postponed. He has heard that the treasury will be moved, and he has left Mandu. I curse this ungrateful Bidaulat. I lose both son and kingdom!"

"You lose nothing when you lose the prince!"

"Bidaulat!" the emperor corrected.

"Yes, precisely, Bidaulat!" said Nur Jahan. She sat restlessly, tugging at the scarf that hung from her neck.

"His army has encamped at Agra's wall," said the emperor, "and he has found it amply defended. My men have aimed cannon from the castle's top, and the gates are bricked up. Agra has not succumbed to his assault; the treasury is safe. My news writers now tell me that thwarted, my unworthy son pillages the nearby towns and even the homes of my amirs to pay his army, as if it were royal privilege."

"This must cease!" cried Nur Jahan.

"Yes, tomorrow I mount my elephant and bring the war to Bidaulat."

"Oh my God, no! You cannot!" shouted Nur, her face registering horror. "By your own admission, you are too sick to fight!"

"Yes, but never too sick to ride an elephant. The sight of their emperor energizes my armies. Besides, I find warfare calming," said Jahangir, "Am I not a Mughal?"

"I cannot allow this."

"My dear, my soldiers must see me and I them."

"No!"

"If you love me, you will not argue."

"But I do love you."

"Is that all you say?"

"Yes, my lord king, my darling, my dearest, yes, I will not argue. I love you more than I can measure," said the queen. She could not hold back the tears and fell to her knees, sobbing on Jahangir's shoulder.

"I will win this battle for you. He is your enemy as well as mine."

"I beg you stay out of harm's way," said the queen, barely able to get the words out through her sobs.

She took the huqqah's velvet snake from the king's hand and placed its end between her lips. She drew the sweet smoke deep into her lungs, then had another pull and another, and soon she lay dreaming at her husband's side.

The emperor's health had taken an uptick and the trembling had nearly stopped when, a week later and in the best of spirits, he sat high up in his howdah with General Mahabat Khan at his side. They were riding Jahangir's prized Ceylon elephant, famous for its courage in battle. The elephant led a company of horsemen, Jahangir's personal guard.

On either side of the massive entrance to Agra Fort stood red stone towers, huge in height and circumference, standing sentinel beneath *chatris* that looked like wide-brimmed European hats. Before them, a staircase of granite slab, specially constructed to bear the weight of elephants, stepped down to a level field. The main force of the army mustered there, all aglitter in long, irregular rows beneath the white yak-tail standards and the lion banners of the Mughal Empire. The army band played a salute as the emperor's elephant stepped, sure footed, down the steps, with the Ahadi horse clicking and sparking in the rear.

Coming to meet the emperor astride his own beautifully dressed elephant was Asaf Khan, who led a troop of soldiers. His drums beat a lively tattoo, and his pennants waved gloriously in the spring sunshine. Asaf had written that Shah Jahan had "torn off the veil of respect" and that Asaf would come to be at his emperor's side.

"Look to the east, my lord. Asaf Khan approaches," said Mahabat as their elephant descended the stairs.

"Ah, dear loyal Asaf," said Jahangir. "He brings an army as well. Are we sure on whose side he will fight?"

"The side that gives him the most advantage, as always, sire," said Mahabat.

"Then it is a good omen that he comes to us. He foresees the winner," said Jahangir, laughing.

CHAPTER 34

After a month of barely profitable raiding, Shah Jahan had turned his army northward toward Delhi, where he hoped to meet the emperor in battle.

"We are sliding toward bankruptcy," said Shah Jahan.

"You pay your men better than they deserve," said Abdur Rahim.

"The monsoon is over. If I give them small money, they will turn back to farming or, worse, to the enemy. Soldiering is a seasonal profession in our parts. No one knows this better than you, sahib."

"I am of the mind that those nobles who have come to our side from Jahangir should bear part of the expense of the war. After all, they will share in the spoils of our victory."

"In time, Abdur sahib, in time. First we must defeat the emperor in a small battle at least; then my hand will be strengthened."

"Did you know that our Asaf Khan marches right now under Jahangir's banner?" said Abdur.

"Only for the present, to keep up appearances. He is still very much my father-in-law."

CHAPTER 35

THE EMPEROR HAD LEARNED THE lesson of the Jain sages and had taken the vow of ahimsa. He had resolved never to do violence to any living thing with his own hand. But now this Bidaulat had raised his head in rebellion, and Jahangir's reasoning had spun around. *I have no choice but to kill,* he thought as his long lines of infantrymen and cavalry marched toward Delhi. *I beg Allah's beneficence; let this war be short.*

For a moment, Jahangir considered leaving the harem behind the walls of Agra Fort. He understood that neither Akbar nor any other emperor had ever done so. They were too fearful of losing their treasure of females to an opportunistic army. But Jahangir had left a large garrison, and he was sure they would be safe there. Moreover, the presence of the harem slowed the army down to a snail's pace, and here speed was of the essence. In the end, though, he did as all Mughal emperors had done before him and took the zanana with him in the slow splendor and comfort to which his women were accustomed.

"News from our scouts, my king," said Mahabat Khan, reading a communication that had been handed up by a messenger on the morning of the tenth day of the march. He was sitting side by side with Jahangir in the swaying howdah. His jeweled turban sparkled in the morning sun. "It is not Shah Jahan who leads the army but Sundar," Mahabat informed the emperor.

"And who might Sundar be?"

"You know of him, I'm sure: the Gujarati warlord."

"Ah, just a moment. Yes, he is rajah. Am I right?"

"You are most correct, Majesty."

"This Sundar, as you call him, has a fearsome reputation. He is bold and intelligent," said Jahangir.

"A superb general," added Mahabat Khan.

"But we will win. I have consulted my oracle. He has given me every assurance."

"Forgive me, Your Majesty, but when have your soothsayers not given you every assurance?" said Mahabat Khan jokingly.

"I defy you to give me an instance when they were proven wrong," said the emperor in good humor. "But that is beside the point. I have every confidence that we will be victorious."

"I too feel thus, sire, but my certainty is based on a sure knowledge of our capabilities."

"Assalaamu 'Aleichem," cried a runner hurrying from the rear.

"What is it you want?" shouted Mahabat Khan, looking over his shoulder, irritated at the interruption.

"The rebels have attacked our rear flank, your grace." The army's slow pace had rendered it vulnerable to such incursions.

"Sundar's men?" asked Mahabat, looking down at the man, who was dressed in only a loincloth.

"Yes, but we have turned them back!" The runner was trotting alongside Jahangir's elephant, squinting up at the sun and the men in the golden howdah and straining to catch his breath as he spoke.

"We have defeated them?"

"Oh yes, Majesty!" exclaimed the runner.

"This is what I mean by sure knowledge," said Mahabat Khan, turning to the emperor and smiling. Jahangir glanced over his shoulder at the runner, whose pace slowed to a walk as he fell behind the elephant.

"'Have faith in your commanders' is how my seer put it," said Jahangir, turning back to Mahabat.

"We will send scouts to find the enemy camp and strike as soon as we have news. Let us get this dirty little piece of business over as soon as possible. Agreed?"

"Soothsayers and tacticians stand as one," said Mahabat Khan, smiling and putting his forefingers side-by-side to show unity.

CHAPTER 36

IT WAS THE END OF March. The mild temperatures of spring had given way to the scalding heat of summer.

At Baluchpur, under a fierce sun, the Mughal cavalry, mail clad and sword wielding, galloped at the rebels. The horsemen rode wild-eyed with yak tails flying out from under their saddles. They wielded the curved Mughal bow as well and shot arrow after arrow as they rode. Behind them, howling like madmen, came the imperial infantry, charging with pikes and English swords. Then the cannon sent shot over the heads of the riders, and smoke rolled through the files. Matchlock men fell to their haunches and aimed their weapons braced on wooden yokes. In the rear were the old adversaries, Asaf Khan and Mahabat Khan, now co-commanding, each of them riding a Ceylon elephant bearing an armored howdah set with a heavy musket. Alongside them a line of mailed elephants advanced to the deep voices of a hundred kettle drums.

The rebel line broke. They were outclassed in both men and weapons. Sundar himself was thrown from his elephant, frightened by a volley of rocket fire. Immediately, he was run through with an infantryman's sword, and another sword separated his head from his body. With their general dead and their salary in doubt, the surviving troops ran from the battlefield to the vicinity of their employer, Shah Jahan. It was a total rout. Imperial forces had defeated the rebel army and killed its commanding general.

Sundar's head, grasped by the topknot, swung like a censer before the emperor, who rested on a portable throne in the imperial tent. Although Jahangir had enthusiastically wanted to join in the battle, Mahabat Khan had persuaded him not to do so.

"My lord, behold the enemy!" Mahabat Khan exclaimed with satisfaction as he raised Sundar's head high over his own head. The enemy leader's mouth and chin were mottled with congealed blood. His eyes were closed and the face peaceful, as if meditating.

"Sundar?" asked the emperor. Mahabat nodded with a great smile. "Even Siddhicadra will forgive my delight. You have done splendidly. And you as well, dear Asaf. From the look of him, it seems that you have dispatched him to Paradise!" said Jahangir jovially.

Asaf Khan bowed and delivered a graceful kornish. Both generals were still dressed in their soiled battlefield *jubbas.* They stood before the emperor relaxed and beaming as Mahabat lowered the head and placed it under the arch of his left foot. The king proffered his hand to Mahabat and Asaf Khan. After Mahabat had taken the emperor's hand to his lips, Asaf Khan bent his brow to the king's knuckles. As Asaf prepared to kiss the back of Jahangir's hand, the emperor said in a low, confidential voice, "Tell me, have you heard from your son-in-law?"

"Nay, sire. I will not communicate with a traitor," whispered Asaf Khan.

"All the same, you should say to him that in view of Sundar's destruction, he should not again gird his loins against his father-emperor. Will you deliver that message?"

"If it pleases you, sire, I shall, certainly."

"Tell him also that the penalty for treason is death," said Jahangir. He paused to fix his gaze on Asaf Khan, who had risen to stand up straight before him. The khan returned a look of complete innocence.

Is it the Persian blood that makes my wife's family so duplicitous? Jahangir asked himself. *Perhaps so*, he answered, *but it is a fact that the empire needs such men.*

"And now we press on in pursuit of Bidaulat. Khuda hafiz," said the emperor aloud and rose from his throne. Spontaneously, the standing crowd of turbaned nobles, some bandaged and bloodstained, shouted, "*Pad shah Sala'mat!*" as the unsteady monarch was led from his crimson tent.

———

In the middle of April, in the deadliest heat of summer, Jahangir paused to wait for his son Parviz at the edge of Keetham Lake. Parviz was to assume command of the army and pursue his wayward brother, Shah Jahan. Jahangir could then return to Agra to recover from the strains of the campaign that had wearied him and further damaged his health.

The Mughal camp was flung out along the eastern shore so that the army could enjoy the cool breezes coming off the water. Campfires fringed the lake, and the smell of broiling kebabs suffused the grounds the night that Sultan Parviz entered camp riding a camel. The prince was drunk and in the company of a group of his amirs, who also rode on camels.

"My most fortunate son has come to the rescue," cried Jahangir, embracing Parviz. The two men were alone in Jahangir's private tent. Outside, the night was still, but the joking voices of Parviz's drunken nobles carried from the lake's edge where they were watering their mounts. A solitary voice from the soldiers' camp traced the arabesques of an ancient love song.

"Tell me, Father, how is it that you picked me? Is it to humiliate Shah Jahan?" asked Parviz.

"Because you are the appropriate warrior, my son. Bidaulat has proven himself unworthy. You will succeed me. I want the world to know of your prowess."

"Has the world changed, then, since you relieved me of command in the Deccan?"

"Enormously so. You are now my favored son."

"But the rumors are that Mahabat Khan is to proceed with the army. Am I to be merely a figurehead?"

"The khan is the senior general. He advises even the emperor. Take this as a soldier without grumbling. I'm giving you the chance to settle scores with your brother."

Parviz stood still for a moment, considering. Then he answered, "Very well, Father, I accept. You want me to bring Shah Jahan to justice, Father, and I shall. I will kill him with the greatest pleasure, of that you can be assured," said Parviz, contorting his handsome features into a mask of hatred. Parviz's clothing still held the dust of travel. His face was wind-burnt and had the look of health, but beneath his jubba was an ailing body much older than its thirty-four years. Even the tent's atmosphere of incense and sweet perfume could not conceal his personal odor of stale alcohol and decrepitude.

"I want him alive!" cried the emperor.

"Alive?"

"I want to see his arrogant face beg for my mercy. Do not take that satisfaction from me!" The thought of torturing his son soothed the emperor's nerves. He wanted to burn Shah Jahan with firebrands until he acknowledged his wrongdoing. Then perhaps they would reconcile, his favorite son and him. He would offer him the empire; he would transfer it to his son as a pure act of love. Then he thought of how Shah Jahan had refused his request to fight in Kandahar, and immediately the image of his son's head splattering under the foot of an elephant came to mind.

"I leave this entire matter in your hands. With Mahabat Khan at your side, I will take my weary body to Ajmer and await your success."

"Let us drink to that, Father," said Parviz drunkenly. He was propping himself against a tent post and hoped his father would ask him to sit.

"Nothing for me. And it would do you good to stop wine yourself," the king said.

Jahangir had been drinking steadily all day, but he could not stop moralizing where his sons were concerned. He did so without the slightest feeling of hypocrisy. It pained him that his son, like himself, was victim to the family susceptibility to alcohol. Jahangir's brothers, Murad and Daniyal, had both had their lives shortened due to drinking. Indeed, the entire male line dating back to Babur had had their troubles with alcohol.

When he thought seriously about it, Jahangir knew that Parviz was too weak to rule. The truth was—and he had trouble admitting it—that Shah Jahan was the only one of his sons fit to administer the empire. He hoped desperately that Shah Jahan would submit to him not only to save face, but to make an orderly succession.

The next morning, Jahangir and Parviz stood outside the scarlet tent watching the long procession of Parviz's cavalry, his rolling bronze artillery, and the files of his motley infantry. Parviz had brought his harem with him, swaying in howdahs and palanquins. Then the camp followers: tradesmen, prostitutes, wives, children, and goats. Housewares were packed high in bullock carts.

Jahangir was saddened that his two sons would soon be at war with each other. He looked up at the brightening sky as if he could find some answer there but cast his eyes down to earth once again in sadness. He spoke to Parviz above the sounds of the drums and fifes. He shouted over the beating hoofs, the noise of the caissons, and the songs of the marching infantrymen.

"Bidaulat's army is moving toward us. Foolish boy. We far outnumber him."

"Go to Ajmer with a mind at rest, Father," said Parviz at the top of his voice. "I shall bring you honor."

"I have no doubt but spare him. Do not allow him to be killed," said Jahangir, but his confidence was entirely in Mahabat Khan. He began to weep. He turned away from the march and walked back into his tent, where Mahabat Khan was waiting.

"It is Abdur Rahim, that chief of deceivers, who is the ringleader of trouble and sedition. He goads Bidaulat on," said Mahabat.

"Abdur Rahim? Bidaulat had him in prison," said Jahangir. His tears had stopped, and he had begun to think clearly again.

"Bars cannot contain his evil. It spreads out like a stain from his cell," said Mahabat.

"Bidaulat makes his own evil."

"I rue the day that you pardoned Abdur."

"He will yet prove useful," said Jahangir.

"He is completely untrustworthy, Majesty."

"Yes, of course," said Jahangir. "We can expect an offer from him at any time. He is more duplicitous than our Asaf Khan. My spies tell me that Bidaulat released him only after he swore loyalty on the Qur'an. Is that not the surest sign that he is soon to change coats?"

"I want his head!" cried Mahabat Khan.

"Why settle for his head when we can have his entire body and half of Bidaulat's army as well?" said Jahangir, laughing lightly. "Patience, my dear Mahabat."

———

The emperor left for Ajmer the next morning. Part of the imperial army went with him. A week later, he received news that the royal forces under Parviz and Mahabat Khan had easily defeated Shah Jahan's small army.

As it became clear that Shah Jahan's was the losing cause, more and more of his rebel troops fled to the imperial banner. As the emperor had predicted, Abdur Rahim went over to Mahabat Khan. With the main body of his troops still intact, Shah Jahan took his family and pressed south to the Deccan, where he stopped briefly at Golconda, outside Mughal territory. Then he went north to conquer Orissa, which was under Mughal rule. He ranged up the coast to take Bengal, then north to Bihar. From there he ventured northwest to lay siege to Allahabad, where he met Parviz and Mahabat Khan. After a prolonged battle on the banks of the Ganges, the imperial army drove Shah Jahan back to Orissa.

Mahabat was relentless. He countered the shah at every turn and forced him finally back into the Deccan. At Berar, Shah Jahan had reached the end of his rope.

———

"I am a cornered rat, and now fever. If not for you, I would be dead," said Shah Jahan, who was shivering and lying on a cot in a garden. Although the morning had become hot, a warm compress lay on his brow, and a woolen blanket was drawn up to his neck.

"Let us not speak of death on this fine morning," said Mumtaz Mahal. She was sitting cross-legged on a brocaded cushion at his side. She was radiant in the sunlight that filtered through the champa trees.

"I have finally received word from your Persian, Abbas. Do you know what he says?"

"No, my lord."

"He says to be obedient to my father! If the fever isn't enough to finish me, I shall laugh myself to death!" Shah Jahan cried.

"My lord, please!"

"This is the end. I have nowhere to go. Even my Sargent-at-arms has deserted me to become a fakir!" Shah Jahan exclaimed. "He says he will lead me to salvation. He too is despondent."

"Then it is time for you to take Shah Abbas's advice," offered Mumtaz patiently.

"Ha, my father will hang me!"

"Not if you are properly repentant."

"I will not debase myself!" exclaimed Shah Jahan.

"It is a small thing to humble oneself before one's father. The reward will be great both in this world and at the day of judgment."

"Is this written in the Qur'an?"

"It is written in the books of the wise."

"It is you that is wise," said Shah Jahan.

"We have no other choice. You must become your father's son."

"If I survive this illness, I will write him for your sake. Do you love me?"

"What?"

"Do you love me?"

"I have given you thirteen children. Is that not proof?"

"But do you love me now?" said Shah Jahan. His series of military defeats had drained him of all self-confidence.

"Sometimes you are like a little boy," said Mumtaz, smiling. "I will nurse you as I would a child. Inshallah, you will get better and not ask such questions."

"I shall need a bit of the afim to drive away the fever."

"Yes, I will bring you some and another blanket to help you sweat."

CHAPTER 37

"My son has written me a letter," said Jahangir.

"Parviz?" said the queen.

"No, my dear, Shah Jahan."

"Shah Jahan? He is no longer Bidaulat?"

"Well, for a short time he was, but now . . . read the letter, will you?"

And so, she read:

Assalaamu 'Alaikum, dearest Father-emperor,

As you may have heard (your ears are everywhere), I have just recovered from the most grievous illness. Only through Allah, most Gracious, most Merciful, the Cherisher and Sustainer of the worlds, have I been diverted from the grave. In the midst of my fever when I thought all was lost, by His Divine Grace, angels came to wrest me from the hands of the Grim Despoiler and by their spotless commentary restored my mind to sanity. They declared that my place is at my father's side augmenting him, not provoking him astride an elephant. In the name of Allah, I beg forgiveness and pray that we can become once more united as father and son. May Allah preserve and protect you and the ever-compassionate Queen Nur.

Khuda hafiz,

Your devoted son Khurram

"The ever-compassionate queen. Ha!" cried Nur Jahan. "That's a nice touch.

"What are you saying?"

"You are not fooled, are you? This drips with insincerity. He is at his wits' end; that is obvious. And he signs himself 'Your devoted son Khurram.' What hogwash!"

"Do not mock his efforts to be a son to me. Do not!" said Jahangir, full of fury.

"My lord, I merely point out what—"

"That is quite enough. This is a happy occasion, and I rejoice that my son returns to me."

"A full pardon?"

"Yes!"

"You blinded Khusro for less, and he has a huge following even now. It is you who mock the memory of Khusro."

"Mock him?"

"Do you not see how this will be perceived among the people? Khusro has taken on the aura of a saint. In the districts of the poor, he is worshiped, even among the Hindus. What I am saying is that Shah Jahan must be punished if you wish to keep faith with your people."

"Ya Allah! Do you think I should blind him for consistency's sake?"

"I say that you must find a punishment, a diminution of his prerogatives, perhaps, something firm that will let the people know that the emperor is not to be trifled with. And do not make the mistake of accepting him here in your midst. However much you may love him, he is a dangerous man. That is beyond doubt."

"You make my head hurt with this. Leave me now." The emperor put his hands to his temples and closed his eyes. His body as well as his mind was reeling.

"My lord, there is more to say."

"And I say leave me now, damn you!"

"My lord!"

"Go. Once and for all, go. I will make my own decision. Get out of my sight. Go!" Jahangir was snarling. He had reached his limit. Nur Jahan had every reason to be afraid. At this stage, the emperor was unpredictable.

"As you wish, my lord," said Nur Jahan, bowing and backing out of his presence as would a slave girl, an action bordering on sarcasm. But Jahangir was rereading the letter and did not notice.

For Nur Jahan, this was merely a tactical retreat. The queen would be back in the morning with fresh ammunition. She had lost a battle, but the war was interminable while Shah Jahan was alive. She could not allow him back at court. She would disenfranchise him. If she were to survive in power after the emperor's death, she must at all costs have Shahryar crowned as king.

CHAPTER 38

"I HAVE RECEIVED HIS ANSWER. You will not like it," said Shah Jahan.

"What says the letter, prince?" Mumtaz Mahal inquired with a look of fright.

Shah Jahan had fully recovered. It was just after morning prayer, and the audience room was sunlit and full of the prince's retainers. The letter had come the night before. They sat at a divan while the morning meal was served.

"All our sons are to be sent to court, and we must go into exile."

"What?!" she exclaimed.

"Our sons are to be kept as hostages. He will accept nothing less."

"How can I part with my children?" Mumtaz said with tears rising. "This is her doing. There is no doubt. I will not permit it."

"I must surrender Rohtas and the fort at Asir."

"What will we have left?"

"He will allow me the province of Balaghat."

"Ya Allah, I would rather be dead than live in that godforsaken wilderness. Are you to be prince of the Gonds? She humiliates us."

"She is your aunt."

"I spit upon her! She will not take my children from me!"

"We must comply. The boys will be safe and well taken care of. You must look at this in perspective. Jahangir's time is short. This exile will give us time to breathe. It is better for our sons to be away from turmoil. In any case, we cannot hold out against an imperial onslaught. Then we are all doomed. As always, that diabolical woman rubs my nose in filth, but your father is loyal, and in the end, we shall win. Patience," Shah Jahan said without conviction.

"I will not have my children held hostage!" Mumtaz was stricken. She placed her head on Shah Jahan's shoulder and wept. He cradled his wife tenderly in his arms and brought her close to his chest. After all their years together, it still gave him pleasure.

He knew her well enough to know that she would acquiesce. He kissed her brow, and his heart sank with hers in a sense of powerlessness and defeat.

CHAPTER 39

1626

"I HAVE NOT BANISHED HIM, my lord. That he has chosen not to come to court is his own doing," said Nur Jahan. "He has nothing to fear from me. I have sent him messages of welcome."

"He has taken his wife to Nasik. Oblivion! What could he possibly find there?" asked Jahangir.

"He is ashamed to see a father whom he had so much injured," said Nur Jahan.

"I am told that he is actually afraid of the machinations of the favorite sultana," said Jahangir.

"Gossip, rumors. The court is awash with such nonsense."

"You mean him well?"

"He is your blood, and I love him as such."

"And Shahryar is mine also, and you love him as well . . . more, I think," said the emperor with a sly smile.

"Is it not natural that I prefer my son-in-law, as my perfidious brother prefers his?"

"I am sending Asaf to Bengal, though I will sorely miss his company. That should please you."

"Yes, my brother has quite turned against me. He will like the climate there," she replied sarcastically.

"Is that all?" said Jahangir.

"I'm well aware that you have kept him in Agra as a hedge against my ambitions for Shahryar. Why do you change now?"

"Shah Jahan is not at court. Why should I suffer his proxy? He will only stir up trouble. Shah Jahan will make the superior emperor when it is time. But he will have to come to the capital to claim his throne."

"You have entirely bypassed Parviz?"

"Parviz is weak. He will not fight for his place. Unlike the more sensible English, the Mughal line must make war for its inheritance; it is our curse. Roe tells me that the English throne goes to the eldest son; *our* kings are soaked in the blood of their brothers."

"And fathers! Even did you scheme to steal your father's crown!" the queen said.

"Astaghfirullah, my father was in such good health that I thought that I might die before him! I am still ridden with guilt and regret. But Shah Jahan knows my frail condition and that I will soon leave him the empire, yet he rebels. He resents your power. He fears you, if you want the truth. Tell me, Queen, what will you do when I am gone?"

"My lord Jahangir, please!"

"Even with your support, Shahryar will not be king. How do you propose to rule through an imbecile? The nobles will not countenance him, nor will they acknowledge you. If you had any sense, you would encourage Shah Jahan. Only he has the qualities to rule," said Jahangir.

"He opposes me. He is headstrong and wants no advice. Is it not true that, Mashallah, the empire now flourishes? You have not misplaced your confidence in me. The coins with my image speak to your wisdom. The nobles are aware of my role, and they will respond to Shahryar as well. Together, my lord, you and I have made them rich!"

"That does not satisfy them. They are dispirited that their saint is a woman. They are convinced that it works against their honor," said Jahangir.

"They have mothers!"

"It is not only you but your family that displeases them."

"My family? My mother has died, and Father has followed. Only Asaf Khan survives, and you are sending him to Bengal."

"Yet their memory lingers."

"As cream that rose to the top, my lord," said Nur Jahan, "nothing else."

"I had no argument with your family. They served the empire well. But my amirs are resentful."

"Is there no solution?"

"Shah Jahan only," said the emperor.

The queen began to twist on her haunches. *This can't be my end. I will fight with everything I possess*, she thought. *I cannot allow Shah Jahan to finish me.*

"Shahryar will make a fine emperor. He will have the benefit of my guidance," she said with desperation.

"He won't do!" The emperor spoke with finality. There was no more to be said.

CHAPTER 40

"In time, Mahabat Khan will have your head and mine too." Nur Jahan was speaking to her brother Asaf. "He has been so bold as to go before the emperor with a complaint."

"Yes? What did the man say?"

"That all the world is surprised that such a wise and sensible ruler should permit a woman to have so great an influence over him. History, he said, has not recorded a king so subject to the will of his wife."

"And the king? What was his reply?"

"I am told that he laughed at the khan. My husband loves me so that if a thousand men would address him in the same way, his confidence in me would not be shaken. Yet I fear Mahabat!"

"Yes, he has gathered too much power. We must we cut him down to size," said Asaf Khan.

"And how do you propose to do this?" asked the queen.

"Our first step is to separate Parviz from his mentor, and that will have to be your doing."

"I have the idea that Parviz would flourish in Gujarat," said Nur Jahan.

"And the khan?"

"Has not this valiant soldier earned himself a governorship? I have spoken with the emperor. Bengal would be the appropriate honor."

"My brilliant sister! Yes, put them at opposite ends of the universe where they can do no mischief."

"Well that you say so, but I am not fooled. You posture as the emperor's friend, and I aid you in that deception because you are my brother and I love you. But you champion my enemy!"

"Yes, but here our interests intersect. Shall we leave the question of Shah Jahan for another day?"

"Pray that your head remains upon your shoulders, for no matter how much I love you, I will not allow my will to be thwarted! The emperor is sending you to Bengal as well; did you know that? You will be in the territories of your old friend Mahabat Khan," said Nur Jahan.

Asaf broke out laughing. "You are truly the master politician. I bow to you, my queen-sister," he said. After delivering the kornish, he flippantly backed out of Nur Jahan's presence, still smiling.

CHAPTER 41

Zamana Beg was an Afghani émigré, the son of a Persian noble, who had entered military service under Emperor Akbar. Zamana Beg joined Prince Salim's personal guard and soon became the friend of the crown prince. Upon Salim's ascension to the throne, he awarded Zamana Beg the title Mahabat Khan—Great Lord.

Mahabat Khan was an effective general and longtime Jahangir loyalist. It was he who had blinded Khusro in Agra Fort at Jahangir's request. Ultimately, he became commander-in-chief of the Mughal army. Fiercely loyal to the king, he was the perfect model of military decorum and a true patriot. In an age of betrayal and deceit, Mahabat remained steadfastly faithful to the crown and his emperor.

But then the game changed.

"After so many years of loyal service to the crown, I am now accused of the most dishonorable of crimes," said Mahabat. He was speaking to his eldest son, Mirza Amanulla. He held in his hands a scroll with the king's official seal summoning him to Lahore.

"What are the charges the emperor lays?" asked Mirza.

"Not the king . . . she!" said Mahabat. "It is she who puts the seal and makes the policies. I'm to account for the pickings after the war with Shah Jahan. She wants the gold I have taken. And, by God, she wants even the elephants! It is her object to humiliate me, to break my honor and disgrace me."

"You cannot go, Father, with the wedding to be performed."

"I shan't ruin the wedding! On no account will her wedding be spoiled. I was just on the point of sending a messenger to the emperor seeking permission for Fatima to marry, but now we will go ahead without royal permission."

"Is that wise, Father?"

"Not wise but called for. I will no longer be Nur Jahan's vassal."

"That is rebellion, Father!"

"After the wedding, I will go to Lahore and speak to the emperor. I seek only justice, nothing more!"

"You dare to marry without royal permission? Answer me!" cried Jahangir. His face flushed with rage.

He was sitting on the throne in the Hall of Public Audience at Lahore Fort. A young officer was standing before him, trembling. He had been brought from Bengal tied to the back of a camel. He had not slept throughout the long journey, and his eyes were red with sleeplessness. His jailers had not allowed him the dignity of a turban, and his dark hair fell in long dusty strands. His mustaches drooped carelessly; he had not been permitted to groom them into the formal curl of the soldier. His cheeks were overgrown with dense black beard, and his military tunic was stained with sweat and the filth of the road. He stood before the emperor barefooted; his boots were now on the feet of his jailer.

"My lord, my father-in-law-commander assured me he had obtained permission," the young man said, beginning to sob. He had been taken from his wedding bed in the middle of the night by agents of Asaf Khan. The rich gifts given to him by Mahabat Khan had been confiscated, and his fine Iraqi stallion had been sold. "I had no intention of deceiving you."

Ordinarily, the emperor might have relented at the sight of this wretch who was so obviously innocent. But Nur Jahan had goaded him to such a pitch of vindictiveness that he could not think clearly. She sat behind the purdah screen demanding that an example be made of such grievous insubordination.

With Mahabat Khan out of reach, her vengefulness had centered on this poor young man.

"I will listen to none of your arguments," said the emperor. "An officer of our army has an obligation to his emperor to be dutiful, to be truthful and obedient. You are none of these."

"I am a loyal soldier!" cried the officer and broke down into unabashed weeping.

"Kill him," whispered the queen from her box behind the screen. Her abhorrence of Mahabat had no bounds. She was willing even to execute this young man to satisfy her hatred. This last command from the empress finally brought Jahangir to his senses.

"Prison will suffice!" he shouted into the screen so loudly that the entire court was made aware that the empress sat hidden at the king's shoulder.

"Take him away. Two years at the fort." Even that was a severe punishment, but the emperor was in a most disagreeable mood. Mahabat Khan, his old friend and most important general, had defied him.

CHAPTER 42

"MUSTAFA ALI IS IN JAIL and we do nothing?" said Mirza Amanulla.

"Keep your tongue!" demanded Mahabat Khan, irritated at his helplessness.

"What is your plan, then, Father?"

"I will answer the emperor's summons."

"At this late hour? After what has happened? Fatima will not leave her room. She is heartbroken."

"Certainly. He is still my lord. He has only fallen under his wife's evil influence."

"He is a lazy king!"

"You know nothing of Jahangir. He is a well-disciplined man, a brilliant soldier, and a scholar. He chooses to turn the reins of government to his wife's hands while he pursues his scientific and aesthetic interests."

"And you support this?"

"Him, not his wife!"

"What will we do, then, to save my sister?!"

"The emperor leaves for Kabul shortly. I will meet his camp."

"Father, beware!"

"I will have five thousand brave Rajputs in my train. Will you come with me?"

"I would gladly die at your side, Father."

"Astaghfirullah, Beta, we go not as warriors but as supplicants."

CHAPTER 43

In March of 1626, the Mughal emperor, on his way to Kabul, established a camp on the east bank of the River Jhelum. Mahabat Khan rode there to greet him, but the emperor was so displeased with Mahabat that he was not allowed to appear at the imperial camp until called for.

Humiliated, Mahabat Khan and his son sat on horses observing the army in the valley below while they awaited an imperial summons that would never come. They watched as the army tramped across the narrow boat bridge that rose and fell on the Jhelum's dark currents. A train of camels, infantry, and cavalry, the entire army, was moving through the narrow corridor of torches that lit the creaking bridge.

"Just the army will be crossing tonight," said Mahabat Khan, the seasoned general. "From the look of it, the emperor's entourage will not begin crossing until late morning."

"Then let us seize the day, Father!" cried Mirza.

"What do you mean?"

"The time is now. The emperor will be unprotected."

"Attack the emperor? Your imagination runs wild."

"Not attack, Father. Since he holds you at arm's length, let us make our way into his presence under our own initiative. Not war—merely a bold move to gain an audience, a brief breach of protocol to make your point. We will have the emperor's ear unobstructed."

"What you describe is insurrection."

"Father—"

"Let me finish. The idea has crossed my mind as well. The condition of being under the thumb of Nur Jahan and her brother is unbearable. Let us strike at daybreak when the army has crossed the river!"

"Alhumdillah!" cried the mirza joyfully.

When the sun rose, before the mists had cleared from the valley and only the tops of the river's willows had been touched by sunlight, Mahabat's Rajput horsemen thundered onto the boat bridge. The men at guard had been sleeping, and the first man awakening to give resistance was skewered through the throat by a Rajput lance. The two others scrambled quickly to leap into the stream below and dog-paddle furiously to the eastern shore.

Beneath an awning outside the emperor's tent, the officer of the day, had just risen from his prayer rug and was bending again in the morning prayer when he heard a sentinel cry, "Mahabat Khan arrives!"

He looked down the avenue of white cantonment tents to see the stern figure of the old general at the head of a phalanx of Rajput warriors. A servant walked behind, holding the reins of his white Arabian. They moved rapidly, armor clashing, raising a cloud of dust.

"Forgive me, General, but you are to halt here while I report to the emperor," said the officer firmly, and as Mahabat stepped up to him, "Inshallah, you are to wait until the emperor sees fit to see you." He spoke sharply as he was quite irritated that his morning prayer had been interrupted, just as he was nearing the end, and that he would have to repeat his ablutions and do the prayers all over again.

Sinews of anger strained at officer's throat. The old khan smiled contemptuously. He motioned to his men to stand fast.

A moment later, Jahangir appeared from his tent and was helped to the palanquin waiting to carry him across the river. The emperor stared imperiously at his general. His glance demanded to know the cause of this invasion. At the sight of the emperor, the general's mood changed. Humbly, Mahabat stepped to the emperor and threw himself on his knees. He hung his head as if presenting it to the emperor's sword. At his back, however, stood one hundred Rajputs in full armor. The emperor's troops were across the river.

"I am the victim, sire, of Asaf Khan. I suffer under his malice. It is sure that he will put me to death in shame and disgrace," said Mahabat, careful not to implicate the emperor's wife in his indictment. "This is the cause of my presumption. If I deserve ignominious death, I beg you, deliver it by your own hand. My lord king, I throw myself on your mercy," Mahabat said.

The emperor was beside himself with rage at Mahabat's impertinence. Twice he put his hand impetuously to his sword. At that moment, nothing would have given him greater pleasure than to deprive Mahabat of his head. But each time, his hand was stayed by the advice given him by the Mughal amir who stood at his side. The man spoke to him in Turki, the language of the Central Asian steppes, the Mughal homeland; a language that Mahabat the Pathan, did not understand.

"This is a time for wisdom and fortitude. Allah will punish this wickedness on the day of judgment. Leave this traitor to God." The amir, of course, had included the troop of fierce Rajputs in his calculation. Any action against Mahabat's head would mean that theirs would roll as well.

Jahangir's inaction was a capitulation and Mahabat's victory. Mahabat rose to his full stature. The white scar on his cheek glowed against the deep tan of his weathered face and the stubble of his beard. There was triumph in his eyes.

"Ride out with me, sire," Mahabat said, "as if we go to the hunt." The emperor was totally in his power. "Give the orders that I may go as your slave, that I go at your direction. And take my Arabian as a token of my love."

"I ride my Iraqi mare. Only she is suitable for an emperor," Jahangir declared arrogantly. Mahabat nodded. He knew that the emperor could be pushed only so far.

It was midmorning now. Mahabat could see that the emperor was beginning to sweat under the ascending sun.

"But Majesty," said Mahabat, "if we ride on the backs of horses, will we not swelter?" Mahabat was looking at the sky with a hand over his brow. "Would it not be more pleasant to ride under the cool shade of a howdah?"

Mahabat's motives were transparent. He wanted the emperor to be most visible high up on an elephant so that all would be considered normal. Jahangir, who was sweating from the heat of the wine he had drunk, nodded. He was all too willing to ride on the back of an elephant, his favorite mount. Thus, the emperor on an elephant, his captor, and the Rajput cavalry went ceremoniously through the salaaming crowds of the villages and over the clay paths and through the dry yellow fields back to Mahabat's camp.

But where was Nur Jahan? How had he forgotten her? In the commotion of the morning, he had overlooked her. His arch-enemy was now free to rally the imperial forces to his destruction.

"And the queen, sire? She is well?" said Mahabat when he and the emperor were seated among his nobles in Mirza Amanulla's tent. They were eating the emperor's favorite meal of roasted chicken and naan.

"Yes, as well as can be expected. It is a bit indelicate, but I think I can tell you, Mahabat, my beloved suffers from the swollen foot trouble," said Jahangir in a fanciful lie improvised on the moment.

"Is she not young for this?" said Mahabat, somewhat astonished. "And a female with this malady, most unusual!"

"And trying. The queen is not a patient sufferer. Her foot swells so that it is painful for her to walk," said Jahangir. "Our hakim has cautioned against eating lamb in excess but has not, as yet, proposed a cure."

"Ya Allah, as it happens, the Venetian doctor is in Agra at this very moment," said Mahabat in an untruth.

"Belmonti is here?" the emperor said skeptically.

"Yes. He will cure her. But time is short. Inshallah, he leaves for Lahore in two days' time. But where are we to find the queen, my lord Jahangir?"

"Astaghfirullah, the queen is her own mistress. She comes and goes as she pleases," lamented the king with a sigh.

"Majesty, we must find her. It is important for her health that she be seen by this marvelous healer," insisted Mahabat. Jahangir nodded his permission, aware that this theater would go on interminably if he did not acquiesce.

After dinner, the emperor and Mahabat remounted the elephant and set out for Jahangir's camp on the east side of the river. Although it galled him, the emperor finally had to acknowledge that he was Mahabat's hostage. At the boat bridge, the general stopped to question the guards about the queen. A small group of Rajastani soldiers had set up camp on the embankment. They squatted in a circle at the bridge, holding their muskets upright.

"Yes, my lord," one said in response to Mahabat's question. "Queen Begum crossed to other side in afternoon."

"You bloody fool!"

"But orders were to stop Jahangir's army coming east only. Nothing was said of the queen," the guard said.

Mahabat was too wise a general to punish a man who had simply done his duty no matter how faulty his judgment. He walked away from his soldiers without saying another word. Now, he was in the thick of an insurrection that he could not keep up. It was only a matter of time before the emperor was rescued. His meager corps could not stand up to the ponderous force of the imperial army. Then Shahryar came to mind. Yes, Shahryar was in the vicinity. He would make a far less dangerous hostage to keep than the emperor. He could let the emperor go, and that would relieve the pressure. Shahryar was Nur Jahan's most precious possession. Mahabat laughed. Yes, Shahryar was her possession and her key to the empire. *I will take Shahryar*, he thought.

"Excuse me, sire, but I must ask you to accompany me to Shahryar's camp."

"But I know nothing of his whereabouts," said Jahangir, surprised at the direction Mahabat's thoughts were taking. He sensed Mahabat's desperation. His most important general, usually so cool and decisive in battle, was falling to pieces before his eyes.

"Yes, but I know precisely where he is encamped," said Mahabat. The moment he uttered the words, he wanted to take them back. Would Shahryar's abduction make the situation any better?

"Well, by all means, then, let us proceed," said Jahangir. Taking Shahryar would be yet another blunder, thought Jahangir. What would Mahabat do with the captured prince? Obviously, if challenged, he could not kill him. His death would only strengthen the hand of Asaf Khan. Mahabat's only hope was to run.

"Yes, let us proceed," Mahabat said flatly. To stop now at the beginning of an action would make him look like a child. His mind was besieged by a multitude of plans, all of them hopeless.

By a slave's torch, the imperial elephant was mounted, and Mahabat's party set out for Shahryar's camp guided by a bright moon in a clear sky.

CHAPTER 44

ON THE WEST SIDE OF the river that night, the petite queen stood regally in her brother's tent at the center of a circle of twenty nobles, whose turbans inclined in deference. She had never been more queenly and self-possessed than at this moment of crisis.

"You have allowed the unimaginable to become a reality. Never has such humiliation been heaped upon the empire." Her voice was firm and even in tone, as befitted a queen. "Who are the real soldiers among you? And what will you do to fix this calamity? Inshallah, by morning I want a plan put before me."

The amirs stood with heads bowed in agony and shame. Not one had the courage to raise his head as the queen made her way out of the tent's stifling heat into a warm night full of sparkling stars.

The following morning at first light, Asaf Khan and two amirs appeared before Nur Jahan.

"Our only recourse is to storm the boat bridge," said Asaf Khan.

"But you are too late. I saw the bridge go up in flames last night!" said Nur Jahan.

"Ya Allah, a calamity! When? At what time?" he said but then realized that it made no difference,

"Inshallah, there are other places to ford the river," said Asaf Khan after a moment's reflection.

"Yes but, be aware it is not only river crossings that matter. My husband sends the message that his army will not fight with resolve without his presence to rally them on."

"Let us not be naive. The army fights for profit, not love of king or country," said Asaf Khan, "from whence comes this communication?"

"From our agents on the other side of the river."

"Can you not sense that this letter rings false? Why would the emperor want to discourage his own liberation?" said Asaf Khan. "This letter is obviously a forgery. My men will find a suitable place to cross, and once on the other side, we will overwhelm them. It is a simple matter."

"Then cross while the morning is still cool and bring my husband home to me," said Nur Jahan.

The crossing was a disaster. A ford was chosen that was too wide. The army was disordered and, as the emperor had warned, without fighting spirit.

The imperial army had been so confident of success that Nur Jahan herself and her daughter and child had begun to cross, riding in an armored howdah.

"We must turn back! Turn back, Mother. The crossing is too difficult," said Nur Jahan's daughter, Ladli. The river had suddenly and inexplicably surged so that the current raged at the elephant's waist. It ran so powerfully that even under the repeated goading of the mahout, the animal could make little headway. It stalled, raised its trunk, and trumpeted in frustration, inaugurating it seemed, a fusillade of arrows from the other shore.

"Oh my God!" cried Ladli in horror. Somehow, an arrow had found its way through the metal plates of the closed howdah and lodged in the breast of her infant daughter's nurse. The elephant took a coordinated volley of musket shot and then, screaming in pain, turned of its own accord, and made for the safety of the western shore.

Mahabat's men, standing in a single file on the river's edge, sent another wave of arrows against the invaders. On the embankment above the archers, his musketeers calmly fired, reloaded, and fired again at the elephants and the men crossing in boats.

Already intimidated by the turbulent river and confused at the sound of the rifle fire and the booming of Mahabat's cannon, the imperial elephants stopped dead in the water. They then turned away in panic under a hail of musket fire that tore through their skins. The river ran with their blood.

On the imperial shore, the generals ranged their muskets and shifted big-bore cannon into place. But it was too late. The army was in tatters, and the bulk of the soldiers had fled from the battle in a dispirited mob.

Chief among the deserters was Asaf Khan, the author of the debacle. Although he was a master of court intrigue, he was no soldier. He had failed in every military adventure he had ever undertaken. Now he ran to save his life without thought of his sister or his emperor. He feared Mahabat Khan's vengeance more than he regarded his duty.

"He is a sniveler, sire, a coward and a base adventurer," Mahabat announced with his face in a hateful contortion. He sat in Shahryar's tent, where the emperor occupied a divan next to his son. Mahabat sat at his side.

"But he has served me with distinction, you must admit," said Jahangir.

"Sire, he has deserted his sister," said Mahabat. "What distinction lies in that?"

"You fought as colleagues against my rebellious son. Was he not a valiant and sober general?"

"Majesty! He cowered under the umbrella of my protection. Could you not see? Were you not aware? In return, he has brought me disgrace!" said Mahabat, still careful not to indict Nur Jahan in his bitter rhetoric.

These were things that Jahangir had known of but had left to Nur Jahan's discretion as he had so much of the administration of the empire. He had never trusted Asaf Khan or his valor, but he loved the cultured Persian's company and his brilliant scheming. And of course, Asaf Khan, the son of Iti-mad-ud-daula, was above all his wife's brother.

The disaster at the Jhelum and her brother's departure had left Nur Jahan in a predicament. On the one hand, her hold on the ragged imperial forces was fast deteriorating as part of the army marched off under a white flag. Even the officer of the day had crossed the river to kiss Mahabat's hem. On the other shore were the disciplined Rajastani forces, waiting to do her harm. She would have to act quickly to save herself and her emperor.

"It is rumored that Asaf has left the battlefield," said Aisha, Nur Jahan's lady-in-waiting.

"Bah, my brother is no coward. He thinks logically, and logic shouted that he leave. He has no instinct toward martyrdom. Mahabat Khan has vowed to kill him," said Nur Jahan, trying to salvage her brother's reputation.

"But he has left you unprotected!"

"My dear Aisha, you forget that I am the queen."

"I have not forgotten, but Your Majesty, you are . . . we are, if you will forgive me . . . in a fix."

"That will change tomorrow. We leave for the east bank immediately after morning prayer. Mahabat Khan has accepted my letter of surrender."

"Surrender! My queen!"

"Yes, the king has turned over command of the army to Mahabat Khan, and I will join him in captivity. But all this is secret; the empire will carry on as if nothing has changed."

"Astaghfirullah!"

"I wouldn't worry, dearest. Things will be made right."

When Asaf Khan's courage was called into question, Nur Jahan thought of the story her mother had told of her children's encounter with a lion:

"Sunset prayers had been said, and the royal women leaned on a fence, looking down at the sentinel fires that shone like jewels embedded in the black fabric of the jungle. I stood among them watching the bare-chested bearers emerge, skins glowing under the torches like old brass. On their turbaned heads and firm shoulders were borne the artifacts of the hunt: the cookware, the knotted hemp nets, and the rolled wooden slats used for fences. A file of beaters wandered out, their sticks finally still, then came the soldiers bearing their muskets and bows. Officers strode out, coolly unencumbered, their weapons jogging on the backs of slaves.

"My husband had followed Akbar on the hunt. All officials were obliged to do so. For Ghiyas and me, this was an imposition, but my children rejoiced, you especially. You had insisted on joining your father and brothers in the jungle. For an older girl, this would have been a breach of purdah, but at ten years of age, your presence among the men was permissible if not totally embraced.

"My husband's gait was unmistakable. My two sons preceded him. *But where was Mehrunissa?* I thought.

"My heart stopped when my eyes went to the litter behind them. It was carrying you. Immediately, I raced down the hill. I was comforted slightly when I saw that my child was smiling. I thought, *her kamise is stained with blood and she smiles?* So were my two boys smiling, and I thought that I glimpsed a look of pride on my husband's face.

"My God, what has happened?! I shouted as I bent to embrace you with all the fierceness of my love.

"Our little girl has killed a lion today, praise Allah," said Ghiyas.

'A lion, Mama, with the face of a king,' you said.

"Mashallah, a lion!" I said, and hugged you again, "Oh my God, he bit you!" I said as I looked at your legs.

'No, don't worry. It is small scratches only,' Ghiyas said. 'After taking two shots from our daughter's musket, he leaped at her and ran his paw down her leg as he fell. She did not flinch but watched the beast die at her feet,' said my husband jubilantly. 'We treated her scratches as best we could, but it is painful for her to walk. Inshallah, we will send for our hakim to dress her wounds properly,' he said.

"Oh, my poor child," I cried, "I promise that you will never have to hunt again." Then I remember covering your face with kisses."

What mother didn't know was that I had put myself between the attacking lion and my brother, who was frozen with fear. When my first shot didn't stop the beast, I took hold of my brother's weapon and fired again. The queen smiled ironically when she thought that she and her brother differed so much in the quality of courage, that it was as if they came from different parents. But it did not matter. She loved him with all her heart, and she worried about him now that his life was in jeopardy.

———

After I had tasted the blood of my first lion, there was no power on earth that could restrain me from hunting, thought the queen. *And then there was the glory*, she thought. *That night, our tent rocked with laughter and feasting. Many visitors came to pay their respects to the little lion killer. People looked at me with awe and took me by the hand with love and congratulations and commended me to Allah. Throughout the camp and later throughout Hindustan, I came to be known as a person of unequaled bravery. No, I knew then that I could never stop hunting.*

———

The next morning, the queen's new elephant transported her, Ladli, and her infant granddaughter across the Jhelum at the shallows near the repaired boat bridge. On the eastern side of the river, Jahangir and the ever-present Mahabat Khan awaited with white yak tails flying on the lance heads of the emperor's private guard. Trumpets and a roll of the kettle drums announced the arrival of the queen.

———

"Your brother has been given amnesty on condition of swearing fealty to Mahabat," said Jahangir, wrinkling his nose in disgust.

"And your blood boils," declared:'the queen, sharing her husband's disgust at her brother's behavior but at the same time relieved that he was now out of danger. Nur Jahan was lying with her head on the king's lap in the privacy of Jahangir's tent.

"I will do more than boil once we are out of this quagmire," said the emperor.

"You have persuaded Mahabat to proceed to Kabul?"

"Yes, he will go, if only for relief from this accursed heat. He thinks he will find security there. It is, after all, his birthplace," said Jahangir.

"Kabul plays into our hands. Mahabat's support lies in Rajastan."

"What do you see?" asked Jahangir.

"Already the nobles are tortured with envy at his assent. His Rajputs hold them in check. But what will it be like in Kabul, far from his base? His court will be a comedy. Mahabat is a soldier, not a courtier. Even his servants find him clumsy. He is way out of his depth."

"He is a lamb, my lady, awaiting slaughter. No match for your cunning," said Jahangir, grinning.

"And I have a plan," said Nur Jahan, tickling the emperor's neck with her delicate fingers. A wry smile was on her face.

"A plan? God help poor Mahabat!" said Jahangir, laughing heartily.

"They swagger like conquerors, sire," said the commander of the Ahadi guard, "They even walk like kings among the bazaars, taking what they want without thought of payment." He was speaking of Mahabat's Rajput soldiers, who were relishing their newfound superiority as his main supporting army.

"Yes, I know. They have become troublesome. My amirs are filled with complaint at their behavior, and the common people bristle always."

"What will you do, sire?"

"It is a question of what *you* will do, sahib," interrupted the queen, who had been listening behind the purdah screen. "Are you aware that Rajput horses graze the emperor's fields?"

"No, my queen!"

"It is your sworn duty to stop it. Are you an Ahadi or just a common soldier?"

"I swear by the Prophet's beard that this shall not happen again!" he exclaimed.

"And if it does?"

"Then we will burn their camp to the ground."

"Go, then, and look to your duty," said the queen.

"I was not aware of these infractions!" Jahangir announced after the officer had left.

"Nor was I," said Nur, coming out of purdah and smiling. "But you have only to invite the Rajputs to graze upon your land to make it a reality."

"To what end do you start this mischief?" asked Jahangir.

"To see what Mahabat's heavy hand will do in response."

"Oh, how I weary of these intrigues," said Jahangir, shaking his head.

"If you want our freedom, you must allow me my game of chess."

"It is your father who has taught you this chess, isn't it?"

"And well he has taught me," declared the queen with a look of self-satisfaction.

CHAPTER 45

"This is the emperor's private land!" a royal trooper shouted at a Rajput whose red turban identified him as an officer. The trooper's horse snorted and dug at the ground with a foreleg. The trooper called out again across a swatch of grassland, "It is forbidden to the uncircumcised!"

The Rajput laughed and cupped his hands over his mouth and shouted back, "Our horses graze where they please!" He rode without a saddle. With bare feet poking outward, he goaded his horse with his heels. He waved his men in closer to the black-clad Ahadi horseman.

At the lone Ahadi's back, the field went to a road filled with bullock carts, harnessed camels, and parties of men on horses. Peasants in white cotton robes drove sheep and geese. Men, bearded and not and some wearing turbans in brilliant colors, crowded the road and strode before the open stalls of the bazaar. Beyond were the brown buildings of the town and the high white-tipped mountains stark against the concentrated blue of the sky.

The Rajput cavalry men now closed in on the Ahadi. There were hundreds of them. Slowly, they formed a menacing circle around him.

"So, Mughal, what did you say?" said the Rajput officer, cocking his head forward and cupping his hand to his ear with comic exaggeration.

"I say that you are not allowed on imperial land," said the Ahadi, holding his lance upright.

"Not allowed, you say?" said the Rajput and shot a wry look at his men, enjoying his role as tormentor. "By whose order?" Other Rajputs rode up to reinforce the circle. "Is it your God who won't let us graze?" said the Rajput with a knowing glance at his men.

"Yes, Allah prohibits all Hindu dogs from our lands!" shouted the Ahadi with passionate sarcasm.

By now the Rajput ranks had swollen to hundreds, and more horsemen appeared on the horizon. With a motion of his hand, the officer held back his restive men and leaned forward on his mount. With a wild yell, he galloped at the Ahadi, pointing his English sword with a straight arm.

The Ahadi lowered his spear. That was a signal. From behind the tents of the bazaar, from the right and left flanks, Mughal cavalry suddenly appeared. Hundreds of men armed with composite bows advanced on the Rajputs. With deadly aim, they shot them down with volleys of arrows. The Rajputs, who were mostly unarmed, resisted with their usual valor, but it was futile. The Rajputs were surrounded. Hundreds fell before the raging Ahadi troopers. The officer in the red turban was run through by the lone Ahadi.

From the street and the bazaar, hordes of townspeople who had been the objects of Rajput arrogance closed in on the fallen warriors and stripped them of their possessions. Hundreds were captured. With their hands bound behind them, they were then led single file to be sold as slaves to the highest bidders in the bazaar.

After the battle had ended, a naked *sadhu* stood at the edge of the green meadow. With great sorrow, he beheld the dead and the patches of sunlit grass glazed with human blood. When he walked away, vultures flapped to the ground to stride arrogantly among the corpses and do their work.

CHAPTER 46

"OVER THREE HUNDRED DEAD, TWO hundred captured and sold into slavery on that very day," said Mahabat's son.

"How could this be?" asked Mahabat.

"Hatred is a powerful force."

"Then we must meet force with force. Calm must be restored, or we are lost."

"Father, we are lost if we punish the Ahadis. It is the townspeople who must feel our wrath. Only the emperor can punish his guards."

"Yes, we will punish the townspeople, but recognize that we will bring even more hatred upon us," cried Mahabat Khan.

Mahabat issued orders, and his Rajput horsemen swarmed down on the roadside bazaar and burnt its tents to the ground. Townspeople who stood in their way were slaughtered. Order was restored, but it was the end for the Rajputs. They could not walk the streets of the town without being cursed by the Afghans. The entire population despised them. In town, shopkeepers would offer the Rajputs only inferior goods at unreasonable prices. If shopkeepers had advance warning that Rajputs were in the bazaar, they would close their shops altogether. Even animal fodder was difficult for the Rajputs to obtain, and sometimes their mounts would go hungry. The Rajputs themselves longed for their desert home, and Rajput officers had trouble keeping their men under control. Desertion was high, and mutiny was on every soldier's lips.

"It seems your game is prospering," said Jahangir.

"This displeases you?" asked Queen Nur.

"Not in the least. I await the checkmate."

"The queen cannot checkmate without a move by the king."

"I would be delighted to participate in the queen's gambit. What do you suggest?"

"That you calm your general. Show him goodwill and appear to be his friend and my enemy."

"Will he not suspect my motives?"

"Mahabat does not know which way to turn. He is a blunt man immune to subtlety, but you know this. Give him a shoulder to rest on, a light to guide him through his long night. Show him a way out."

"And then?"

"And then the queen advances to checkmate."

CHAPTER 47

"AH, MAHABAT, IS IT NOT like old times? There is something about being among army men and warriors. Let us count the times we have been campaigning. Do you not remember Khusro's rebellion? Then you were at my side," Jahangir reminisced with tears forming.

"Majesty, I have never left your side."

"You have wandered, let us be frank. I understand. If it were not for this woman, you would never have wavered."

"What woman do you describe, Majesty?" said Mahabat, leaning in closer, astounded at the implication.

"Must I mention her name?!"

"Surely you—"

"Do you for a moment think that I am her pawn? I had lost control, yes, but only for a moment. A moment's inattention and she has taken power. Finally, the scales have fallen from my eyes, and I see her clearly now."

"Majesty!"

"Yes, I know, Mahabat, that you have been faithful to me. I was a fool not to see it before. But that shall soon be remedied."

Mahabat fell on his knees and with tears in his eyes kissed the emperor's feet. "I have never wanted more than to serve you, sire," he said.

"And you shall. She has set afoot plans to kill you. But we will overcome her."

CHAPTER 48

Even Jahangir was not quite sure how she had done it, but Nur Jahan had gathered an army bit by bit that had become numerically superior to Mahabat's shrinking forces. His original army of Rajput warriors had diminished to just above three thousand after the debacle at Kabul. Nur's army now numbered in the four-thousands and outstripped the khan's forces in weapons, equipment, and most importantly esprit de corps.

Mahabat had lost faith in his enterprise and now hungered to be forgiven by Jahangir and received once again into his good graces. This was a hope eagerly encouraged by the emperor as Nur Jahan went about quietly building her army with the nearly unlimited resources of the royal treasury. The rebel army also had lost faith because Mahabat could no longer pay his men with any regularity. Homesickness had taken its toll as well. A goodly number of Mahabat's Rajput soldiers had run back to their desert home.

It was a brilliant day, the sky blue and the temperature perfect. The Jhelum ran golden under an afternoon sun. The emperor and his entourage were returning from Kabul. The emperor himself was being carried in a gilded palanquin on the damp rim of the river.

"My dear general, would you be so kind as to take your men ahead so that I may look upon my queen's troops?" said Jahangir.

Mahabat was perched upon a white Arabian trotting restlessly at Jahangir's side. The animal was in the mood for a run along the river's cool bank.

"My lord, you ask too much," declared Mahabat, restraining his mount with a strong arm on the reins. His face was a mask of suspicion.

"It is for the most fundamental of reasons. How are we to judge her strength? If you ride with me, she will never allow an inspection."

"Majesty, please do not ask me to leave your side!" said Mahabat.

"Then our plan will be stymied. You must allow me to inspect her troops. Really, I must insist."

Still eager to maintain the fiction that the emperor was in charge and to keep faith with him, Mahabat reluctantly agreed.

But all was not well with the khan. He was plagued with doubt. His instincts told him that this was a trap. In the deepest agony, he went ahead as Jahangir had suggested. He took his troops a day's march in advance of the emperor, but then, overwhelmed with suspicion, he bolted, taking with him Asaf Khan as hostage.

CHAPTER 49

"THAT DAMMED FOOL HAS RUN away with your brother. My nephews were taken as well," said Jahangir.

"I am aware, my love, but not worried," said Nur Jahan. "Yesterday I issued an ultimatum: release my brother and the children or the imperial army moves against you."

"Will that idiot comply?" asked Jahangir.

"He has moved two days distant but left your brother's children behind. After another day's march, he says, he will release Asaf Khan."

"Good. His fright is increasing to panic," declared Jahangir, grinning.

"Shah Jahan has sent you a message," said Nur Jahan. "I have taken the liberty of reading the letter myself."

"What does he say?" asked Jahangir, somewhat surprised.

"He marches to your rescue!" declared the queen, laughing. "Your loyal son!"

"Should I hide?" asked the emperor with bitter sarcasm.

"Only if you fear a man riddled with fever at the head of a few dozens of cavalry."

"Inshallah, I will ask Mahabat to intercept him. That should keep them both busy and give Mahabat a chance to reingratiate himself with me as well," said the emperor.

"Ah, the perfect endgame. Really, Your Majesty, you should occupy yourself more with politics," said Nur Jahan.

"I am content with your policies. After all, you are the true Persian."

"But will you allow me the checkmate in the emperor's name?"

"If you wish. You and I are as one. We walk together as the shadow of God."

CHAPTER 50

"Parviz has died," said Jahangir. He had tears in eyes. The news had come from Burhanpur. "He collapsed at his throne. He lay unconscious for a week."

"Ya Allah, wine will cause us all to collapse," declared Nur Jahan. Inwardly she rejoiced. The death of Parviz narrowed the field of contenders for the throne to two. "There is nothing more hurtful than the death of a child, and you have lost two these past months," said Nur Jahan in a soft voice. She took the pipe away from the servant, loaded it herself, lit it, and put the tip of the snake into Jahangir's mouth. "Draw deeply, my love. Take all the pain from your heart."

"We are an accursed family, drawn so disastrously to wine," he said and inhaled deeply, holding the smoke in his lungs. He turned his head onto his queen's shoulder and sobbed softly, sputtering out the sweet smoke against her breast. "My handsome son is dead. My heir is gone," he sobbed. "Only Shah Jahan remains."

"My lord, do not discount our Shahryar!" Nur Jahan exclaimed.

"He is no emperor. He is weak and incompetent."

"I shall make him into a king, I pledge that."

"Even you cannot make an elegant robe from cheap muslin. Where is my son?"

"He has gone to the Deccan, where he can do no harm."

"He does no harm here. He belongs at my side!"

The wine had made the emperor sentimental and forgetful of the danger presented by Shah Jahan. The opium made him dreamy and full of pleasant images of his son that contradicted his good sense. He clung to these as he avoided the horror in contemplating Parviz's death.

"Mahabat has blocked him at Sind as you ordered," Nur Jahan announced.

"And where is he now?"

"As I said, he has withdrawn to the Deccan."

"Send Mahabat to find him. I must see my son."

"Mahabat has fled once again, my lord," Nur Jahan said with a tone that implied that Mahabat was a hopeless case. "He attempted to seize the treasury en route from Bengal."

"That old scoundrel has attacked my treasury? Why had I not been told?"

"Your nerves are on edge, my husband dear. Forgive me, but I have kept the worst news from you. The truth is he has gone to join Shah Jahan."

"Against me?"

"Nothing is clear, my love," said Nur Jahan, although she wanted to tell the emperor the truth, that the two were conspiring against him.

As this last news sunk in, Jahangir sunk with it. His world was collapsing. He had hoped to settle the issue of succession, but a solution seemed as elusive as ever.

His health was failing. It was something Nur Jahan fretted over daily, but now he himself could feel death in his bones, and his mind went to the towering cliffs of Kashmir. He longed to escape to the clear mountain air. His hakim had recommended the crisp breezes to relieve his asthma. At last, he thought, he must act on his hakim's advice. Within a week he had commanded his court to leave the dust of the Punjab behind to journey on to the high valley.

"Before we leave, my lord, I have good news. Mahabat has released my brother!"

"Why should I receive that news with a happy heart? Moreover, why should you? That man is the very soul of deceit."

"Yes, but he is my brother, and I love him. It is my weakness," Nur Jahan said. As the familiar crafty look crept into her face, the emperor sighed heavily.

"I am not fooled. You have plans for him, I see," he said.

"It is only that now that illness has befallen you. We need someone to look after the needs of the empire."

"Your brother, then?"

"Why not appoint him your deputy and take him with us to Kashmir? Inshallah, then the worries of administration will be over."

"I am too weary to resist," lamented the emperor. More cheerfully he said, "But why not? I suppose one Persian more or less will do me no great harm."

"And you like my brother."

"Yes, yes, he charms like a snake, and if he doesn't steal with both hands, he will be satisfactory. Send for him and I will, Astaghfirullah, invest him," sighed the emperor.

"Brilliant! We shall leave for Kashmir with clear minds."

And so, the long caravan of the emperor's nomadic court marched across the burning Gangetic Plain and, for the last time, journeyed to the white mountains of Kashmir.

CHAPTER 51

JAHANGIR'S ILLNESS HAD PROGRESSED TO such a pass that he could not walk. The wooded trails he had so enjoyed climbing in the past, he now needed to transverse carried flat on his back in a litter. The mountain air that his hakim had promised would bring him relief only increased his wheezing. His lungs had become so weak that he could no longer smoke the opium that had been his comrade for 30 years. He had lost his appetite for food, and Nur Jahan could comfort him only with wine,

The mountain trails, never easy, were treacherous in springtime. The four men carrying the emperor's litter were augmented with four more at the bank of a stream rushing with melting ice. The men shivered as they strained to cross the freezing water. One man, shorter than the others, lost his footing and was driven away, bouncing off a rock and disappearing downstream into the turbulent gorge with a scream. After the emperor had passed over the stream, parcels went from the backs of camels and elephants to the turbaned heads of coolies, who crossed through the water in loincloths. The unburdened animals crossed beside them. On the other side of the stream, bare-chested men stood warming their shuddering bodies before the flames of a huge bonfire. Others loaded the backs of the trembling beasts, who would journey on through the pine forest that led to the valley.

Late in the afternoon on the valley floor, the emperor's palki passed through a scarlet field of saffron glowing with the fire of a declining sun. A tract of white roses spread before him and then a field of cool blue Kashmiri irises. Beyond, the face of Lake Dal shimmered in pink light. At its distant shore were the tall poplars of the Shalimar Garden and the rush of a waterfall high on the face of the mountainside.

In the declining light of the evening, the emperor and Nur Jahan boarded an elegantly decorated lighter to cross to the garden they had both created. Darkness seeped in among the cypresses and plane trees. It saturated poppies and lilac. Lanterns twinkled on the poplars along the canal's rims. At its end, a pavilion glowed with the light of forty torches.

Forty soldiers stood at parade rest, and forty light cannon sounded in slow succession as the festooned boat floated majestically up the canal. When the emperor counted the reports of the cannon, he said, "Ah, they anticipate the forty days of mourning my death."

"Oh no, my lord king," cried Nur Jahan with a worried look. "It is recognition of the forty hadith of the Prophet . . . an auspicious welcome."

"Or forty days of the great flood, perhaps?" asked Jahangir ruefully.

"Forty days of the Arabian nights, my lord . . . forty days of joy."

At this, the emperor broke down. "Ya Allah, if I have forty days left, it will be a miracle." His eyes were full of tears. Jahangir hated the idea of death.

Inside the garden's wooden pavilion under the gilded dome, oil lamps flickered. Lines of Persian calligraphy—Rumi's lines—ran along painted walls. Saffron curtains ruffled in a breeze that puffed down from the mountain.

To welcome the emperor, still in his palanquin, an orchestra struck up as he entered. The queen walked solemnly behind. The emperor was too ill to sit up to greet his Kashmiri nobles. To make matters worse, as soon as they were situated in the royal apartments, news that Shahryar's condition had worsened came from across the lake. That the prince had contracted a type of leprosy that had caused the hair on his head and eyebrows to fall out could no longer be kept quiet. Over the last week, he had become entirely bald. His facial hair had gone as well. His cheek was as smooth as a boy's.

"This is disastrous," said Nur Jahan. This was the worst news that she had received since Shah Jahan's insurrection, an enormous step backward. How would she retain power once Jahangir was dead? And that dreaded event was now as close as a week? A month? But it would happen soon; there was no doubt.

"Yes, proper treatment is not available here," said Jahangir. The emperor was propped up on a divan, picking at a plate of dates. Dates were the only thing he could digest. Like the Prophet, he thought. The Prophet loved dates. He also loved perfume and women. In this too he was similar, mused the emperor.

"You cannot expect the people to accept a leprous ruler, poor child," said Nur Jahan.

"My amirs won't want him either. It is sunnah for an ordinary Muslim to have whiskers; an emperor *must* have them!" said Jahangir, stroking his own luxuriant mustache. His complexion, always a wheat color, had become an astonishing yellow. The whites of his eyes had turned yellow as well. His hakim had seen patients with jaundice many times before and was treating him with a Unani compound that was usually effective. Only time would tell.

"I will persuade Shahryar to find treatment in Lahore," said Nur Jahan.

"Is such a thing possible?" said Jahangir.

"Treatment?" asked Nur Jahan.

"A cure."

"Inshallah."

If a cure could be found, she would find it. She would ransack Hindustan to find it.

Nur Jahan sat deep in thought among the women of the harem in the zanana pavilion. The answer to the dilemma of the royal succession was near at hand. If only *she* could inherit the crown. But that was not possible, she reflected. There must be an answer. There must. She was not ready to let go. Her work was not yet done.

The queen moved about like a crazy woman, as if her tent were on fire. Her servants did not dare approach when she was in such a mood.

Then it dawned on her: the answer was for the royal entourage to proceed back to Lahore. Of course! Shahryar would then be close to the emperor when he died. This embarrassingly bald man, without eyelashes or beard, would be made emperor at the very moment of Jahangir's death. Wherever Shah Jahan was encamped, he would be too far away to forestall this. The imperial army would be in her hands. Her victory over Mahabat Khan had won the respect of the generals, and Shah Jahan would be powerless to oppose her. He would have to accept, as would the amirs, a fait accompli. She smiled for the first time that afternoon and ordered a banquet that night to celebrate both the emperor's arrival and his imminent departure.

The dinner was a grand event. The emperor enjoyed himself, although he could eat almost nothing, and wine, his former lifeblood, he could barely accommodate. Stimulated perhaps by the music of the sitar and the graceful movements of his dancing nautch girls, he found that he could eat a dose or two of opium and a few dates.

The harem had been transported along with the army as usual, and the emperor sat among his perfumed women, dreaming. The intricate moves of the dance inspired memories of his first love, Anarkali, his father's Hindu dancing girl. She was the epitome of grace and sensuality. Even as a young man, the prince had had his harem, but there were none among his women as beautiful as Anarkali, no one who lit his sexual imagination in the way that she had.

Jahangir's father was, of course, an obstacle. Akbar had had over five thousand women in his zanana, but Anarkali was a different matter. Anarkali was the emperor's favorite, her dancing perfect in both classical and sensual execution. Underlined with kohl, her black eyes glowed as her head turned from shoulder to shoulder, exhibiting the three superb planes of her face. The palms of her arched hands pushed rhythmically at the air and sent her bangles clashing. Her hips undulated as if she were in sexual ecstasy (she was, as she later confessed to Salim). The tambourines jangled, the sitar implored, the drums pounded a symmetrical rhythm, and a chorus of women sung an ancient lyric. She used the music of her silver ankle bells to keep time as her tiny feet leaped over the polished floor. The swirl of her silken *dupatta* perfumed the air and cloaked her face as she ended the dance and bowed before the emperor with the deepest humility. That too, Salim found intensely stimulating. The young prince vowed that he would have her. Whatever the consequences, he would have her.

The dying emperor recalled the insolence of her nipples, her acid sweet taste, and how he had entered that yielding sweetness, intoxicated by the odors and flavors of her body and the euphoria of her submission. She had been the love of his young life, but she was a commoner. His father would never have agreed to a marriage on those grounds alone. He would certainly never have agreed to his son's taking his favorite concubine.

When Akbar discovered the clandestine affair, he was outraged at his son and furious with Anarkali, who by law was his property. Prince Salim begged for dispensation to marry her, but that only increased the emperor's rage. Akbar was so incensed that he had the woman bricked up alive in a palace room, where she suffocated to death.

Jahangir's reverie ended with tears. The old emperor was lost in the past and had no appetite for the future or even the present. So, it was no challenge for Nur Jahan to persuade him to return to Lahore, where he had built a tomb for Anarkali.

Alongside the ninety-nine names of Allah, Jahangir' craftsmen had inscribed on a wall of Anarkali's sarcophagus the Persian couplet:

"I would give my thanks unto Allah on the day of resurrection,

Ah! that I could behold the face of my beloved."

And later he had added the words:

"The one profoundly enamored, by Salim, son of Akbar."

CHAPTER 52

THE EMPEROR WAS IN A state of delirium as his palanquin descended through the pines. Despite the fresh mountain air, his asthmatic wheezing had increased. While the doctor's treatment had conquered Jahangir's jaundice, even his most optimistic hakim had lost all hope for his life. Nur Jahan had insisted he keep his prognosis from the emperor's ears.

When the imperial entourage had reached the sunshine of Bairam Kala, known as "the place where one enters India," Jahangir felt a surge of energy, a brief recovery, and had himself attired in the traditional green jubba and turban of the huntsman.

"Why do you wear the green today, my lord?" asked Nur Jahan suspiciously.

"Because today I shall hunt," Jahangir announced. Hunting was his favorite pastime, and he wanted one last hunt before the shadow of death closed in upon him.

"Oh no!" cried Nur Jahan, in a panic that the emperor might die before reaching Lahore. There was no question that she loved Jahangir and was genuinely concerned about him, but one had to be practical.

"I will hear no objection. My fever has gone. I'm in fine fiddle. The mountains have finally done their magic. Order my gamekeeper to thrash the forest."

"I shall do no such thing. I will not allow you to commit suicide."

"Must I make the arrangements myself?" The emperor's voice was menacing. He rose from his divan and stood to his full stature. He cocked his head and stared down at his little queen with full imperial visage. When Jahangir truly wanted something, contradiction was not possible. This the queen could only acknowledge.

"Darling king, I will do as you wish," said Nur Jahan, bowing her head so as not to show her tears. Her voice shrilled through the imperial tent for the chief eunuch, who summoned the gamekeeper, who hired beaters from among the village poor.

The emperor was carried to a hilltop and helped to sit cross-legged under an umbrella held by a slave. Jahangir looked up at his servants and smiled paternally as a musket inlaid with gold was put into his hands. The end of the long, engraved barrel was supported on the shoulder of another slave, who sat on the ground just before the emperor. They looked down into the ravine.

When the beaters drove a cotton-tailed buck up to Jahangir's gunsights, the emperor, who had been at that same moment adjusting his posture, fired and only wounded the animal. Jahangir watched as the deer ran over the cliff before him. A villager, trying desperately to please the emperor, took an incautious step in pursuit and plunged screaming off the cliff. The emperor shook with terror.

Jahangir had always had a morbid fear of death. He feared the day of judgment when God would take him to task for all the pain he had caused in the world, all the sins of excess, all the injustices he had administered. The demise of this poor man crystallized his fear. Jahangir took it as an omen of his own impeding death. He stared, blinking in horror, at the place where the man had fallen, bloody among the rocks and entangled with the wounded stag. They both murmured softly as their lives drained slowly away.

Anxious to get away from this misfortune, the emperor ordered the tents struck. The imperial entourage started again on the march to Lahore.

Just outside Rajauri, the emperor, riding in a palki and compelled to travel completely prostrate, signaled for a stop. Sickness and old age can often make a person disagreeable. An autocrat could tend to irritability, but Jahangir became patient and humble. He would request rather than command and treat all his servants and underlings with gentle understanding.

"Please help me up," Jahangir asked of the manservant who now accompanied him everywhere to do his ablutions, to help him in prayer, and even to attend to the performance of his bodily functions. "I am parched. A drink is what I need. Call for some wine," the emperor rasped.

"Yes, Majesty," said the servant.

At that point, Nur Jahan appeared and looked deep into the emperor's eyes. "Hurry!" she shouted. She saw death there, and tears rushed to her eyes. With the help of servants, she propped Jahangir up and supported his fragile body. "Hurry with that wine!" she shouted again. When a servant rushed to her with a crystal flask, she poured some of its contents into a jade goblet and put it to the emperor's lips.

"It will not go down," Jahangir said quietly. He swished the sweet wine around in his mouth, then spit it out onto the hard earth. He could barely speak; his throat was so constricted.

"Make camp here. Now! Right on this spot!" ordered the queen. She broke out crying.

All through the night, after the emperor's tent had been speedily erected, she cradled her man in her arms and tearfully hummed his favorite melodies until she herself fell asleep.

As dawn was breaking, the queen awakened from a dream of monstrous human forms and growling jackals. She shuddered and instinctively rolled to Jahangir's side for comfort. When she put her lips to the cold flesh of his cheek, she rose in horror. Jahangir lay on his back with fixed eyes. She shook him and spoke in a voice quaking with fear. She called his name and, lacerated by his silence, put her hands to her temples and shrieked. She fled the tent wearing only a loose robe that fell from her shoulders. The sun cracked the horizon behind her and, as she ran, cast her porcelain skin dark in shadow and rendered her black hair red. She halted on the hilltop with no consciousness of her nakedness. Deep from inside her came a long shivering wail that went down to the valley floor, where the army had just begun to stir. Every waking soldier lifted his head to the stark figure on the hill and knew that their emperor was dead.

Nur Jahan's servants approached and quickly covered her. Others formed a circle around her and led her back to the chief eunuch's tent. She leaned her head against a shoulder and repeated Allah's name until it caught in her throat and she could find relief only in sobbing.

Then servants ran out from Jahangir's tent shouting, "The emperor is dead!" spreading the news through the still not completely awakened camp. Within minutes, Asaf Khan emerged sleepily from his tent and ordered his sergeant at arms to send runners to all points of Hindustan and most especially to his son-in-law in the Deccan.

Jahangir's reign of twenty-two years had been short as compared with his father's fifty and not nearly as productive. On October 28, 1627, it was over. Nuruddin Jahangir Padshah, fifty-eight, had died one year to the day of the death of his son Parviz.

There was no official heir, and the struggle to win the throne began immediately.

Barely had she dried her tears when Nur Jahan ordered an assembly of nobles to test the waters for Shahryar's accession. But it was not to be. Asaf Khan put her in his custody before the meeting could take place. He ringed her tent with a troop of his loyalists, and not a single noble expressed an interest in freeing her.

Nur Jahan paced before her brother in her tent, which had become her prison. She had been crying once again, and her hand clutched her dupatta, which she had lowered to her neck.

"You are my brother, my dearest love. I have no other. But you have betrayed me!" She stopped before Asaf Khan and began to cry once more.

Her brother pushed her away. His look was severe and totally unmoved by her tears. "No one will countenance Shahryar. It is he that turns me away from you. I love you still," said Asaf.

"Then let me out. I will not go against you!"

"There will be time enough when Shah Jahan is crowned. Like me, you are the child of Ghiyas Beg, filled up to the throat with cunning. You cannot be trusted. You would plunge the empire into chaos."

"I serve the empire well; you cannot deny it!"

"Sister, you serve yourself well. No, upon my word, I will not free you."

"Bah! Your motives are far from pure! You wish your daughter's husband to become emperor!" she exclaimed.

"Should I not, when you support an imbecile?"

"But he shall have my guidance," she pleaded.

"No, Sister, I will not set you free!"

In compliance with Islamic law, which requires a quick burial, Jahangir's corpse had to be washed immediately. With Shahryar at a distance in Lahore and Shah Jahan far away in the Deccan, the honor fell to Asaf Khan. As brother-in-law, he was male next of kin. He was obliged to wash the corpse and wrap it in plain cotton cloth as prescribed by the Sharia. It was then placed in a plain pine box and consigned to a wagon to be rushed at breakneck speed to Lahore for burial.

Thousands of men had entered the funeral procession from among the throngs that lined the streets of Shahdora, a suburb of Lahore. Hundreds had fruitlessly clamored for the honor of assisting in carrying the bier that could ride only on the shoulders of the emperor's closest amirs.

Muslims consider flowers to be unbecoming at a funeral. Women are thought to be prone to hysteria; thus, the presence of females is proscribed as well. But at the very rear of the long procession, at a decorous distance behind the marchers, strode the lone figure of Nur Jahan. Asaf Khan had placed guards at her sides, and others walked discreetly behind her.

The empress was dressed in mourning clothes of pure white. At certain moments, the sun would catch a tear that shone beneath the sheer fabric of her veil. Otherwise she was the very picture of the calm dignity demanded by Sunni custom. Her own Shia religion would have allowed her to give full expression to the emotions that were churning in her breast. But that outlet was not available to a Mughal queen.

In the late afternoon, Jahangir's body was buried in a plain pine box alongside the Ravi in the sumptuous garden that Queen Nur herself had created. The reign of the fourth Great Mughal had ended.

CHAPTER 53

Nur Jahan's power in the world had come to an end. Asaf Khan had blocked what little support she received from the amirs. He had also persuaded Dawar Bakhsh, Khusro's son, to take the throne while allaying the young man's doubts and suspicions with his smooth talk. Asaf Khan had presented his case so adroitly that Dawar himself began to believe that his accession on the day after Jahangir's death was real. But as even the dullest courtier could see, his rise was just an excuse to hold the throne until Shah Jahan could return and claim it for himself.

After the funeral, Nur Jahan's house arrest was continued. The three sons of Shah Jahan, whom she had held as hostages, were set free. Her isolation was almost complete.

A swift runner had been sent to the Deccan to summon Shah Jahan home to his destiny. It would take the prince three months to journey to Agra. Meanwhile, Nur Jahan had sent a secret message to Shahryar bidding him raise an army to assert his claim to the throne.

CHAPTER 54

"YOU SAY THAT I SHALL be king, but Ya Allah, I do not look like a king," said Shahryar, standing before a mirror.

He wore a striped turban that cleverly wrapped his head to hide his baldness. Eyebrows had been delicately cut out of mouse skin and attached with *char gund*, although in wet weather or when the prince sweated profusely, they would curl at the edges and migrate to comic locations on his forehead. Black kohl was traced along his eyelids to offset his lack of eyelashes. But none of these subterfuges fooled anyone. It was quite clear that Shahryar was completely without hair.

"The truth is that I look like an infant, not an emperor," said Shahryar, squinting and trying to look important before the mirror.

"If it were hair that made a king, then every bearded man in Hindustan would have a kingdom," said Ladli, his wife, a woman nearly as cunning and self-possessed as her empress mother.

"Then I am destined to be king?"

"The first step is to declare yourself king," said Ladli. "You are your father's heir. My mother's message to you is to arm yourself. Raise an army!"

"War requires more than words. It is gold that moves men to action," said Shahryar.

"There is a treasury here in Lahore with no one to protect it."

Shahryar thought for a moment. "How many men would it take to seize it, do you reckon?" he asked.

"We have sufficient men. The question is, do you have the will?"

"My will is iron!" shouted the prince.

"Then you cannot be defeated," Ladli said with a shrewd face.

After the noon prayer, Shahryar stood in the mosque before the minibar addressing a group of nobles. Ladli and the women of the harem sat, veiled, behind them.

Shahryar delivered words that his wife had written. "I have brought you here to talk of your prospects, to tell you that the emperor is dead and that a new ruler must be chosen. In the Deccan, a dark prince purposes to make himself king. If you will not abide this, then the time has come to act. We must build an army while Shah Jahan gathers his in the southland. Only bold action brings victory, and yonder lies the treasury. If you love freedom, cry its name and know that our war will bring success!"

The nobles sprang to their feet and shouted, "Freedom!" over and over again.

Ladli thrilled when the cry thundered against the walls and sounded out into the city, where the burning sun had left the lanes bare and the bazaars deserted.

Hawks glided in the air above the sun-scorched roof of the treasury. Sultan Shahryar stood in the dust before its doors with the lances of five hundred soldiers at his back. The sultan was dressed in white robes and turban, and he struck a martial pose before his men. Ladli was sitting on the back of an elephant. At her signal, a log was brought forward, placed in her elephant's trunk, and slung until the teak doors were battered open. Ladli's mount ambled before Shahryar's armed men and entered the high hall of the treasury.

Bronze lamps hung from the heights, and long bars of sunlight cut through the shutters and lay across the marble counters. Three clerks froze behind the form of the chief diwan, who stood before Ladli's elephant with calm dignity.

"What brings this intrusion? By what right?" the diwan said.

"You must know that the emperor has died, and here is Shahryar, the new king. The treasury is his!" shouted Ladli as soldiers filtered in around the diwan. "Lead us to the vault!"

The diwan pulled at his beard for a moment and allowed his bright eyes to assess the soldiers and the elephant standing before him. Abruptly, he clapped his hands. Followed by his clerks, he strode to the polished bronze doors at the rear of the building and unlocked them with an enormous cast iron key. Then the clerks, all four in turbans, plain white robes, and bare feet, pushed at the doors' heavy panels until they swung slowly open.

The diwan's men hastened to light the lamps. Before them, glittering in the yellow flicker, were gold and jewels beyond imagining. The diwan stepped to a dais, where alongside pen and ink was a scroll that was the treasury's inventory, sealed with wax and tied with an official red ribbon.

"Excellencies," he drawled in his official voice, "surrounding us is the fruit of the emperor's last weighing and the gifts tallied from this year's session of the royal court at Lahore."

"Proceed with an accounting!" cried Shahryar, quite overcome with the sight of it all.

"As you wish, Majesty. Here are the diamonds," the diwan said, pointing to an open bronze casket filled to the top with large, faceted stones gleaming in the lamplight. He broke the seal of a scroll, unrolled it, and weighted it open with a blue rock of lapis lazuli. He recited, "Five thousand nine hundred seven misqals of diamonds."

Then, pointing to a similar casket, he announced, "An equal weight of pigeon's blood rubies cut and polished at Amber City to the emperor's requirements. "Here are the emeralds, 11,887 Misqals of them," he said, pointing at a basket of stones glowing with green fire. "As you can see, there are stones surrounding us that are so numerous as to be not yet completely counted." Unclassified gems stood in piles covering the marble floors completely except where paths cut through to the rear, where stacks of gold bullion were piled to a man's height.

"And here lie the gifts of the amirs, amounting to one thousand in number." The diwan referred to the gem-studded saddles that were piled randomly around the vault. Also enumerated were boxes upon boxes of jeweled turban ornaments set with diamonds, rubies, and emeralds. A half-dozen thrones made of gold and set with gems were dispersed around the room, and lances set with diamonds leaned against its walls. Shabby by contrast were the stacked pyramids of silver bullion and crates of silver rupees allowed to sit tarnished against the sheen of the marble walls and the brilliance at the vault's center.

The sight of the treasury overwhelmed Shahryar. His eyes went everywhere and blinked spasmodically. He had never beheld such wealth. He became giddy as he realized that this treasure was now his.

Sensing his intoxication, Ladli, who had dismounted, went to his side. "Remember, what you see before you is a tool only. It is the coin with which you will purchase the empire," she said. "The wealth of Hindustan is ten thousand times greater, and that too will be yours, inshallah."

Shahryar was too dazzled for his wife's comments to make an impression. He walked to the pile of emeralds and ran his hands through them. He picked a ruby pin from a box and stuck it into his turban. He posed for a moment with a silver lance and, laughing, made to throw it at his wife.

"Yes, I shall be king. It is my destiny." His self-confidence soared now that he had wealth, and he imagined that he now had the imperial power as well.

Shahryar did not follow his wife's good advice and foolishly gave away a significant part of his wealth to his new supporters. They had flocked to his banner at the first sign of the money to be had. But this did little to ensure their loyalty as he had hoped. Few would recognize him as emperor. "He is too foolish to be king, a boy seeking a man's post," was what many of the nobles had said of him. They continued to accept his gold and give the appearance of fealty, but his position was far from secure.

It looked as if Shahryar's fortunes might improve when his cousin Mirza Bayasanghar, Daniyal's son, the late brother of Jahangir, came down from the mountains. His cousin had the military experience necessary to mount a campaign against the forces of Asaf Khan, who, with his own newly minted emperor, was advancing on Lahore.

The two opposing armies met just outside of the city at a bend in the River Ravi. Miraculously, considering Asaf Khan's military ineptitude, Shahryar's mercenaries capitulated with only a feeble resistance at the very first thrust of the khan's army. Mirza Bayasanghar disappeared, and Shahryar, who stood at Lahore gate with a few thousand horsemen, fled in a frenzy into the fort. In so doing, he stupidly entrapped himself. His fate was sealed when a spy let Asaf Khan's men into the fort. Shahyar's personal guard was destroyed, and he was found cowering in the harem of his late father.

In chains, Shahryar was led before Emperor Dawar Bakhsh, who ordered him blinded. The revenge was sweet. Dawar Bakhsh, whose father, Khusro, had been blinded by Jahangir, was able to inflict the same damage on Jahangir's son. Three days later, the order was implemented, and the self-proclaimed emperor was rendered sightless and politically impotent.

CHAPTER 54

It was cool. Breezes blew down from the top of India, and the sun lingered with a delicate light on Junnair Fort. Banarasi was exhausted from his run. He took refuge with the guards at the wall. The guards, like himself, were Hindu. They poured water into his mouth from a goatskin.

"Allow me to enter the fort. This message must be delivered," said Banarasi. He could barely stand. He had run all the way from Rajauri: twenty days with little sleep. When finally, the vast sandstone rectangle of the fort came into sight, he had relaxed his will and collapsed. Two peasants had taken pity on him, lifted him into their cart, and driven him to the wall.

"The emperor is dead," said Banarasi, gulping the water.

"A blessing," said a smiling guard who wore a dirty shalwar chemise and a khaki turban stained with perspiration.

"His mother was a Rajput princess," said another in response. "Who knows what will come now?"

Banarasi's arms hung over the necks of two guards. They were strong men, farmers most of the year. They bore him tenderly as they would an injured son. Part of the fort was still being used as a prison, and an inmate's derisive cry echoed from its windows: "Bringing us a new one? Whose throat did this man cut? A Musulman's? Ha ha ha."

"Why do you care? You'll be dead at daybreak," squawked another prisoner.

Banarasi was brought right to the doorstep of the royal apartments and presented to the sentry on duty. "Brother, this man brings news of the empire. In the name of Allah, let him pass," said the Hindu soldier.

"Who is he?"

"Banarasi, and I bring important news for Shah Jahan's ears," said the runner.

"The prince has gone."

"Then Mahabat will see me."

At that moment, Mahabat Khan was going out from his apartment to join Shah Jahan for evening prayers. "Who is this man?" Mahabat demanded.

"He says he brings news."

"From whence come you?"

"Lahore, General. The emperor is dead."

"Dead?" said Mahabat. "Who has sent you?"

"Asaf Khan," said Banarasi

"This is a trick!"

"No, no, my lord. Here is my lord's ring!" said Banarasi and produced a signet ring of heavy gold. "He has dispatched me to request the return of Shah Jahan. The kingdom is his, Excellency. Look here," said the illiterate Banarasi, passing a bamboo tube containing a scroll.

"He is genuine," said Mahabat Khan, passing the scroll to Shah Jahan. "He has shown me your father-in-law's ring. Jahangir is dead. Asaf encourages a speedy departure. Khusro's son has been declared emperor temporarily to keep Shahryar from the throne."

Shah Jahan gave the scroll a careful glance and said with an urgent voice, "Time is of the essence. If I know Nur Jahan's mind, she will push Shahryar to move against me immediately."

"Then let us hasten," said Mahabat Khan, glad for a call to action.

They gathered their men and within three days were headed north. By the time they had crossed the River Narmada, news had filtered down from Lahore that Asaf Khan had won against Shahryar and that the blinded usurper had been imprisoned.

"Fortune rides with me this day," said Shah Jahan. "Allah has smiled on me at last. In Lahore, the amirs have called me emperor, and I will be."

"Are you forgetting your brother and your nephews? Nothing is secure while they live," said Mahabat Khan.

"I have not forgotten. I have just sent my message to the *vakil:* 'Send the pretenders to hell!' Mahabat, let the drums roll for the new emperor! We proceed to Agra in triumph."

"All hail the emperor Shah Jahan!" exclaimed Mahabat Khan.

"Hail, too, the brilliant Rasa Bahadur!" cried Shah Jahan, raising an index finger as he spoke.

"Khusro's . . . "—Mahabat paused—" . . . deliverer?"

"Yes, it is he who will perform the Thugee," said Shah Jahan.

"The man is a Thug?" said Mahabat, astonished.

"It is the only way to get such a delicate task done satisfactorily."

"But the Thugs are a menace. I am amazed at your choice. Akbar banished them from Agra years ago."

"Banished or not, the Thugs have continued their trade. They are masters of the art of strangulation."

"Astaghfirullah, and theft," Mahabat lamented.

Eight days later, Rasa Bahadur arrived at Lahore Fort and knelt before Asaf Khan.

"Ah, Rasa," said Asaf Khan, offering his hand to be kissed. "Tell me, how was your journey? Eatawah is a distance."

"Eighty kos, Excellency, but the ride was pleasant enough. We traveled mostly at night to avoid the heat."

"You have made good time, Rasa sahib. Tonight, you will meet Dawar Bakhsh and the sons of Prince Daniyal. Will you see them alone?"

"I have two helpers from my town."

"Splendid. They are in adjacent cells. Inshallah, you will have no difficulty, and you will come to tea with us tomorrow," said Asaf Khan.

Rasa's dark eyes glittered at the prospect of the night's work. "Inshallah," he said, smiling, and kissing the vakil's hand slavishly.

It was Rasa who procured the pine boxes for the bodies of the three princes and then had them buried in the garden next to Jahangir.

CHAPTER 55

Shah Jahan celebrated his thirty-eighth birthday in Rajastan with his old friend Rajah Karan. They were drunk.

"Yes, you will come to my coronation. It will be like old times. Are you still the wild man?"

"I am a king like you. My subjects expect decorum," Rajah Karan declared, and then said slyly with a laugh, "but I still enjoy a good ride. And you? Will you ride?"

"What have you got for me?"

"A *Yabus*, high spirited. He needs a strong hand."

"Let's take him out on the desert, then," said Shah Jahan, delighted.

It was a January night, cool with a light wind tracing the desert floor. Brilliant stars punctured the black sky. The oblong moon glowed like an opal. Only the two of them went out and rode bareback over the dry earth. They howled like prowling wolves and prodded their mounts ferociously.

"The world is mine!" shouted Shah Jahan over his horse's thunder. "Let us ride to the ends of the earth and shout the news." In the moonlight, the wind fluttered his turban ends and spread the tails of his white jacket. They galloped toward the dark mountain until their horses were winded, then stopped and looked up into the starry bowl of the heavens. "The earth is mine, and by God, I will take the sky!"

"You can fly?" the Rana inquired.

"Watch me!" He sprang up to his horse's back and stood gracefully in his bare feet while beseeching the heavens with gestures of the classical dance.

"Majesty, your dancing is breathtaking. Your flying is not."

"Be patient, Beta. In time, everything in the universe will bend to my will," said Shah Jahan with a drunken laugh. His legs parted, and he slipped to the rider's position. He dug his heels into his horse's ribs and hollered at the mountain. Jackals howled a reply. The two men took their horses by the reigns and turned. They raced at the white palace while the mountain echoed, and they churned a scrim of moonlit dust.

"Did you for a moment think that you could outride an emperor?" shouted Shah Jahan back over his shoulder at the rana.

"Challenge only, Majesty," said Karan into the wind. He had been restraining his mount. "It is unseemly for a prince to defeat an emperor."

"Yes, and inshallah, this emperor will never be defeated!"

CHAPTER 56

THE WHITE DOME OF THE tomb of the Sufi saint rose before him. Shah Jahan had arrived in Ajmer just a day after his encounter with the rana Karan and was still feeling the ill effects of that bout of drinking and hubris.

Shah Jahan stepped within the tomb and beheld a thick fog of incense. He stooped before the golden cenotaph and lavished it with rose petals from a golden charger. Then he dropped to his knees. With his palms uplifted, he readied to receive the saint's guidance as he recited the *Fatiha*. He begged the *kwajah's* blessings and pledged that he would never drink alcohol again or defile the air with his boastfulness. Peace and justice would distinguish his rule. In time, he would be known for his good works. That he promised the saint.

The sun had just set, and outside a muezzin called the faithful to prayer, to prosperity, to the one God. Long lines of pilgrims bent, prostrated themselves, then rose to chant a prayer, then prostrated themselves once again. Then they sat all in a line and murmured a prayer. The deep vibrations of their devotions resonated throughout the grounds.

The courtyard smelled of the *khichri* that was being prepared in two enormous cauldrons. Years ago, on the anniversary of the kwajah's death, Jahangir and Nur Jahan, with their own hands, had made food for over five thousand in those same *deghs*.

The square was crowded with hundreds of pilgrims. Torches blazed along the outside walls of the tomb and along the enormous height of the gate.

When the prayers finished, plates of food were passed around, and the courtyard became the site of a grand dinner party.

Shah Jahan, Mahabat Khan, and their entourage made their way through the squatting multitude uttering salaams. As it dawned upon the pilgrims who the handsome noble actually was, the crowd shouted, "Shah Jahan, zindabad!"

"In their minds I am already emperor," said Shah Jahan, nodding, and patting his hand to his heart as he picked his way through the crowd.

"The will of the people can sometimes make a king but let us wait for our reception in Agra before we celebrate," said Mahabat. As word spread that the new emperor was among them, more people gathered around, saluting them.

"Mahabat, my friend, you are much too cautious. No one stands in my way. Asaf Khan assures that the nobles are with me, in fact, the queen's brother-in-law has prepared his gardens for our use."

"Qasin Khan? He has come over? My God!"

"There is nothing like the scent of power to cleanse the soul of petty attachments," said Shah Jahan.

"The queen's world trembles," said Mahabat Khan.

"And our own rises. We will make camp at the garden in two days' time and await developments."

Shah Jahan's complement of armed men, horses, camels, and elephants entered among the palms of Qasin's garden and spent the night there overlooking the Yamuna. The next day under a bright sun, shining in jeweled clothing, Shah Jahan entered the capital with his soldiers. He held his head high in an open howdah. Every avenue his elephant walked exploded in applause. Ordinary people stood on rooftops and at windows, scattering handfuls of colored grain, and jamming the streets to shout: Shah Jahan Zindabad! And the well-to-do threw rose petals before his elephant's feet, and all acclaimed him emperor.

Twelve days later, on the day when by his astrologer's reckoning the stars favored a long and fruitful reign, the turban of his dead father was fitted upon

Shah Jahan's head and the sword of Humayan placed in his hands. Hindustan had crowned a new emperor. For a week, fireworks lit the skies, and the city's lanes and bazaars were delirious with celebration.

Asaf Khan was also honored. Jahanara, Shah Jahan's daughter, and his own daughter, Mumtaz Mahal, fêted him royally as befitted the man who had engineered Shah Jahan's ascension.

CHAPTER 57

For Nur Jahan, the shadow of evening had fallen. From the heights of power, she was reduced to powerlessness. Not only had her brother deserted her, but the emperor despised her so thoroughly that he did his utmost to obliterate her memory, even to the extent of melting down the coins that bore her image. She was also not permitted to continue on at court, a benefit which was usually allowed a widowed queen.

Money was not a concern for Nur Jahan. As a matter of showing a generous public face, Shah Jahan had endowed her with an extremely generous annual pension of 200,000 rupees. The treasure held for her in Agra's city vaults was prodigious, partially an inheritance from Jahangir and partly profits from her many business enterprises. She was a rich and independent woman.

Shahdara
1635

Walking along the banks of the Ravi, the old queen looked up through the plane trees at the mausoleum Shah Jahan had constructed. The tomb was a low profile of red sandstone pierced with graceful archways and a white domed minaret at each of four corners

Jahangir had left instructions that his tomb be left open to the sky as his ancestor Babur had said, that "the rain and dew of heaven might fall upon it."

The queen and two slave girls walked barefooted in the mud of the riverbank. Behind them an empty palanquin bobbed on the shoulders of four robust men. In the vanguard were Nur Jahan's armed eunuchs. It was her custom to walk the riverbank while the mist rose from the water's face and deodar trees still stung the air with their fragrance. As the sun showed on the horizon, the queen would pass up into the garden she had created and walk with the rising sun to Jahangir's cenotaph.

Today in Nur Jahan's paradise garden, a team of women squatted in bright clothing and scythed a growth of weeds. Men loaded an oxcart with mangoes and another with oranges. A camel stretched to a neem tree and began nibbling the bark until a gardener beat him away with a stick.

Everywhere, roses, marigolds, poppies, carnations, dahlias, and chrysanthemums edged the graveled paths, filled squares between hedges, blossomed in clay pots, and encircled the tall palms.

Nur Jahan still carried herself with grace and dignity, but she had grown pale, and her hands shook with infirmity. She was obliged to use a cane.

It saddened her that during the years it took to build the tomb, her brother had not seen her, although he came frequently to Lahore. Indeed, like Shah Jahan, he had assaulted her memory and defiled her good name.

As she walked into the sarcophagus, she thought of Shah Jahan. *He has erased my name from the public records and tried to take me from the minds of my people. To what end? I have no power, nor do I care for any. That part of my life is over. I want only to honor the memory of my husband. I pray to live the life of a faithful Muslim and to have an easy death. But even in death, Shah Jahan has chosen to assail me. He has forbidden me to lie next to my husband. He wishes me to build my own tomb. And I will be obedient to the emperor. What choice have I? Inshallah, even as he builds his tomb for my niece, I shall construct a tomb of my own.*

Nur Jahan entered the dark room where the cenotaph lay on a pedestal of marble set with gemstones. The ninety-nine names of Allah circled its sides in emeralds and rubies, and the burnished floor and walls of amber marble glowed in the dim light. The queen sighed as she approached. She laid a bouquet of red roses upon its cover. She eased herself to the floor and assumed the posture of prayer. With palms upturned, she recited the Fatiha, the opening Surya of the Qur'an, the prayer for guidance. The murmured Arabic words echoed in the small, silent room. Then she rose with the help of Hoshiyar Khan and lay her cheek on his shoulder. She would come again tomorrow and every day as long as she lived.

The End

AFTERWORD

I HAVE BEEN CAREFUL TO match the narrative of this book to standard histories of the Mughal era. The reader can rely on the accuracy of the story, with only two exceptions. The first is Akbar's description of the warfare of the Brethren in Chapter four. While the method he relates, doubtless, was employed by Gengus Khan in the thirteenth century, there is no evidence that it was used by the Mughal army in the seventeenth century.

In truth, the Mughals never smoked opium, they swallowed it in pill form (as Indians still do). Story wise, I thought it livelier for Jahangir to puff a hubbly-bubbly instead.

In composing "Queen & Emperor", the most referenced historical source was "Nur Jahan, Empress of Mughal India", by Ellison Banks Findly Her book is a reliable account of the Empress' life and the most vivid.

GLOSSARY

Adab	Manners, ceremonies, etiquette.
Afim	Opium.
Agah	A Lord.
Alhumdillah	Praise be to Allah.
Amir	A Noble.
Assalaamu 'Alaikum	Peace be upon you. The standard Muslim greeting.
Astaghfirullah	I ask Allah's forgiveness. Often recited to claim innocence.
Azan	Announces prayer, usually from a minaret.
Baradari	Pavilion.
Banian	Hindu *jati*- a merchant caste.
Banjara	Hindu *jati*- caste of bullock cart drivers.
Beedi	Poor man's very thin tobacco cigarette wrapped in an herbal leaf.
Begum	A term of respect, used for women of high station.
Beta	Literally son. An affectionate term for both young women and men.
Betel	Nut and leaf—the traditional *paan*. When chewed produces red saliva.
Bhang	Marijuana, ground and baked in cakes or mixed into drinks such as wine or lassi.
Caravanserai	Places of rest for travelers. Built by the state or private donors alongside major roads.
Chai	Tea.
Chaiton	Devil.
Chapati	Flat wheaten bread much like a tortilla in shape and thickness.
Choli	Blouse tightly conforming to the breasts, terminating above the navel.
Chula	Brick or earthen stove, found usually in village homes.

Darshan	To see or be in the presence of a highly revered person or God.
Dhobi	Washer and ironer of clothes.
Dhoti	A garment wrapped around a man's waist and tucked up through the crotch.
Diwan	Mughal treasurer.
Diwan-i-am	Mughal hall of public audience.
Diwan-i-kas	Mughal hall of private audience.
Durbar	Mughal court. Also, an official reception held by a native prince.
Fakir	Muslim mystic.
Farman	Edict issued by a Muslim Court or religious authority. Can be a passport.
Firangi	Foreigner in India.
Ghagara	Ankle length skirt.
Ghee	Butter rendered clear by heating and filtering.
Hakim	Muslim doctor. A practitioner of Unani medicine, a Muslim form of Ayurveda.
Howdah	Seat placed on the back of an elephant, often canopied.
Inshallah	If Allah wills or when Allah wills.
Jagir	Land and its revenues assigned by the Mughal government to an official.
Jati	Occupational caste.
Jharokha	Window used by Mughal emperors to listen to public grievances.
Khol	Powdered antimony, employed in Arabia as an eyeliner against the glare of the sun. In India and elsewhere it is also used as a cosmetic.
Koka	Stepbrother, in the sense of having been suckled by the same mother.
Kornish	The customary salute to the emperor.

Kos	1.86 miles (or more depending on the local definition).
Kshatriya	Warrior caste, second in rank after the Brahmans.
Kuda Hafez	Goodbye. Literally: God protect you.
Kurta	Traditional Indian shirt.
Lakh	100,000 of rupees.
Maghreb prayer	Sunset prayer.
Mansabdar	Imperial official ranked by the number of horses and soldiers granted by the Emperor.
Marathi	Fierce Hindu warriors from Maharashtra state in Western India.
Mardana	The outer part of a house or palace reserved for men.
Mirza	A prince. A member of the royal family or the aristocracy.
Mohur	Gold coin worth 15 silver rupees.
Naan	Flat white bread resembling a small bare pizza bereft of all toppings.
Nadiri	A stylish coat designed by Jahangir to honor select nobles.
Nafs	Islamic concept: Incite one to do evil. The lower self. The base instincts.
Namaste	Hindu word saying hello or goodbye
Naqshbandi	A Sufi order originating in Central Asia and an important influence on Mughal governance.
Nautch girl	Dancing girl who can sometimes be a prostitute.
Nilghau	Wild blue ox.
Paan	A preparation made to be chewed containing betel nut and sweet spices, enfolded in a betel leaf. Stains saliva and teeth a bright red.
Punkah	A ceiling fan, in the form of a flat sheet operated by pulling on ropes.
Purdah	Literally curtain. The seclusion of women from public view.

Qaba	A long sleeved coat.
Qawwali music	Love songs or music connected to spirituality.
Rajmata	Queen mother
Shaitan	Devil
Sahib	Sir. Used as a mark of respect.
Sarai	See *caravanserai.*
Shehnai	A small oboe with a brass bell. Earlier versions were used by snake charmers.
Subhanallah	Glory be to Allah.
Sufi	Sufism is the mystical aspect of Islam. Another name for Sufi is Dervish.
Sunna	Actions or activities of the Prophet Muhammad.
Tabla	Drum used in pairs.
Tasbih	Ring of beads similar to a rosary. Usually fingered while asking God for forgiveness.
Uncle	Term of endearment, used for male elders not necessarily relatives.
Varna	Caste. Literally meaning color. A Hindu is born into a Varna, one of the four in the Vedic caste system: Brahman, Kshatriya, Vaisya, Shudra(Sudra).
Ya Allah	O' Lord or O'God.
Zanana.	Harem.
Zhur	Midday prayer.

ABOUT THE AUTHOR

TONY RAOSTO WAS AWESTRUCK THE first time he saw India from the deck of a merchant ship. He has returned to this beautiful country a dozen times since and remains inspired and invigorated by the people and culture.

Made in the USA
Lexington, KY
03 December 2019